THE ACCUSED ARCHITECT

A Ken Knoll Architectural Mystery

by

Christian Belz

For information, email **Cozy Cat Press**, cozycatpress@aol.com or visit our website at: www.cozycatpress.com

COZY CAT
PRESS

ISBN: 978-1-939816-07-8
Printed in the United States of America

Cover design by Karri Klawiter
http://artbykarri.com/e-book-print-cover-art-design/

1 2 3 4 5 6 7 8 9 10

To Alex

Acknowledgments

Above all, I'd like to thank my son Alex for his love and support. Words can't express how grateful I am for the many hours we spent plotting this book. Remember how we kicked around ideas over the course of weeks and weeks, searching for motives and just the right murderer? You have my gratitude for editing the novel, not to mention your energy and enthusiasm in our marketing endeavors. Your confidence means the world to me.

Thanks, Mom, for all the years of love and encouragement which brought me to this published novel. I love you.

Thanks Pop, though you're no longer with us, for showing me the way and always affirming that, no matter what, we can accomplish our dreams.

A special thanks to my writing mentor, Iris Lee Underwood, for ten years of support and inspiration and your constant reminder that it all begins with poetry.

I'm so grateful to my Taking Leaps writing group. Thank you all for your steadfast critique, weekly encouragement, and a *decade* of inspiring, joyful Monday nights. I continually look forward to hearing your stories and poems. It's the highlight of my week.

Thanks to my new writing friends at Detroit Working Writers and our monthly critique group. What fun Saturday afternoons!

Much appreciation to Sandi Lampiris for editing this book in its early stages. Thanks for years of support and all the notes, stars, and exclamation points in the margin.

Thanks to the Troy Citizen's Police Academy, which taught me so much and revved me up about various aspects of police work.

A heartfelt thanks to everyone else who has supported and inspired me through the years.

Finally, a joyful thanks to the authors who have inspired and delighted me through the years, beginning with Carolyn Keene and Franklin W. Dixon. Nancy, Frank, and Joe started it all when I was a kid. Thank you to Sue Grafton, Michael Connelly, Lawrence Sanders, Erle Stanley Gardner, John D. MacDonald, Rex Stout, Janet Evanovich, and my new (delightful!) discovery, Emily Giffin.

Finally, thanks to Patricia Rockwell for your hard work in bringing this book to press, and to the Cozy Cat family for welcoming me with open arms.

Christian Belz
Berkley

Chapter 1
Edison's Folly

"Ken," he wheezed, "I have to talk to you. I tried to reach you last week, but I didn't get any answer at your house. I couldn't get through on your cell either."

I'd returned from a year-end vacation to find my latest intern visibly shaken. Extracting information, however, was painstakingly slow.

"Ken, listen. This is serious. Dead serious. We have to talk." The black circles under Edison's eyes drooped an inch. His chubby cheeks, normally telegraphing a joyful outlook, appeared hollow and desperate. Fresh perspiration glistened on his forehead. His dark eyes darted with a nervous twitch.

"Edison, relax and tell me what's going on. You don't look so good."

His rotund mass filled my guest armchair as Edison nervously poked his pudgy fingers through my candy dish. It was a relief to be back to work, after a rough holiday week. I surveyed the orderly stacks of files and rolled drawings in my modest eight-foot cubicle with satisfaction, delighted that I'd taken the time to straighten things before leaving on Christmas Eve. With a prolonged sigh, I shrugged off the previous week's miseries.

Standing up hastily, Edison raised himself on tip-toes to peer over the partitions, scanning the room's dozen or so grey fabric-covered cubicles. "Maybe we should go into the conference room. There's...um...something I have to tell you."

The moment his words stopped drumming on my ears, Edison withered away from my thoughts. Memories of the unceremonious tongue-lashing I'd received from my girlfriend the week prior gnawed at me like graphic images of some third-world catastrophe. The message light on my phone blinked incessantly, further blurring my focus, so I didn't immediately register the panic in Edison's voice. I shook my head to cast off those thoughts and return to the moment.

"Just spill it, Edison."

His eyes skipped from one point on the floor to another. "No, I can't do it at your desk. Someone will hear." He swayed from side to side, rust-colored shirt straining at the button above his black leather belt. Several moments passed, then he motioned for me to follow. Reluctantly, I stood and trudged behind. Shuffling down the aisle between cubicles, the toe of his hiking boot caught on a loose carpet seam.

Shutting the oxblood-colored metal door, Edison sank into a brown padded roller-chair. Anxiety pinched the muscles of his face, pulling his mouth into a nervous pout. Where had Edison's familiar joviality disappeared to? He sucked in a long breath, then shifted forward toward me. "Ok, Ken. You know how you asked me to do that job inspection at Flamingo Shores, right before Christmas?"

I remembered all right. Days before I blew town, we'd received the contractor's monthly Application for Payment for the thirty-six million dollar addition to Flamingo Shores.

Our firm had designed the two story mall addition, the upscale department store Crystals, and the parking deck in-between. The owners of Flamingo Shores hired our firm to review the contractor's monthly payment requests. Our task: to ascertain that, for each of the twenty trades, the amount of completed work agreed with the dollars requested. We'd been late on the previous pay app and I'd resolved to return this one on time.

He continued, "Well, everyone was off work anyway, and I still had some shopping to do. For Jeanelle. I didn't get around to the inspection until last week."

"Edison, that pay app should have gone out two days after I gave it to you. We talked about this. The critical timing on that paperwork must be adhered to. Last minute Christmas shopping for your girlfriend is not an excuse I can give the client."

"Yeah, I know, I know. You're right." He lowered his eyes in apology. "But listen. I went there on the twenty-seventh. The contractors must have had Monday off for Christmas. The place felt deserted. I went step-by-step through the project, reviewing the status of completion of the various trades and taking pictures. Like you and I did for The Shops at Silver Pond. I knew what you needed done."

Blood rose up the back of my neck. "Wait, didn't Wally go with you?"

"Yeah, we were going to meet, but issues flared up at Brighton Mall and Wally's wife's aunt landed in the hospital. He told me to click off a bunch of pictures and he'd check everything out before I shipped it."

Wally had promised to accompany Edison to the site, review the paperwork, and stand on Edison's head until it went out. Mental Note: ask Wally why he'd abandoned his commitment to help out on this.

"Anyway," Edison said, "I went through the whole job, comparing the trades line item by line item. Only, there was a snag."

"What kind of snag?" I said reflexively, my patience evaporating. I was only half listening to Edison's rambling. Those blinking messages awakened a dozen little nagging thoughts in the back of my mind. I had eight projects dancing around in my head; urgent tasks and duties niggled at me for attention. "Edison, tell me the problem so I can deal with it. I need to move on."

"Look, I know you'll be mad at me, but it was the right thing to do. It went horribly wrong, that's all." Perched on the edge of his seat, his hands grasped his knees as his body tensed. The fresh scent of a cherry Lifesaver on Edison's breath seemed incongruent with the strain in his voice. His dark eyes glistened, and ragged eyebrows poked out in all directions.

There's nothing difficult about traversing a construction site and noting the status of construction. Our job simply concerned checking the contractor's breakdown sheet and verifying the work completed. Edison had been with the firm almost a year. Though this constituted his first architectural job out of school, his age of thirty-four years suggested he should have been able to handle those duties. "Quit stalling, Edison. Tell me what happened."

He licked his lips. "When I first saw him, I would have sworn he was asleep. I mean, he looked like one of those homeless guys you see in the city. He had, like, three layers of rumpled clothes on and a week's growth of a beard. I thought he'd wandered onto the site to get out of the wind." He wrapped one hand around the other, but despite this, they shook like leaves in a windstorm.

The panic creeping into Edison's voice began to grow a knot of apprehension in my stomach.

Edison began talking faster. "Well, he sat right in the shot I wanted to take. I needed a picture of the elevator and he was blocking the view. I had to do something."

"They finally got the elevator in?" Even as an ominous feeling in my stomach grew, I noted this development with pleasant surprise. After weeks of delay, not only was the elevator delivered, but somehow the installation had been coordinated during the notoriously slow construction month of December.

Edison fidgeted in the chair, shifting his weight from one bun to the other, wringing his hands until the fingers became red as popsicles. "This is what I'm saying. I knew you'd be really upset if I didn't get a picture. I tried to change the angle to get the shot without disturbing the bum, but his body leaned right up against the door jamb." Edison's eyes pleaded.

"So what did you do?"

"I yelled at him. Tried to wake him to get him to leave. He didn't move. I thought maybe he'd fallen asleep or passed out. Or, I thought, maybe he pretended to sleep so I wouldn't kick him out of there. Finally, I figured I'd better shake him awake. When I touched him, he slumped over."

I bolted straight up in my chair. "Did that wake him?"

"No. He was dead."

"What!" I jumped up.

He nodded and stared at me. "Edison. How could this be?" I took a breath. "What was he doing there? Why didn't you call me? Crap!" I wished I'd listened more closely. "Why now? On the parking deck?" I paced back and forth. "A dead man on the jobsite. Who was he? How did he get there? We're so far behind already. I bet the cops will have the place shut down for a couple of weeks."

"Exactly my thoughts. That the police would get their hands in everything. They'd be poking around, and keep the work from getting done. And you constantly remind us how the job's a month behind already. If they found a dead body on site, the project would never be completed on time. So I thought, well, it's just a homeless guy anyway. What difference is it if they find him on the project site, or out in the woods somewhere? He'd be easy to, er, relocate. The work could continue and the project would have a chance of opening on schedule."

I couldn't believe the words hitting my ears. "What? You decided to move the body?" He stared quietly in my direction, his weepy eyes seeking approval. He certainly wasn't getting that from me. "What were you thinking?" I screamed.

"I thought, this job's never going to get finished with a murder investigation going on."

"*Murder*?" I shuddered. "No, some lost soul made a place for himself sitting up against the elevator. He died in his sleep. Probably of exposure...maybe he had a heart attack."

"No, Ken. It was murder. A broken neck tells a story. Maybe I didn't learn much at the morgue, but one time, Uncle Gary let me help him with the prep. I'll never forget how it felt. There's a certain change in the quality of the muscles. Anyway, I could tell something didn't align properly. Oh, yes, his skull was fractured, too."

My head spun in tight circles. A dead man on our site. My heart beat faster. How could this happen? And why would Edison move the body? Didn't he have any common sense? Doesn't every adult know that you don't *move* a dead body? Doesn't he watch TV? *Don't leave the scene of an accident. Don't touch fallen electrical wires. And don't move a dead body.*

His eyes continued their erratic motion. "Let me tell you what happened next."

"There's more?"

"Yeah, I moved the truck over underneath the edge of the parking deck near the body. I found a pile of cardboard and some plastic sheets at the site and laid them in the back of the pick-up truck. Then I went back up there. Luckily they haven't put that rail up yet next to the stairs. I kicked him over the edge, into the back of the truck. He didn't have far to fall from the second level, only a few feet to the truck. I pulled the bed cover over the top of him and snapped it on, so that no one would see."

"I didn't know your truck had a bed cover." The moment the words were out of my mouth, the realization hit me. Forcibly trying to stay calm, I lowered my voice. "You put the body into our *company* truck?"

He nodded sheepishly.

"I just thought...it seemed like...I just thought I'd drive him a few miles away, and dump him into the woods over by Stony Creek."

"You touched a dead body. You didn't call the police. Then you moved a body. Do you know how many crimes you must have committed? As if that wasn't enough, you put it in the company truck."

Edison nodded his head up and down slowly.

"I can't believe this. You go out to do a simple job inspection, and now.... Not only did you get yourself in trouble, but you've put the company in an untenable position. Who's going to believe we weren't involved in moving the body off site?" Edison exhaled a weighty sigh. Moments passed. We looked at each other silently. "You might as well tell me the rest of it."

"I went back to see if anything needed cleaning up."

"Was there?"

"I noticed a little smear of blood on the wall. Not so the casual construction worker would observe. That elevator wall has yet to be painted anyway. And the guy had relieved himself. Did you know you do that when you die? A small stain marked the location. It didn't seem like enough to bother with. Well, when I got back downstairs, Robert was there."

"Robert?"

"Westin. He almost gave me a heart attack."

Having your boss, not to mention an owner of the firm, appear when you're moving a dead body would spook anyone. I closed my eyes.

"He and Andrew had come out to look at the project. I guess those guys don't take any time off." Andrew was the senior partner in our firm. What were they doing at the jobsite two days after Christmas?

Edison continued, "They started asking me questions, and so I was dragged into showing them around the project. All the while, I was desperate to leave and dump that body. Finally, they'd seen enough and I thought I could get on with it. All of a sudden Andrew explained that he was late picking Smartain up at the airport. Robert suggested that Andrew go right to the airport from there, and he would catch a ride back with me."

I stared at him incredulously. "You drove Robert back to the office with the body in the truck?"

Edison nodded. "What could I do? It wasn't like I could tell him 'no.' Back in the office, I kept looking for an opportunity to sneak out to the truck, but things kept coming up. Around four o'clock I finally dropped everything and went out there. The truck was gone."

"*Disappeared?*"

"No, not like that. Wally had signed out the truck. He was gone for the rest of the day. I guess Wally sweet-talked Rita into giving him the other set of keys."

A drop of sweat rolled down my back. Slumping back in my chair, I said, "Edison, I can't take any more. Where is the body now?"

"It's still in the truck. Gwen took it home over New Year's. As soon as she gets here...."

I was shaking. I didn't want to move. It was hot. My

eyes closed. I could feel the vein in my neck pounding against the collar of my shirt. "I passed Gwen at the coffee pot as I came in." I braced myself and stood on unsteady knees. Edison looked disoriented. He sat expectantly in his chair, hands braced on the armrests. "Let's get out to the parking lot now," I said with a dry mouth, "and take care of this business before somebody discovers what's in that truck."

We walked deliberately through the office, grabbing our coats along the way. As we approached the back doors, I peered out the window. There sat the white company pick-up truck on the opposite side of the lot. The truck's bed cover was pulled back. Gwen stood at the side of the truck, reaching into the bed and fiddling with the contents. I pointed out the window. "What is she doing?"

Edison looked dumbfounded. "I don't know."

"Let's find out." It was the last thing I wanted to do, but what choice did we have? My stomach convulsed as I opened the door. Gwen had moved to the back end of the vehicle, her petite body bent over, reaching into the truck bed with her gloved hands. For a moment my sensibilities were overcome. Gwen's layered, copper-colored hair barely touched her shoulders. I admired her athletic back, which accented the the lines of her stylish winter coat. My eyes were drawn to her tight black skirt, which played intriguingly at the edge of her three-quarter length coat. Edison and I stepped up on either side of her as we approached and looked into the bed. Arranged neatly side-by-side were sixteen full-sized gold shovels and three large boxes of white hardhats.

There was no sign of the body.

Chapter 2
Grim Groundbreaking

"Are you ready Ken? Everything is set on my end." Gwen turned her startling blue eyes up at me, while spreading her velvety lips into a disarming smile.

Gwen Hillsdale was an associate in the firm and one of the treasures of the office. Three project managers, including Wally Johnson and yours truly, reported to her.

But I barely heard her melodious voice through the fog in my head. What happened to the body? Ready for what? Where did it go? Did someone move it? How could this be happening? Did someone find it? If so, why wasn't there some big commotion at the office? What the hell did it mean?

Cold pecking at my cheeks brought me back to the present. A light dusting of snow had appeared overnight, and now gusts of wind were driving the hard little snow pellets every which way. It was oddly refreshing.

"Edison, can I help you with something?" Gwen leaned against the back of the truck, tiny snowflakes peppering the fuzzy edges of her charcoal coat. The feminine lines of her petite dark figure contrasted against the hard white truck behind her.

The groundbreaking, of course. Olsen House. Monday, January 3. Today. "Yes, Gwen, we should be going. Um...I thought it would be good for Edison...you know, as part of his training, to come along and see one of these ceremonies in person." I struggled to concentrate, speak normally. Maintain the facade.

Gwen pursed her full lips, giving him the once-over, then turned a narrow glance to me. Her dark upcurled lashes balanced tiny snowballs. As if arriving at a decision, her broad smile returned. "Wonderful! Edison, I'm thrilled that you want to take this opportunity to learn. It'll be a bit snug in the truck, but hop in. Robert and Andrew will meet us on site after their breakfast meeting with the folks from Olsen House." Gingerly, Gwen stepped around to the driver's side. I opened the passenger door and maneuvered into the cab, sliding across the bench seat next to her, while Edison parked his ample carriage to my right. Though I was happy for the cozy seat next to Gwen, in my disoriented state it was difficult to completely enjoy her presence.

"Of course, they'd do some schmoozing beforehand," Edison observed.

"Think of it as allowing our glow to remove the shadows from their faces. Our excitement and enthusiasm can remove the doubt and hesitancy," Gwen responded. "Groundbreaking for a new, one point eight million dollar home for abused children. Politicians. City officials. The Press will jump in on this one too. A tremendous occasion to make a change."

As Gwen cut through traffic and began our twenty minute drive from our Southfield office to the Troy project site, I mentally reviewed the events that Edison had described. When he visited the construction site on the twenty-seventh he found a dead body, put it in the company truck and returned to the office. While Edison was busy with—whatever—Wally checked out the vehicle.

Wally's abrasive personality put many people off, including me. Opinionated, stubborn and tactless, his manner incessantly grated on my nerves. Yet, he was one of the firm's most effective project managers. Tough assignments found their way to his desk. I knew that with six kids he'd wanted to take some time off at the end of the year. I had to twist his arm with an old favor to gain his agreement to look over Edison's shoulder and review the payment application before leaving for the holiday. It sounded like something big had come up on the Brighton job. I remembered my Mental Note (#1) to inquire about it.

Gwen took home the vehicle for New Year's weekend. Where was the truck between the twenty-seventh and the thirty-first? It was company policy that no one was to take the truck home overnight unless there was an extraordinary reason for it. What caused her to bend the rules? Mental Notes #2a and 2b: question the two people who had possession of the truck during the last week, Wally and Gwen.

I sighed. My unchecked phone messages wouldn't let go of their grasp on my awareness. Those calls had to be returned soon.

Gwen and I began our employment at BPW Architects one autumn, two weeks apart, some eight years ago. We became acquainted quickly and were frequently assigned to the same projects. We often worked late into the evening. Gwen's husband Douglas, a mortgage loan officer, worked extended hours as well. Gwen would coordinate with Douglas, or one of her neighbors, to assure that her two pre-teen boys were cared after. After the office cleared out, Gwen and I would remove a few courses of brick from the professional wall between us and share with each other. We'd talk about music, fitness, and movies. I enjoyed adventure and spy thrillers, completely taken with *The Bourne Supremacy*, a movie she couldn't care less about. She was intrigued with period pieces like *Being Julia* and *Finding Neverland*. Those movies bore me, and our verbal sparring grew from amusement to absorption. On occasion, we'd find agreement in cinema that blurred genre lines such as *Million Dollar*

Baby or *50 First Dates*. Then again, who wouldn't be taken with Adam Sandler seeking romance with Drew Barrymore? The gut wrenching twist left us both breathless.

During this time, I shared an intimate detail of my life which I'd previously tucked away in a secret mental vault. Three years after my divorce—I was married for six years during my twenties, no children—I fell deeply in love with a co-worker. Sheila and I basked in two-and-a-half years of bliss before suffering an abrupt ending that cut me to the quick. One day she dragged me into the conference room at work, no privacy, no intimate moment, and told me that we were through. She'd changed her mind. Done. Finito! Having suffered unforgiving torment at the hands of a co-worker-turned-lover, and then forcing myself to remain courteous during our workdays, caused me to endure months of anguish. Through circumstances not related to the job, I left the firm a short while later. I swore that I would *never ever* involve myself with a co-worker again.

Gwen's caring compassion soothed a bit of the old scar and my vulnerability opened up new personal ground between us.

Four years ago, devastation occurred. Gwen and Douglas miss-coordinated, and both were working evening hours, neither tending to the kids. Gwen received a frantic call from the neighbor. No one had come home to relieve her, and now she was late preparing for a family dinner. She was willing to help out, but wouldn't be taken advantage of on her family's special night. Gwen called Douglas, and, though speaking in hushed tones, I could tell it was something of an argument. Gwen insisted she couldn't leave work, as our project was due the next morning. Douglas lost that exchange, and agreed to dash home. An hour later, the neighbor called again: where was Douglas?

Irritated, Gwen phoned her husband to no avail. An outraged Gwen left for home. En route, she received a call from the hospital. Douglas had been broadsided and arrived at the hospital in critical condition.

Douglas died the next day.

At the funeral, Gwen appeared composed and proper, but her emotions were veiled. Understandably unavailable, we traded superficial words. I offered her my listening when she was ready. The real Gwen didn't reveal herself until several weeks later.

One night she telephoned and I invited her to my home. She arrived shaken and morose. It was her time to fall apart. She had been strong for her children, but now she needed to find her own ground. Gwen blamed herself for the accident, for her temper, for her career, most of all for causing him to rush home. The finality of it left her aghast. She longed to explain to Douglas, apologize, come to understanding. But there was no such availability. A stupor enshrouded her, from which she couldn't rouse herself.

During the ensuing months, I watched her regain her balance and care for her two boys. She took them to a support group for children who had experienced loss. During this time, she and I resumed our late night connections, and I grew to think about Gwen in more personal terms. *Very personal.* Perhaps we had the kind of connection that could ripen into love. But how long after a woman experiences the loss of her husband is an appropriate waiting period? And did I dare break my long-standing rule about not dating co-workers?

But I missed it.

As I finally convinced myself to move forward, Gwen involved herself with Robert Westin. At fifty-eight, he was the youngest of the firm's principals. The evening I planned to broach the idea of an "official" date, Gwen revealed her new relationship. I was flabbergasted. Jealous. Angry.

Of course, they kept it low-key.

I awoke from my pondering to realize that Gwen had been talking, and tuned-in as she said, "Ken, I believe a lunch outing will seal the deal, don't you agree?"

"Of course, Gwen." My glance of her soft cheek and sweet lips was held a moment too long.... Who had I agreed to have lunch with? No matter, my top priority was to find my way out of the mess that Edison had plunged us into.

"How was your New Year's?" I probed.

"Oh it was legendary!" She smiled. "The boys had some friends over, a rambunctious crowd, four boys and a couple of girls. I smile at their innocent bravery. They set up an impromptu jam session in the garage, and ran around the back yard laughing and joking with each other, from all appearances unencumbered by the frigid weather. I invited a half dozen couples, including two of my high school girlfriends, and we had a blast sharing adventures we've had through the year. I haven't seen Becky and Sandi for about three years, but it's astonishing how it feels true and honest, as if the shadow of time has not touched us." Her eyes slid my way. "I heard that yours wasn't so good."

Her words smacked me in the face like a cold mackerel. "I've had better." Truth was, I'd watched the New Year's Eve TV coverage from a mattress on the floor of my new bedroom, with a 13-inch screen sitting on the floor next to me. I'd moved into my latest home renovation project on Christmas Eve, leaving my freshly completed project behind. Relocating myself into a handyman special precipitated the *Christmas Incident*. After that nasty argument with my girlfriend, I wasn't about to hang around and put myself through anger, resentment and guilt while Mary celebrated Christmas with her family. I pointed the car toward

South Carolina. A few days away from everyone, cell phone turned off, and I almost forgot about Mary and the aggravation she caused me.

Perhaps cutting myself off from all communication was an exercise in poor judgment (Mary would have called it childish), but my mind called for peace.

After that knock-down-drag-out fight, there wasn't anything keeping me here for the holidays. My sister, Karen, took time off from her radio show and, husband and kids in tow, had driven to Pennsylvania to visit her in-laws. My widowed father (it's been six years since Mom passed on) flew to New York to check out "the greatest legs in the world."

Myrtle Beach welcomed me. The fourteen hour drive itself was cathartic. Time to re-evaluate my relationship, my priorities, my dreams of improving the neighborhood. What did I really want, and what was I willing to give up? The beach was serene, though chilly. Buns against the sand, watching the sun rise and hearing the ocean waves break soothed my nerves and righted my head.

I returned with time to celebrate the New Year on the mattress, a glass of Piesporter in my hand. It tasted a little flat as I bemoaned my state of affairs. But how could I reveal my misery to Gwen today?

What I offered was, "I hope you weren't working like Wally was, over the holidays." Morning sun, streaming through the windshield, glanced off her copper hair, accenting the natural angles of her tender cheekbones. Time to act on Mental Note #2b. "I heard you had the truck checked out. With so many of you working, I'm feeling disproportionately guilty for my ten-day vacation."

Gwen's face froze for an instant, her head held still as an opossum. Then she re-animated. The pause was so quick I almost missed it. "No," she said, "my car was in the shop and I needed some wheels for the weekend."

"Wheels? I had some great *wheels* last week." Edison constantly heckled Gwen about her use of '60s language. Suddenly excited, he said, "A '69 Cady DeVille. Factory pink—*Wisteria*. White leather interior, 472 engine. That ride was boss!"

Gwen smiled stiffly at Edison's tease, yet the underlying film of tension remained.

Desperately, I wanted to quiz her on the facts surrounding her taking the truck, but I didn't dare press my luck. Why was her BMW in the shop? And why had she hesitated? MN #2b's resolution was incomplete.

We pulled up to the groundbreaking site, a two-and-a-half acre parcel of land on Crooks Road, two blocks north of Maple in the booming city of Troy. Three years ago, it had been dozed clear to make way for development. Before construction began, local residents filed a lawsuit that pleaded NIMBY—Not in My Back Yard. What were they afraid of? The new building would house abused children, not murderers. As one motion countered another, the case dragged on, the lawyers playing a game of *would/would-not*. Both sides plead emotional arguments. A judge brought the case to a close and here we were, ready for the groundbreaking.

Jumping the curb, we parked adjacent to the contractor's job trailer. A dozen vehicles were lined up already. We picked up the first load of hardhats and shovels. The ceremony ground was a bit contrived, as the contractor had scraped off the snow and put down 12 inches of clean sand. A small stage, "red carpet," and an American flag completed the set. To one side, a plywood sign displayed a vibrant, brightly colored rendering of the one-story contemporary building. Edison designed that sign. Perhaps he was an idiot. Maybe he had absolutely no common sense when it came to moving dead bodies, but he was a graphic artist with a sense for color, proportion, and style that coaxed a project sign to nearly sing. Perhaps it was *that* graphic, visual talent, illustrated in his interview presentation, I found so impressive that I hired him on the spot.

I won't employ anyone lacking the basic qualities of initiative and common sense. Everything else can be learned. Somehow, Edison's graphic skills overshadowed the fact that he had only a modicum of common sense. Having hired him, it was incumbent upon me to prove that I'd made a wise decision. The project sign in front of me was a positive affirmation of that hire. Edison's periodic botches and the stunt *du jour* revealed not only his incompetence, but reflected on mine.

Snow crunched underfoot as we lugged hardhats and shovels across the field. For a moment, a small crowd garnered my sympathy as folks stood there in the snow, cold wind whipping at their skin. Cynically, I wondered how many were in support of this project, and which ones were there to catch a glimpse of the celebrities.

Weaver Construction's job trailer was generously proportioned, a wide-bodied unit, boasting a huge conference table two steps inside the door. I smelled coffee brewing as we hurried inside. My taste buds snapped to attention, and I realized that I hadn't had my first cup of java yet. I perused the surroundings. The table before us was set-up to seat eighteen on metal folding chairs. Four feet across, the table pushed chairs nearly to the walls. Overcoats, briefcases and planners lay about on the sparse furniture. A plan rack was located to the right. Long metal binders were clamped to thick stacks of drawings and hung on the metal framework. A separate "stick" was used for each work trade: plumbing, electrical, and so on. The coffee machine and bottled water sat beside the project plans. A small office opened to the right, with two men standing by the desk motioning excitedly to the third, who spoke on the phone, an exasperated expression on his wrinkled, sun-hardened face.

To the left, a clerical desk, the toilet room, and another office, this one larger than the first. Men in tailored pinstripe suits and women in elegant outfits bustled around. The scent of expensive perfume slapped me in the face. Several smaller groups had crowded inside. Voices blurred together, hurried phrases competing for attention in unintelligible layers. Gwen shimmied back to join them while I set my sights on the coffee. Edison watched me silently out of the corner of his eye, then reminded me of the additional shovels in the truck. Reluctantly, I agreed to postpone my indulgence.

Two men in black overcoats and a smartly dressed woman entered as we exited into the cold. A few minutes later, we returned, depositing the gold shovels on the platform stage. We squeezed into the trailer to find Gwen returning from the rear office, a stunned and perplexed look on her face.

"What's the story, Gwen?" I asked.

"Oh, it's the usual mad rush coordinating the details prior to an event like this." Her face expressed more exasperation than her words admitted. "Isabelle was tasked to phone each of the speakers to verify they would arrive on time. She never arrived at work this morning, and now we have three VIPs in the no-show column. I swear, I'll never schedule an event like this again, coming right off a holiday week." The small gathering in the back room broke up and everyone came out, ready for the ceremonies to begin. Twenty people crowded around the table and introductions were made.

Charmaine Holstrum, Olsen House Director of Community Relations, explained briefly the order of events. Her olive green suit played nicely against her coffee-colored skin, an orange and black silk scarf loosely circling her neck. She recounted the missing VIPs: Barry Hart, the well-known entrepreneur who had contributed significantly to the project; State Senator Henderson; Isiah Thomas, Detroit Piston champion point guard, most recently head coach for the New York Knicks. Crisply, she directed the re-ordering of the speeches to accommodate the missing VIPs.

Afterward, Howard Birch, president of Olsen House, took the floor and said, "This day marks a milestone in the life of Olsen House. The new facilities will not only act as a refuge for sixty children, but a place where they will receive love, tenderness and compassion. This delineates the beginning of that retreat. Shall we proceed?" Mumbling acceptance. "Let's fire it up!"

Senator Henderson arrived in time to present his speech in the desired order. Isiah Thomas pulled up in his green Hummer shortly after the event began. I learned from the discussion on the platform that he'd contributed heavily in time and money to this project. One hour later, the program concluded without an obvious hitch.

Edison and I rambled over to join the crowd as the dignitaries arranged themselves in a line-up, wearing hard hats and leaning on gold shovels. In front, our own Robert Westin and partner Andrew Pieks. Eleven men. Four women. Fifteen hard hats. And fifteen gold shovels. What a sight.

And still no Barry Hart.

Photographers from the *Tribune*, the *Free Press*, and *The News* took in the ceremony, as well as a reporter and cameraman from *Channel 4*. A couple of patriotic songs, sung by local sensation Michelle Wilson, roused the crowd. She's blonde, beautiful, and has a dynamite voice. More words about people helping each other. Doing good things. One kind act leading to another and changing the world a step-at-a-time. It all made you feel good inside, despite the cold weather. The azure sky and dainty white clouds would make for perfect publicity photographs.

A sudden wind shift sent a pleasant chill up my spine. Gwen's vanilla scent, from twenty yards away, caught my attention. Interesting how the wind can carry fragrance over a distance. Olfactory stimulus traveling through the air. I wondered about the dead man. Wouldn't a body, several days old, begin to smell? Of course, it had been bitter cold. If the truck were kept outdoors, would the body be frozen and therefore not stink? If someone had parked the truck in an attached garage instead, would that environment be warm enough to thaw a body?

Photographers took dozens of photographs. Newsmen and -women asked questions. Everyone, including the audience, was invited to walk a block north and across Crooks Road to O'Shea's for a reception. The crowd began to amble away en masse. A social reprieve would also give me an opportunity to act on MN #2a and question Wally about the truck.

Most of us took the pedestrian route, hoofing it to the restaurant. Edison wandered over to catch Isiah Thomas, the pair climbing into Isiah's Hummer. It never ceases to amaze me that Edison is personally acquainted with so many celebrities, from sports stars to TV personalities to divas and rap artists.

The O'Shea's banquet room awaited us, with an elaborate arrangement of hors d'oeuvres, tropical flowers and the aroma of my delayed coffee. A bartender was available too. After checking my coat, I noticed that Edison and Mr. Thomas were still giggling together. In the corner of the room, Gwen was engaged in an animated conversation with Sally Jenkins. Deciding to use the free moment to my advantage, I wove my way over to Wally, who was engaged in conversation with Michelle Wilson. He seemed to be listening in rapt attention, eyes, jaw, and head focused on the stunning blonde before him. His fingers played and twisted idly behind his back. Finally, he spoke a few words which had the effect of causing her to drop her smile, do a quick "Hmpf," and turn on her heels.

Wally moved in my direction, and with a sideward glance and a dirty laugh, muttered, "Sorry, Cannoli, I couldn't resist telling her how much her performance moves, underneath that outfit, turned me on."

I let the comment pass. I ignored the nickname too. Several years earlier, someone at BPW Architects had taken my name—Ken Knoll—and coined this unflattering nickname. The reference alluded to my pot belly and six-foot-one-inch frame. I took the positive approach. "Hey, Wally, happy New Year." We shook hands. "How were the holidays?"

Wally was one of three project managers under Gwen's stewardship. His team was currently engaged in a number of projects, including the six million dollar renovation of Brighton Mall.

"Busy as hell. All the family dropping by the house. Final shopping. Decorating the rec room. I finished the bar in the nick of time. Lots of kid stuff. When you've got six, there's always something. Of course, you focus on having the older ones help the younger ones. But Trevor is so stubborn and independent anymore that he's in punishment more than he's able to help out.... I hear you had a rift with your honey."

Crap. How did he find that out? "Well, Christmas tends to stimulate the emotions," I said acerbically.

"Cannoli, I'll give you some advice. For free. Get

yourself a real place, and stop living in a construction zone. Women don't like to put up with all that shit. There's beautiful houses all over town. A single guy like you, you should have a grand old place, with a big country kitchen that opens into a greatroom. One of those humongous stone fireplaces, and a doorwall that leads onto a redwood deck overlooking a landscaped yard, with a little waterfall spilling over a stone wall into a lily pond.

"And another thing. Dig into your wallet and shell out for some nice furniture. None of that garage sale stuff that you keep carting around."

The veins in my temple throbbed. "Wally, I got enough of this from Mary and her parents. Do I have to listen to it from you, too?" I glared at him. He opened his mouth, then apparently thought better of it. He took a deep breath.

I decided I'd better change the subject to MN #1. "What happened on that pay application for Flamingo Shores? I was counting on you to help Edison with the job inspection."

"I was going to do that, wasn't I?" His edge disappeared. "Shi-it," he said in two syllables. "So many emergencies came up last week. Claudia's aunt was shuttled to Beaumont the day after Christmas with her high blood pressure, and all hell broke loose at Brighton Mall. I told Edison to walk the project and take a boatload of pictures. Afterward, he and I could go through the numbers at the office. If anything sounded off, I'd stop by the site myself."

"Sounds like you had a busy week during the holidays. That must have been tough," I said.

"Oh, you don't know the half of it. Grissim Construction began their work way out on the perimeter, to stay out of the way of holiday shoppers."

"Yeah, it's surprising that we have all this

construction going on during the holidays anyway."

"With the schedules we've got to meet? Don't tell me about options. They don't exist. If they don't have that multiplex open for Memorial Day weekend there'll be hell to pay. Of course we're starting a month late due to that permit hiccup. Thank God for the mild weather, well, up until today. Anyway, they were running the backhoe along, digging out for the foundations, and ripped up an eighteen-inch storm line. Busted clean through and all that water drenched the excavation. The existing drawings weren't accurate and all of those pipes led to who-knows-where. So I spent half my holiday week on-site sorting things out. That was a real trick. I couldn't reach the surveyor who'd originally done the utility survey." He paused, a grotesque frown taking over his face. "Then in the middle of it, that damn truck broke down on me."

That rose my attention. "Truck? What happened to the truck?"

"That piece of shit up and quit. I'm cruising along and it starts shaking like a wildebeest. Suddenly, it won't go over 50. No matter how much I stomp on the accelerator, the speed starts creeping down and I'm thinking it's going to stall right on the freeway. So I cut through two lanes of traffic, made the exit ramp, and coasted into a repair shop on Wixom Road."

I struggled to hide my excitement. "What day was that?"

Wally peered at me through narrow little chicken eyes. His skinny, shriveled, face and hook nose completed the image of an unhappy fowl. "It was holiday week. The Monday after Christmas. I went with Claudia to the hospital to see her aunt in the morning. I didn't pull in to work until after one o'clock. Checked out the truck and then that shit happened. What a stinkin' day."

"What happened at the shop?"

"They were backed up. I had to leave the damn thing there. I talked Tony Grissim into sending one of his guys over to pick me up. It's a real hassle trying to get around without a vehicle."

"Yeah, so you got the truck back the next day?"

"No, turned out it was the transmission. It took them all week to fix. God-damn truck!" Wally glanced behind me as he spoke, and began shifting his weight from one foot to the other.

"All week? Didn't you get the truck back?"

"They didn't finish 'til midday Thursday. I was taking Friday off. There was no way I was missing New Year's Eve with my kids. Joshua and Sam had been looking forward to that for a month."

"I see. So how did the truck get back to the office?"

"What is this, twenty questions? Cannoli, I'm otta here. See ya."

He was off. His story left more blanks open than it filled-in. If Wally was telling the truth, he didn't have time to find a body in the truck bed. And now there were new people to consider. MN #2 was growing by the minute. What about the repair shop? Did they find the body? Who picked up the truck on Thursday? Someone from the office? Did they find anything? Let's make MN #2c checking with the repair shop to see what they know.

Edison!

I sighed, realizing that I was hungry. I hadn't availed myself of the goodies yet. My watch said one-fifteen and I hadn't had a cup of coffee or my midmorning snack. I made a beeline for the food table. On my way, I glanced over to the corner of the room where Gwen had been five minutes earlier. No Gwen. Scanning the room briefly, she didn't seem to be anywhere among the guests. I continued to the buffet table. Fresh salad, cabbage rolls, string beans with almonds, broiled whitefish, broasted potatoes, fried mushrooms, fresh hard rolls. On the dessert table: cheese cake, chocolate truffle torte, peach cobbler. My stomach was delirious with anticipation.

The moment I picked up a plate, Gwen appeared at my side. She slid her hand into mine and pulled me away from the table. Steering me silently through the crowd, she led me out of the banquet room into an unoccupied office. She shut the door behind me, raised her baby blues to mine and put a hand on my chest. My heart raced in expectation, then I registered her pasty white face and trembling lip.

"We've got to go now," she whispered hoarsely. "They've found a dead body at the Crystals job site."

Chapter 3
Dead in a Doorway

The upscale department store Crystals was under construction at the tail end of Flamingo Shores. Located in the high-end part of town, the shopping venue was miles from a shore of any kind. So why the name? Perhaps the image of a hundred pink flamingos on a sunny beach made shoppers feel comforted somehow. Residents didn't want the ugly mall image in their town. The project was not a *mall*, not a *shopping center,* simply a collection of fine mercantile establishments and posh specialty stores.

The Crystals site was choked with activity. A uniformed police officer blocked entry to the Coolidge construction entrance, his car parked crossways on the gravel driveway. Post-holiday shoppers attempted to enter through this side approach, seeking to avoid the heavy traffic jamming up the Big Beaver Road entrance.

I tried to make sense of the current situation. What was the body doing back at the jobsite? Or was it someone else unfortunate enough to end up dead? I found it difficult to imagine two deaths on the same site within a matter of days. In my twenty years as an architect there was only one fatality at a construction site with which I was even remotely connected. It happened almost a decade ago, involving the tragic demise of a construction worker knocked unconscious by a steel joist which struck him in the head as the crane was lowering the joist into place. The cable slipped—a mere thirty-six inches—as the workman walked underneath. He fell to instant death.

Flamingo Shores was barbell-shaped in plan, an anchor store at each end connected by smaller stores in a straight line between them. This follows classic mall theory: one of the anchor stores will attract the customer. Completing his trip to the first anchor, the shopper will transverse the mall to the other anchor store, shopping at the smaller businesses along the way. The barbell was laid out east-west, parallel to Big Beaver Road, with a surface lot between the stores and the street. Macy's stood to the east, built as a Hudson's around 1960, when the Detroit-based merchant branched out from its downtown location into the suburbs. JCPenney anchors the west end of the mall. Originally built as two stories, JCPenney was expanded to three floors as the suburbs expanded in size and pocketbooks grew. At that time, a parking deck was constructed to the north.

Today, shopping designers believe the more anchors, the better. Three, four, five, even six. Flamingo Shores' latest addition provided a new leg to the original mall area, extending perpendicular from the center of the mall, and the new Crystals department store, at the end of the new mall leg for a total of three. Had the site not been landlocked, a fourth anchor store would have been added. The new parking deck, with pedestrian bridges to Crystals and to the mall, was located between Macy's to the south, Crystals to the north and the new mall leg to the west.

Construction traffic was directed to access the site from the Coolidge Road entrance at the northwest corner of the site, continuing east along a gravel construction road that circled around to the north of Crystals, then turned south to pass on the east side of the new parking deck. The deck jutted out beyond the

Crystals building. It was in the "L" formed by the east edge of Crystals and the north edge of the parking deck that contained the elevator where Edison had found his dead man. The most remote part of the site, this area was separated from the occupied mall by 230,000 square feet of uncompleted retail area and parking structure.

The police officer ahead of us was in heated discussion with the driver of a black van. Graphics on the van's exterior told me Elvis Electrical would get me "All Hooked Up." White-jump-suited Elvis watched expectantly as his microphone was energized by an electrician on his hands and knees plugging in his power chord. Cute.

Emphatically refusing to let him pass, the policeman motioned the workman to park on the unpaved strip of property to the left. Twitching the hand that hung out the window, the contractor gestured impatiently.

"This is a country mile from Crystals!" Edison noted, "The workers have a real hike to carry their equipment to the construction." Gwen and I nodded our agreement.

The policeman calmly held his ground. In the end, the electrician gave up and pulled off to the side. Accelerating quickly through the turn, his truck fishtailed angrily, spewing snow in front of us. We advanced and Gwen lowered her window.

"Hello, Officer." Gwen handed him her card. "We're from the office of BPW Architects, the architects for the project. I understand a body's been found."

The police officer studied the card. "Yes, Ms. Hillsdale. I'm afraid I can't admit your vehicle. We're in the process of investigating the scene. You can go on around by foot, but mind the taped off areas." Beyond the police car, I could see a portion of the road was encircled in bright yellow police tape. I noted the luminous yellow ribbon was remarkably similar to "Caution" tape used in the construction industry.

My mind was numb. I felt weak, glad Gwen was driving. I longed to go home and crawl into bed, even if it was a mattress on the floor, pull the covers over my head and enjoy numb sleep for a good three days.

"Officer, who can we check in with to discern the details of your investigation here?" Gwen sighed heavily.

"Lieutenant Coogan is in charge, ma'am." The policeman pointed toward the new Crystals department store. "He's up on the second level of the parking deck."

"Thank you, Officer," she smiled tentatively.

Gwen pulled off to the left, in line with a dozen other vehicles in the crunchy snow. The electrical contractor had opened the rear doors of his van. He and his lanky assistant were grappling with a couple of large coils of wire, attempting to extricate them from the van.

Edison announced his departure, then went over to give the two contractors a hand.

Gwen and I gave each other knowing looks.

Alighting from the vehicle, Gwen's fashionable black boots broke through the snow's crispy crust to the soft powder underneath.

We trudged through the snow, past the JCPenney parking lot, to Crystals. Much of the center portion of the gravel construction drive was removed from service with the "Police Line Do Not Cross" tape attached to poles anchored by sand bags. The four-story Crystals building was faced in buff-colored oversize brick punctuated by horizontal bands of Indiana limestone. A protruding stone coping angled to meet the sky. Our expected point of entry, the vestibule entrance on the corner near the truck well, was blocked by a trim uniformed policeman standing guard as if he were a sentry at Buckingham Palace.

Disinclined to engage the staunch guard, we walked around behind the building, to a skylight-topped drop-off entrance. Blasts of wind whipped through our clothes. Gwen shivered. Peeking through the glass entry, we discovered a policeman there also.

"The police presence amazes me. Do they have the whole building blocked off? How will the contractor get any work done?" I complained.

"They're not."

I turned around to see Robert Westin, who must have followed us from the groundbreaking reception. Robert's short salt and pepper hair lent credibility to his position, while his classic well-chiseled face and Robert Redford smile suited him for marketing duties. Clients tended to like him and his stories always brought the house down. Somehow, even the white puffs of cold air that escaped from his lips today enhanced his air of distinction.

Yet his take-charge attitude and inability to mince words when correcting an employee didn't endear him to me. Neither did his treatment of Gwen. After two years together, an unpleasant quarrel had recently— days after Thanksgiving—led to the disintegration of their union. Rumor had it that Robert retaliated by trying to remove Gwen from the office, but she was an Associate and had the allegiance of Andrew Pieks, the senior partner at BPW.

Robert ranted, "This police presence will tie the job up for weeks. With all the areas they've cordoned off, working to any degree of efficiency will be impossible." He was dressed in a grey overcoat with a black wool scarf.

Gwen favored Robert with a dead stare. When she briefly caught his eye, he responded by looking away.

A man wearing a charcoal peacoat appeared from around the corner. In his mid-fifties, he was of medium build with a round, red, face and a fringe of white hair. With deliberate steps, he approached our group and came to a stop.

"Hello, I'm Lieutenant Coogan. And you all are?" His face, open, available, looked from one of us to the next. His pink cheeks reflected the chilly environment.

Robert said, "Are you in charge here? How long do you expect to have things tied up? We have an aggressive deadline on this job and you've shut down all of these areas."

Lt. Coogan responded matter-of-factly, his brown peepers taking in Robert's features. "I'm sorry, but I didn't get your name." He paused.

"It's Robert. Robert Westin. I'm the chief architect." His azure eyes twinkled in persuasion. *I'm in charge,* they seemed to say, *give way to me.*

"Mr. Westin, what we have here is a murder scene. I didn't create the murder, or precipitate it on this property. It occurred here and this is where it will be investigated. We will do our work efficiently. We will execute our investigation in a professional and thorough manner. Perhaps you didn't ask for a murder to be committed here, certainly we didn't. But we all must conduct ourselves according to the conditions that we encounter. Is that clear?"

"Well, I didn't mean that you could do anything about it." Robert brought out one of his charming smiles. *Let's get along,* it said. *Do things my way, and life will be easy.*

Lt. Coogan waved his fleshy hand in dismissal.

"I simply meant that this is going to tie us up. The construction schedule has already been delayed, and this is going to hamper us further."

"Mr. Westin, I've been through all of those

implications with Chuck Hagar. Understandably, he exuded apprehension, and I accept your misgivings as well. At the moment, the most expedient course of action is to perform the investigation. Work through it. Then you and your people can get back to work. In the meantime, I'm going to miss my wife's legendary peanut pot roast."

For a moment, Westin stood and stared, then he turned his smile up a notch. *Play it my way and we'll both get what we want.*

Chuck Hagar, the senior associate at Pontile Construction, was known for his temper. In a meeting once, Hagar brought his fist down so hard that he splintered the wood table. Without a doubt, he'd given the Lieutenant some grief over the delay in schedule this investigation would certainly cause.

Lt. Coogan turned to Gwen and me. "If you people would please wait for me in the construction job trailer, I believe Jason has some hot coffee brewing. I'm going to have a few words with Mr. Westin so he can return to his busy schedule. Would you mind a moment, Mr. Westin?"

Robert's eyebrows pinched together to close his face down, soft blue eyes turning hard as forged steel. "Do whatever you wish to get this jobsite untied and rolling so that construction can continue as soon as possible."

Gwen and I occupied ourselves in the job trailer. Jason Tyler, a rather nimble and spirited superintendent, made a quick pot of coffee before being summoned out to the job by the drywall subcontractor. Gwen slid out her cell, and made her way to the back office. Edison trudged in, stomping snow from his hiking boots. In a puzzling move, he pulled up a stick of architectural drawings and studied the project details. Mighty industrious of him, considering the kind of day we were experiencing.

Two cups of coffee later, Lt. Coogan's lumbering body appeared at the door. No sign of Robert Westin. For a moment, Coogan paused, stubby fingers pensively rubbing his ear.

"Will you all follow me to the parking deck?" His voice was firm.

Silently, we stomped through two inches of snow, up the stairs beside the elevator, to the parking deck's third floor. The railing encircling the third floor stair opening had not yet been installed. As we walked past the elevator, Gwen stumbled. I caught her elbow before she went down. As I helped her regain her balance, I glanced back with a chill, realizing that this would have been where Edison had discovered the body on the floor below. He and I exchanged nervous glances.

We approached a glass-enclosed breezeway connecting the deck to Crystals' second floor entrance. Yellow police tape crisscrossed the glass and bronze-anodized aluminum doors. Inside, two men knelt, examining the vestibule floor.

"Let's go through here," Lt. Coogan pointed to a flush metal door off to the side. Eventually, this door would admit employees into the bowels of the shopping center.

We entered what would become an office area, steel studs exposed, metal conduit snaking through the framing to the electrical outlets. The floor, littered with cardboard boxes, screws, sheet metal scraps, and wire cuttings, required strict attention beneath our feet. Soda cans and foam coffee cups dappled the work area as well.

We wound our way through the maze of offices until we reached the sales area. It continued on for almost two hundred feet in either direction. Galvanized metal ductwork ran along the roof in a rectilinear pattern, enormous trunk lines with smaller branches feeding off perpendicularly. Ceiling grid had been installed in about ten percent of the space. Steel joists and metal deck could be seen throughout. Our footsteps echoed as we continued to the left, toward the public entrance we had passed outside.

Lt. Coogan spoke. "I'd like to show you the body, if you're up to it. It would help in the identification process."

Edison, Gwen, and I looked at each other tentatively.

"He had no I.D.?" Edison asked as we followed Lt. Coogan to an area on the opposite side of the entrance.

Lt. Coogan stopped. He looked at Edison and paused briefly. Finally he answered, "There was no personal identification to be found."

The investigators had set up a makeshift work space, with folding tables and chairs. There were hard black cases filled with tools and, I imagined, "detecting" equipment. One of the tables held a laptop, which Lt. Coogan now opened.

He pushed a button and an image came on screen of aluminum framed gurney, on which a white sheet was draped over a body. The outline of the sheet prompted me to imagine the lifeless person beneath. Instinctively, I gulped.

Edison walked over to the laptop. Lt. Coogan stopped him. "Hold on there," he said, intercepting Edison's arm. "Let's do this one step at a time."

Edison froze.

Lt. Coogan motioned for Edison to move back. We stood there, the three of us lined up, ready for the image about to fill the screen. Imagination flooded my brain. I half expected the man that Edison had removed from this site.

Lt. Coogan picked up a radio and said a few words to the person at the other end. I steeled myself. The corner of the sheet was lifted, revealing the head. The blonde hair alarmed me. A young woman, she exhibited fine, delicate skin, with long straight shiny hair that fell away from her finely featured face.

Gwen let out a small gasp and put her hand to her mouth. I turned toward her. The color drained from her face and I expected her to keel over. As her knees buckled, I reached around to grab her waist. Lt. Coogan closed the laptop and shoved a folding chair it in my direction. I lowered Gwen into the chair. She bent forward, putting her head in her hands.

"It's Isabelle," Edison said softly.

Chapter 4
Desperate Decisions

That was Isabelle? My God, she was only 24 years old. I swallowed hard. The curtain of doom closed on a now unalterable future. No more bright dreams lying ahead. No husband. No kids. No chasing the bright star in the sky.

What was she doing dead?

Lt. Coogan barked an order to one of the uniformed policemen. The officer scooted out, returning to pass a paper cup of water to Gwen. Droplets splashed onto her lap as the cup shook in jittery hands. "Thank you."

Lt. Coogan may have softened a notch. "Did you know the young lady?"

"She worked as an admin in our office," I choked out.

Gwen's eyes stared straight ahead, her white face stiff, mouth set into a stony grimace. Her hands twisted up in white-knuckled balls, in her lap. She sat motionless. In shock or in fear, disengaged from the moment. My impulse was to slide my arms gently around her, and settle her into a deep restful comfort. I would act as a shield, protecting her from the pain. Cradle her in a safe cocoon insulated from the worries and concerns the world lay at her feet. I would reassure her that—

"I see," Lt. Coogan interrupted my reflection. "We'll have to ask you a few questions." He signaled two assistants, who bustled over forthwith. Coogan stayed with Gwen, who sat limply on the metal chair.

A serious faced young woman, with peacock eyes high in her head, blonde hair fashioned into a simple pony tail, was assigned to Edison. Her petite muscular structure contrasted starkly with Edison's large, sedentary frame. Straight hair pulled tightly against her head accentuated her unadorned ears. Edison's dark curly locks sprung in all directions. He followed as she pushed through an exit and bounded up a stairway.

A tall man in his late twenties approached me. Closely cropped dark hair topped his bony head, his facial features carved to extremes. Eyes deeply socketed, thin nose protruding like an eagle's beak. Small mouth atop a pointed chin. He led me downstairs to the floor below. Effortlessly, he guided his lanky body through the building. Wordlessly, he directed me to a corner with boxes of building materials, which we used for seats. A hand motioned me to sit down.

I wondered how Gwen, in her dazed state, would manage the questioning. I'd witnessed her commanding an assortment of difficult meetings. Settling conflicts with powerful contractors. Situations with tens of thousands of dollars at stake. Resolving incidents involving the company's liability with grace and diplomacy. Always, she remained calm and able to participate with the rhythm of discourse. It was unusual to see her overcome by circumstances.

I considered Edison, and wondered if he'd remain true to the secret of the body he found. Edison responded to situations along random lines of thought I could never decipher. Surely there must be logic to his actions, but I was at a loss to explain it. Would it occur to him that the missing body would have relevance to the current situation? But divulging our secret meant incriminating himself. Would he?

I wrestled with that question myself. What justification did I have to conceal the first murder?

Surely it was information the police needed. And yet I hesitated, perhaps to protect Edison, perhaps myself. After all, I found out about the murder that morning, six hours earlier. Why hadn't I reported it then? Conversely, what was there to report? I had seen nothing. I had done nothing. For all I knew, Edison had made the whole thing up. The fact of the matter was, I had no firsthand knowledge of a murder, or a dead body, or a crime scene.

I decided to keep it to myself, at least for the moment.

The officer's questions were simple, asked matter-of-factly, his voice emotionless. His face registered no reaction to my responses. He took notes. Did I know the victim? How well? What would she have been doing here? What was her position at the firm?

"When was the last time you saw her?" he asked.

They thought of me as a suspect, I realized. I focused on remaining calm, answering evenly, as a chill ran up my spine.

"Before Christmas. I've been off work, out of town the last ten days."

He jotted notes carefully in his little book. "Do you own a handgun?"

"Gun? No, why? Is that how she died?"

"Humm," said the Officer, nodding. "That's all we need. I'll be right back."

He left me sitting, pondering. I couldn't help but think of the first murder, the body Edison found. Suppose I also was to regard everyone as a suspect. Who could have done it? Who had the opportunity? Isn't that the line of inquiry? This gained me nothing. I had no details to work with. I didn't even know the time or what day, for that matter, the murder had been committed. My limited info was only that Edison had found the body on Monday, December 27th, in the afternoon.

An hour later, we were reunited. Gwen's tentative footsteps revealed her equilibrium was shot, so I assumed the chauffeur duties and drove us back to the office.

Pulling into rush hour traffic, I resigned myself to a forty minute ride. No one spoke; Gwen was in shock, Edison unusually quiet. I had halfway assumed that the body found today would be the same one that Edison had moved last week. Two murders at the same location only a week apart put a whole new spin on things. What was the connection between an architectural admin and a homeless person? Edison and I alone were aware there had been another death on the jobsite. The advantage this provided would not endure. I decided to proceed quickly while that small fact remained unknown to everyone except the killer.

I remembered (MN #2c) I'd have to talk to the garage mechanic tomorrow.

We arrived at the office just after six. Gwen felt a trifle better, and a bit of color had returned to her cheeks. Her eyes found mine when we spoke and I was heartened by the sign of life. Gwen's son Dwayne was waiting to pick her up. Relieved that she had a ride, I made my way back through the office, while Edison went to scout for scavengables.

I phoned Valley Auto Repair and Parts, identified myself, and asked if the mechanic who worked on the truck would be in the next day. They told me that would be Joel, and yes he would be in on Tuesday.

Edison's portly figure appeared in my cube, his left hand cradling a pile of sugar cookies.

"Edison, have a seat. Let's talk," I said. "Is anyone else around?"

"Nah-uh" he mumbled, munching. "Looks like everyone went home. Cookie?" he offered.

How could he eat? I shook my head. "What did the police officer ask you about?"

Edison recounted the questions, essentially the same ones I was asked.

I said, "Did you happen to mention anything about...what you told me this morning?" Voicing the words *finding a body* was impossible.

Edison appeared puzzled for an instant, and then said, "No, I didn't." He stopped eating, holding the remaining three cookies in his open palm. "Partly, I was afraid to admit I'd moved him. Then, I thought she'd ask me where the body was now. How could I explain that I'd lost it?"

We were silent. Edison looked at me with doleful eyes.

"Edison, don't worry. Why don't you go home to Jeanelle and try to take your mind off this for a while. We're going to figure this out." I had no idea how.

Until some resolution came, I knew both our minds would be occupied with the deaths. He left and I checked my phone. Five new messages, one of them Mary, sounding rather wistful. I took that as a positive sign. I dialed.

"Mary, hi, it's Ken."

"I tried to call you last night, but there was no answer." Her voice was guarded, but with a touch of optimism.

I could have kicked myself. I had unplugged my phone over the holidays, not wanting to be bothered. Why hadn't I reestablished the connection?

"Oh? I must have been out back or something." It was one of those split-second decisions. Why did I avoid telling her the truth?

She hesitated. "I called several times. I would have called your cell, but I didn't want to interrupt you. I thought maybe you were out to dinner or something."

The unspoken *with somebody else* hung in the air like a fresh spider web. I pictured her dark brown eyes flashing accusations at me.

Images of death filled my head: the lifeless body Edison had found, and the scene of Isabelle laying there on the metal table underneath that sheet. My impulse was to blurt out the news to her, explaining the trauma of my day, but she wouldn't understand. One foot in quicksand, I struggled to pull myself out of the muck. It seemed wiser to change to a lighter note. I said, "If I'd known you were going to call, I'd have stuck by the phone."

"Really? It's been a while since we talked." She seemed to thaw, and I pictured her doe eyes framed in thick lashes, open in expectation.

"Yeah. It's nice to hear your sultry voice. It's like opening a box of rich creamy chocolates." It was true.

Her spirit picked up, and she said, "Something on your mind?" I could see the edges of her full mouth start to turn up.

"Yes, I...." Wally came galloping around the corner, an intent look in his little chicken eyes. He grabbed my arm. "Ow!" I exclaimed into the phone.

"Ken?"

"Mary, hold on, it's Wally." I put my hand over the receiver. To Wally, I said, "Please, I'm having a conversation here."

Wally released his grip on my arm, only to clutch my shoulders with both hands. His dark little eyes skittered with wild excitement. "Hang up," he commanded. He lunged for the receiver.

"No, I'm not going to hang up." I slapped at his arms.

"Hang up." Wally repeated. "Trust me on this. Just hang up." His head bobbed up and down like one of those bobble-headed dogs you see in a car's rear window.

I couldn't let Mary get off the phone without making plans for reconciliation. "I will not. Get out!" I gave the aggravation in my voice full reign.

I returned the phone to my ear. "Sorry about that. Wally's playing games here. How about getting together for dinner soon? That new Japanese place in Novi, Yaki-Gyoza, opened last month. I hear they have astounding chefs that cook right at your table, with an entertaining little culinary show."

"Oh, I've heard the beef sukiyaki is scrumptious. Tell me more," she said, hope spread thick through her expression. I could see her hugging the phone to her ear, beneath soft waves of her dark silky hair.

Robert came striding around the corner, "Cannoli. I have something I need done." His face was hard, intense. Eyebrows strained, mouth set in a straight line.

"Robert, I'll be right with you," I said with a sigh. To Mary, I said, "Shall we make it a date? How about tomorrow?"

"Well...."

Robert pressed his fingers together and pursed his lips. "Cannoli, look, we don't have much time."

I was now outnumbered. With a quick sigh, I said, "Mary, Robert is standing here waiting for me."

"Can't we just finish this conversation?" I visualized her beautiful tawny face pinching together in distaste.

"Mary, let me take care of this right now," I said reluctantly. "I'll call you later and we'll arrange a divine evening—"

"Ken, we're having a private conversation. Just tell Robert and Wally to give you five minutes to finish up with me."

The heat from Robert's eyes bore through me like a laser. The situation had disintegrated into hopeless chaos. "Mary, something's going on here. Just give me a few minutes—"

"Oh, why do I bother with you?" Her voice had turned hard and cold, both pitch and volume picking up. "It's either your home remodeling or your work."

"Mary, I...."

"Don't bother calling me back," she screeched and hung up the phone.

I didn't care what kind of situation had come up, or what reason Robert had for this interruption. I couldn't control the glare in my eyes.

Robert continued with his finger exercises. "Cannoli. I know we've had a rough day with all the excitement at the jobsite, but John Dotsun will be here momentarily. I need you to put together some sample projects."

He referenced Isabelle's death like it was a malfunctioning water heater. I never met a man so cold. One of his employees was killed, and now he wanted a last minute throw-together?

"Then, when Dotsun gets here, I've got tickets for the Piston's game. Milwaukee."

"You made me get off the phone for a basketball game?" I said in disbelief.

"No, Cannoli. For a business dinner. A very important meeting. I've been after Dotsun for months to give us an opportunity to introduce ourselves. Gwen isn't feeling well so she isn't able to join us. I need you to represent the project management aspect of the firm. I don't need to tell you what the Crispy Greek account would mean to us."

"Sorry. I'll put together a presentation for you, but I've got plans for tonight. I can't make it to a ball game."

"Business dinner."

My head spun like an Olympic figure skater. Dead bodies. Mary upset with me—again. "No, no. Sorry.

Can't do it. Take Wally. He'd love to go, and he can tell Mr. Dotsun all about how we manage our projects."

Robert scowled. Wally was not the best person to represent the firm at a business meeting, but he certainly could talk basketball. Wally nodded with vigor, his Adam's apple bouncing up and down like a rubber ball on a paddle. He was elated; Robert was pacified.

As I assembled renderings, presentation plans and sketches, I thought about the conversation with Mary. What could I have done differently? I listened, I tried to accommodate her schedule. It seemed like we were from different worlds, like that popular book, *Men are From Mars, Women are From Venus*. Why is it that we deal with women from Venus anyway? Are there no women on Mars?

There. Presentation complete. I looked it over; it should please Dotsun.

Returning the rest of my calls could wait until tomorrow. I headed for home.

My latest housing project was located in the Nine Mile Road & Woodward area known as *Fashionable Ferndale*. The city had become rundown, an extension of Detroit's inner city decay that had been ongoing since the nineteen-fifties. Fifteen years ago, the city of Ferndale began reversing the decline by improving the public areas. They freshened up the sidewalks with pavers and ornamental lighting. They established an "appearance review committee" to act as a watchdog agency over mercantile development in the downtown district. Some concerned citizens, including *moi*, were buying run-down houses, refurbishing them, and then either renting or selling them—mostly to stylish young people who gave the city a new energy.

I felt I could help counteract the decline of this country's infrastructure one house at a time. This was my effort toward social responsibility.

My last two projects were located four blocks east of the Woodward/ Nine Mile intersection. I had purchased a three-bedroom bungalow eleven months earlier. The paint was flaking off the aluminum siding. The stairway carpeting was worn to the threads. Plaster was cracked or missing chunks. The 60 amp electric service was seriously outdated.

I stripped out the flooring, including the original kitchen linoleum (green with black flecks). Repaired floors and steps. Replaced large portions of plaster walls. Fixed the broken door bell and back porch light. Refinished the hardwood floors. Updated the electrical service and lastly put on new hardwood siding. It was a beauty of a house, completed and ready for entertaining for the holidays.

Mary and I planned a wonderful Christmas weekend with her family. She adorned the house with a variety of tasteful decorations: a natural Christmas tree, a majestic nativity scene with twelve inch hand carved figures from Bavaria, a fresh evergreen garland all around the living room and up the stairway, blinking lights in the window, a Christmas village displayed on a long side table in the dining room.

Mary invited her family, both parents and an uncle, to my newly improved house for Saturday Christmas dinner. They were to see my handiwork and Mary's resplendent decorations.

Meanwhile, I'd bought the house immediately adjacent, lining it up as my next project. It was in a more distressed condition than the one I'd just finished.

An unexpected rental started the trouble. A grade school buddy of mine was moving up to Detroit suddenly; he'd been dismissed from his office job in Knoxville in September. After three months of job searching, he interviewed at a branch bank in Livonia, and was offered the position, but only if he could start immediately. With two little kids and a jobless wife, he needed a place to live and needed it right *now*. I had a place to go, but Earl didn't. So I consented to move out of the nicely renovated place, and relocate next door to my new project. It seemed like the Christmas-minded sort of thing to do. I agreed to let Earl and his family move-in two days after Christmas, on Monday the 27th. I'd have to start moving out during the weekend, so Mary and I relocated the family Christmas dinner to Mary's house in Sterling Heights. Mary was not pleased.

I set up the phone service and started moving my belongings to the new house on Friday (yes, on Christmas Eve). I moved a few things on Christmas Day, too. Mary was perturbed by that. I had planned to finish moving the next day because Earl and Margie Bostian were arriving to move in on Monday.

The straw that finally broke Mary's back came during Christmas dinner. In the middle of carving the turkey the Bostians called. They had arrived from Tennessee, with all their belongings and the kids. Would it be ok to start moving in a day early? Yes, they knew it was Christmas, but they had made good time on the road and thought how nice it would be to get settled in their new home on Christmas. No, they really didn't have anywhere else to stay. Of course, they offered a thousand apologies.

What a pickle!

How could I leave my girl and her family at Christmas dinner? But—

How could I turn away this destitute family, without a place to sleep on Christmas?

So I excused myself from the holiday meal, and went to let the folks into the house. By the time I shuffled my stuff around to give them room to bring their things in, I was in need of a shower and a change of clothes. I went over to my new place. I called Mary to let her know that I'd be on my way soon. She told me to stay away; I had ruined Christmas and I could just spend the rest of the day moving!

So I did just that.

The next morning she told me that my fix-up work must be more important than her, and I could just keep up with my repairs and not bother calling.

Imagine! I was trying to help out some folks—to give them a place to live during Christmas time, and she didn't want to see me anymore. Exhausted from moving furniture, I dragged myself into the car and headed out of town for a few days. Phoneless, companionless, and focused on forgetting *everything*.

The current conversation should have been to make-up, but instead Mary was mad at me again. After a long day of dealing with dead bodies, I entered through the side door of my new abode. A small landing greeted me, with ten steps leading down to the basement, and three steps up to the kitchen door, whose varnish had yellowed with age. The kitchen was a sight as well, its black and orange tile flooring had seen about fifty years of wear and tear and twenty years' of wax build-up.

Funny odors of mold and wet plaster filled the house. Perhaps something had died inside the walls; I wouldn't rule it out.

Other than soda, there was nothing of any substance in the fridge. I'd carted the stuff over from next door, and had not gone shopping since. A container of yellow mustard. A pickle jar containing only the left over juice. Rubbery celery. Taco sauce in little plastic packets. Yuck.

I remembered having some canned goods. Searching

the cabinets under the counter, I came up with a can of spaghetti in tomato-cheese sauce. Reluctantly, I opened the can, poured it into a bowl, and stuck it in the microwave.

As soon as the cooking started, an explosive 'pop' drenched the house in total darkness. I cursed the lack of visibility. The fuse box would be in the basement, somewhere on the north wall. But where exactly, I couldn't remember. And whether or not there were fuses down there, I didn't know. I needed a flashlight. Where did I have one? The broom closet? The bedroom? Probably in the basement, but walking down there would be treacherous, as there was stuff piled everywhere. I remembered a flashlight in the glove box of my Grand Am. I turned to make my way back outside and walked right into the edge of the open kitchen door. My forehead screamed. I touched it and yelped like a puppy. I didn't dare turn or move, for fear of running into or tripping on something else. After a moment of indecisiveness, I groped along the counter top, inching toward the three steps that would get me to the side door. By holding my left hand out in front of my face, I hoped to avert any other unpleasant surprises. No doubt there would be a welt in the morning.

I made my way out. Stars in the night sky provided a little bit of light. I found the flashlight in the glove compartment.

A few minutes later, I replaced the fuse; there were spares next to the fuse box after all. Thankful for the lights, I longed to relax and get some peace. I decided to eat my spaghetti cold.

Should I call Mary? I pondered, picking up the phone. It was dead. Oh yeah, I had unplugged it over Christmas. I reattached the chord to the wall.

I stripped off my clothes and let myself fall onto the

mattress there on the bedroom floor. Adjusting the TV, David Letterman came into focus. Finally, I could let go. Letterman was in the middle of a series of presidential jokes when I fell asleep.

The ringing telephone jolted me from a dream about canoeing on a crystal clear river and banging into rocks. Laughter came from the TV. Letterman was doing "stupid human tricks," so I must have dozed for just a few minutes. I turned the set off and picked up the receiver.

"Hello?"

"Cannoli! Where have you been? I've been trying to track you down all night!" It was Robert Westin.

"Oh hi, Robert. What time is it? I was just sleeping."

"I don't care if you were playing strip poker. I got a call from Jester Cromwell earlier this evening. He said he left four messages for you today, and he has yet to hear from you. I spent at least fifteen minutes trying to calm him down, reassuring him that we value him as a client. Now this business has caused me to miss the three pointer that Stuckey sank at the third period buzzer."

The phone messages! "Robert, I just got back from being off for the holidays. I didn't have a chance to call him today."

"Well, I've got a jobsite that's all but shut down, and right now I'm in the middle of trying to land this Crispy Greek account. I don't need Jester Cromwell calling me in the middle of a business meeting because you're too busy having a vacation and fighting with your girlfriend to service our clients. I want you to call him right now and get him back on our team," and with that he hung up.

Where was my Cloak of Invisibility?

Not only was Jester Cromwell a new client, he also happened to be Mary's uncle. The firm had designed his new chocolate shop, Jester Truffle, currently being built in the expanded mall area at Flamingo Shores. I made the call.

"Hello?" said a sleepy voice.

"Jester? It's Ken Knoll."

"Ken. I've been trying to reach you. I talked to Robert a little while ago."

"Yes. What's up?"

"I've got some major delivery problems. If those cases from Milstone don't ship soon, we're not going to open on time."

Milstone again. I was tired of hearing about this Canadian outfit. "Jester, can we sort this out in the morning?"

"Meet me at the store. Say 10:00 a.m.?"

"Sure, I'll be there."

I hung up the phone and turned over. Closing my eyes, I sunk into the covers, letting the stillness envelop me.

A moment later, the silence was rocked by an explosion: a solid deep 'boom' immediately followed by clattering emanating from behind the house.

Reluctantly, my body allowed me to move it off the bed, grab a robe, and shuffle to the back bedroom to peer out a window. Nothing in the backyard. I glanced at the driveway that extended rearward to the garage, and the abutting grass. I saw no one; nothing seemed out of place. I moved to the kitchen, then down those three steps to the side door. Carefully, I peeled back a portion of the curtain, peeking through the slot just in case someone was lying in wait just outside the door, prepared to bash my head in with a baseball bat.

I didn't see anyone, but grabbed a length of 2x4 from the living room anyway. Again, I checked through the curtain at the side door. Nothing. I slid back the deadbolt, tugged the door open and poked my head out.

Earl Bostonian stood in his yard, next to our chain-link fence. The floodlight on the eave of his house cast harsh shadows through the yard. Heart thumping, I opened the storm door and stepped outside. The cold air pierced my robe. At the back of the house, I saw what remained of my garbage can. The banged up cylinder had been peeled open like a can of sardines. Bits of paper and cardboard littered the grounds. The metal lid had been blown against the house, evidenced by a gash in the siding under the bedroom window.

"What are we going to do about those damn kids? Always blowing things up!" Earl Bostonian stood there in his puffy vinyl blue coat. Arms folded, face grimaced.

I walked over to the fence. "That was rather nerve-wracking, wasn't it?" I said.

"Kids. Stupid kids." The wind had tousled his short brown hair. "Margie got really nervous when this happened to us."

"What happened to you?"

He turned his deeply lined face in my direction. At forty-three, we were the same age but, for unknown reasons, time had left his face severely weathered. "They blew up my cans last week. Same kind of thing as this. Blew stuff all over the yard, only worse. It was just a couple of days after we moved in, so we had boxes and all kinds of crap surrounding the cans when they exploded. Irresponsible kids, trying to get some attention, or impress their friends. Margie has been having trouble sleeping the whole week. Every little noise excites her. I'd have to get dressed and come outside and investigate. Didn't make my day, coming out to check for that kind of trouble. Now with the kids getting into your yard, I don't know if she's ever going to calm down."

Who could sleep now?

Chapter 5
Truffles and Trucks

"I called you last night, but there was no answer." Gwen slid up next to me at the coffee pot. Her delicate hands poked out from silky lavender sleeves, her tender neck encircled by pearls.

My joints were feeling a little stiff. I hadn't slept well after my trash can was ripped to shreds. I hoped that the java would loosen me up.

"Oh, why?" I said, wondering if she was taking an interest, while simultaneously hoping it wasn't something dreadful.

"No. Nothing. I just, um, I've given some thought to what happened yesterday and hoped to divine your opinion about it." Gwen's eyes were ever so slightly puffy. Just around the corners. Not so that most people would notice.

As I turned and reached for the creamer, I noticed Gwen staring at my forehead.

"What happened to you?" she said.

"Oh," I remembered. "A runaway door."

She laughed.

"Gwen, you have a call on line one. Gwen, line one please."

She sighed at the interruption and touched my arm. "Can we talk later?"

I nodded and she hustled to her office, swaying slightly on strappy pumps that matched her suit. I took a sip. Smooth, with a rich nutty flavor on my tongue. A cup of fresh coffee in the morning is a real pleasure.

As much as I thought I'd like to get together with Gwen, I had still not given up on Mary. Sitting down in my cubicle, I picked up the phone to order some flowers. Nothing ordinary. This had to be special. Calla lilies were her favorite. Was there a way to make it more distinctive? I called Kevin at Magic Flowers, which specialized in custom settings. After reviewing options, I settled on a faux-pearl studded, scalloped vase to set off the bouquet, and had it sent to Mary's office at the mall. Perhaps it would make a difference.

As I hung up the receiver, I caught a glimpse of Robert's secretary coming my way with a full head of steam. This could only serve to complicate my life. Rita poked her head in. She wore a plum and red blouse in a lively pattern that clashed with her burgundy hair. The stiletto heels supporting her stout frame no doubt would pierce the wood sub-flooring in a subdivision home.

"Bob would like you to join him in entertaining Edmund Palmer at dinner tonight. Gwen's already turned him down, so think carefully before you answer." She raised her eyebrows in sarcastic superiority.

Robert had been trying to land the Palmer Furniture account for a couple of years. A dinner engagement meant that he was making progress. After turning him down the previous night, I didn't feel I could refuse.

"Sure, Rita. I've got some meetings out of the office. I'll be back around three o'clock."

Her mascara-laden eyes turned to my forehead. "What the heck happened to you? Did you run into a truck, or did you just open the refrigerator door a little too fast?"

I smiled. "I wish that had been the problem. Truth is, there's nothing in my refrigerator."

"Bachelors!"

If I made the Jester Truffle meeting by 10 o'clock, I

could have a discussion with the parties involved, grab some lunch and still make it out to see the truck mechanic by one p.m.

I returned the phone calls that I'd ignored the day before and checked my e-mail. I forwarded three "requests for information"—RFI's—to Edison to research and headed out to my car, stopping at the restroom on the way to check my forehead. A deep red vertical line, offset slightly toward my left side gave me rather a sinister look. Like I was the streetwise sidekick to Jackie Chan or Stephen Segal. I smiled.

It was 9:37. The twenty-three minute drive would get me to the site exactly on time. I pushed my 2004 white Grand Am in and out of traffic. The post-rush hour travel should have been smooth sailing. But no. There was a back-up on Telegraph, just before Maple. This stop and go traffic would set me back at least fifteen minutes. Making my way over to the right turn lane, I pulled onto Maple. When Lahser appeared, I cut over to Big Beaver and was home free. It was 10:07 when I arrived at the site—not bad considering the traffic I'd just managed. Thankfully, there was no snow.

Available parking spaces peppered the surface lot between the JCPenney parking deck and the north mall expansion. This was the employee parking and delivery area. I entered into a service corridor. The gypsum board ceiling was not yet taped, and the block walls were yet unpainted. I let myself into the store via the hollow metal service door.

Jester Cromwell was waving his arms and motioning wildly at the job superintendent. Jester was in his late fifties, salt and pepper hair over his collar, long face with ample, ruddy, jowls that shook when he spoke. He wore a green and yellow plaid sport coat with a brown shirt and dark brown pants.

"Ken, I'm glad you're here. We've got to have the casework here by the 24th of February and Milstone says they can't even ship until March 5th. You know that order will take six or seven days to make it down to Detroit and pass through customs. If we don't have these doors open by Easter, I'm not going to make base rent until Mother's Day." Jester's jowls grew redder by the minute.

"Just hold on, Jester. We're going to sort this out."

Job superintendent Ted Bylund was just standing there, as he always did, with his left hand in his pocket. A slim, fair-haired fellow, his right hand rested on the makeshift plan table.

The cases for the new chocolate shop were to be custom-made glass shelves under a curved glass customer window. Copper top, purse shelf and trim. High end, high cost and long lead time. The cases should have been ordered a month ago. The order was, in fact, placed last week. Jester had hemmed and hawed about the cost; tried to save the expense of having them shipped in from northern Canada by having a local cabinetmaker do the job. Audia Custom Cabinets had suggested a copper-look plastic laminate on the flatwork and revised details in oak. In the end, Jester felt that the genuine copper put chocolates in better company. Now he was going to have to pay the price of waiting.

I dialed Milstone and I spoke to the owner. Yes, he'd heard this plea before. No, he couldn't speed things up. It took what it took. Curved glass alone added ten days to the schedule, as he had to out-source that material. The glass company was backed up. If we changed to straight glass? Yes we could cut the 10 days off the schedule. That would simplify the joining too. Yes, etched glass was an available option—that procedure was done on site. Look for some samples in the overnight mail. Yes, there would be a price break as well.

Jester looked relieved, the red fading from his face. While heartily shaking my hand, he commented about the fresh wound on my forehead, then excused himself to tackle some paperwork before going off to have lunch with the mayor.

After we'd sorted out the casework snafu, Ted took the opportunity to ask me about three other "little things" that had come up during construction that he was unsure how to handle.

A short while later, I was almost out the door when Jester called me into his office. A temporary work space had been set up: desk and chair, telephone and oversize plastic calculator.

While he thanked me again for straightening out the cabinetwork, I noticed that among the sparse office items was a photo of Jester and Mary.

"That picture was taken outside my cabin in Gaylord. Mary has taken such good care of me since my Annie died two years ago. Mary has always been a darling to me. You know, I never had any children of my own. Even when she was only seven or eight, she hugged me like the world would end the moment she stopped. Every year on my birthday, she makes me a Black Forest Cherry cake. Such a dear."

Hearing Jester speak so lovingly about the girl who just broke up with me made me feel like a jerk. I sensed I should stop by her office—it was literally just around the corner—but our conversation would likely (hopefully!) be a lengthy one and I was determined to get to the repair shop. With any luck, Mary would see the flowers as a true measure of my feelings for her.

I finally embarked for Brighton at noon. Coolidge south was the straightest shot to I-696 in Oak Park.

Traffic was somewhat heavy, but I assumed it was due to the lunch hour. Just past Maple, traffic all but stopped. During the next stop-and-go mile, I worked the brake gently, lost in concentration about what to do next about the murder.

Wally had dropped the truck off late Monday. It remained at the shop for the next three days. What did the mechanic know? What did Edison do about the truck being gone? Didn't he try to locate it? Didn't he try to get the body to a secure location? I made a mental note (MN #3) to follow up with Edison.

As I sat idly reflecting, my phone rang.

"Ken Knoll."

"Just what have you done with my Payment Application?" The voice was familiar and female, but I couldn't place it.

"It should have been processed a couple of weeks ago. Jason Tyler says he hasn't received it. Need I remind you that your review of the pay app was late last month as well? If this keeps up, we're going to have a serious problem here." It was Margaret Humes, controller for Pontile Construction.

Edison! With all of the commotion, I forgot about the report. It was the reason Edison had gone to the job site in the first place. He had taken the photos. Why hadn't he and Wally completed the paperwork and sent it out?

"Margaret. We've reviewed the app and walked the site. I shall track down the report to see where it got hung up."

"Ken, there's no excuse for this. This is the second month your review has been late."

A mumbled apology came out of my mouth, and I hung up, resolved to get to the bottom of the delay.

I punched Gwen on speed dial. "Hey Gwen," I said. "Rita invited me to one of Robert's business dinners tonight and I hear you're not going."

"Oh, hi Ken. The dinner meeting with Edmund Palmer? No, I can't make it. I've got a proposal to finish for Gundry Schools. The work plan needs writing, and consultant proposals aren't here yet. I'm only halfway through the project approach. All of this must be on Rita's desk before I leave tonight, or she won't have a prayer of getting it done tomorrow." She sighed. "You know Robert prefers schmoozing with the guys anyway. Of course, Donna is going too."

"Well, we'll miss you tonight," I said. "By the way, how are you feeling?"

"Feeling?" Gwen sounded a bit detached. "Oh, you mean after yesterday? It's a shock. Truthfully, my stomach is tied up in knots. But, I've got a call, I have to run." She hung up...more hastily than I preferred.

Traffic moved up, slowly, a bit at a time, but not fast enough for me to make the next light. A Burger King beckoned on my right, so I thought I might as well hit the drive-thru and eat my lunch as I was plugging along in traffic. I was soon wrestling with the question of lower calories or better taste. Taste won out. I opted for the two cheeseburger combo meal with onion rings and a coke. Placing the paper bag in the passenger seat, I pulled into traffic, still running stop and go along Coolidge. By juggling the drink with my left hand, I was able to clean out the cup holder to make room with my right.

Suddenly, we were all moving again. A couple of blocks up, I saw the two wrecked cars off to the side of the road. Within ten minutes, I made it to the freeway, munching the last of my onion rings.

It was a forty minute ride.

I pulled off the Brighton exit and saw the auto repair building immediately. Valley Auto Repair and Parts. An "L" shaped building, sitting on a rise along the roadway. The concrete block walls were painted white with a red wainscot, and had five glass-and-aluminum overhead doors along the road side. The aluminum doors were painted blue. As I looked through the all-glass service doors, I saw an equivalent five doors on the opposite side. The other leg of the "L" was a solid block wall, no windows, with a red sign painted above the door that said simply "Parts." Beyond the building, I could see a heap of rusted out, wrecked cars. That must have been the junkyard visible from the freeway. Bordering the rusty collection stood an eight foot high chain link fence with intermittent redwood slats that only attracted attention to the eyesore.

I headed toward the white door marked "Office" in blue letters.

Walking up to the grimy counter, I introduced myself and said, "I called yesterday. I'd like to speak to Joel, who worked on our office vehicle."

A thin man, in t-shirt and overalls, looked up from behind the counter as he rubbed the grease off the inside of a round cylinder. "Joel's not here today."

He looked up at my forehead. I felt no compulsion to respond to his look of curiosity.

"But, yesterday I was told that he's in on Tuesdays."

He stared blankly, apparently not identifying with my dilemma. Muted grey irises unresponsive; the permanently creased zigzag wrinkles across his forehead set.

The phone rang, jolting him from his trance. "Hold on," he said to me and picked up the phone. He proceeded to have a conversation, apparently with a supplier, about the availability of a particular engine part.

When he finished, he went back to working his rag along the inside of the metal part in his lap. I knocked on the counter to signal that I was still there.

"Oh, sorry. Joel called in sick today," he said and returned to his work.

Anger welled up inside me and didn't know which way to turn. I was determined to get some answers. I closed my eyes briefly to focus.

"Did anyone else work on the vehicle?" I said steadily. I wanted an answer now, so I spit out a description of the office truck, and explained its condition. As the words left my mouth, a thin boy of maybe seventeen slid to the wall behind the desk where a row of clip boards hung.

The counter man said to him, "Sean, check the battery on that Jeep in bay three." Then he continued with his work, glancing up to say, "No, that would have been Joel. He's the transmission man."

I took a chance. "I'm looking for something that I left in the bed of the truck. It's missing. I was hoping that you could help me locate it."

The man looked up, greasy blond hair falling into his eyes. He reached his arm up, turned and referred to the sign behind him. "NOT RESPONSIBLE FOR PERSONAL ITEMS LEFT IN VEHICLES," it announced.

"Oh, no, I'm not pointing fingers," I said. "I just want to get it back."

"Well, no reason for us to be poking around in the bed of a truck. No work back there."

"Of course," I said and left the office.

As I walked toward my car, I heard footsteps at my back. The skinny boy was ambling along behind me. His ears stuck out from his head, a feature made more pronounced by his buzz cut.

"You lookin' for Joel?"

I nodded.

"He i'n't sick. He's at McKinn'y School. His boy's got a play and he wan'ed to see 'im. Som'tin' about the

Mayflower."

I looked at the boy. Blue jeans worn through at the cuffs where he'd walked on them. Red plaid flannel shirt, unbuttoned at the collar exposing a dingy white t-shirt. "Thanks. I appreciate the information."

"Ain't nothing. Take this road up about five miles." He pointed toward the north. Make a right turn at Waldon and then right again at Little Birch. It'd be on your right."

I thanked him again and got into my car.

"He's got a Cruiser," he called after me. "A silver PT Cruiser."

I nodded. My cell phone was ringing.

"Ken, it's Edison."

"Hey, Edison. What happened to the payment app you were reviewing on the Crystals job? Why didn't it go out? Maggie Humes just called and she's hopping mad. Wally told me he was too busy to visit the project site with you on Monday, but I wasn't aware that the report never went out at all. What can you tell me about it?"

"Ken, listen to me. Ken." He had that worried tone in his voice again.

What happened now?

"Edison, relax. Now let's take this one thing at a time. First, explain to me about the pay app."

I could hear him take a breath and change gears. "Ok, Ken, I had that report almost ready to go last week. I had all the papers put together. I gave Serenity the chip out of the camera last Thursday so she could put the photo sheets together."

"So why didn't the package go out last week?"

"She was almost done with the photos on Thursday. I told her to print out two sets—one to send and one to keep."

"Go on," I was getting impatient.

"When we came into the office on Friday, we couldn't find them."

I paused and took a breath. "What do you mean you couldn't find them?"

"We arrived in the morning, and Serenity came over to me and asked if I'd taken the photos. We went through all of the papers on her desk including her in-box. You know that thing hasn't been cleaned out since Thanksgiving? There was an invitation to a turkey trot at the Detroit Zoo. You know, I had intended to go to that—"

"Edison!"

"Oh, sorry. Anyway, we looked all around her desk and mine, through all of the papers and found zilch. We asked around the office and no one knew anything either."

"So why didn't she just print out two more copies?"

"They disappeared."

"What do you mean they disappeared?" A dark feeling crept into my gut.

"The chip disappeared off Serenity's desk, and the pictures are gone off the computer."

"Off the system? How can that be?"

"They weren't on the system. Serenity had them on her 'C' drive on Thursday. The next morning they were gone."

"Did you check with IT?"

"Sure, sure. Her computer's clean. They couldn't recover anything."

I whistled low. Now the photos that Edison had taken on the parking deck where he discovered the body were missing?

"It's like the photos and everything just disappeared. Say, you don't think...." I could see the light bulb go on over Edison's head.

"Bingo."

"Whoa. That means someone was inside our office and wiped them off the computer."

"Yeah, and that also means someone knew that you were out there taking photos of the jobsite."

We were both silent for a moment.

Edison spoke. "Robert is looking for you. He checked with Jason Pontile and Jester Cromwell, and then he called your cell phone but didn't get through."

"What's going on?"

"I don't know, but he's in a huff. He thought you'd be back after the Jester Truffle meeting. Maybe it's because the cops were here."

"The police?"

"Yeah, that Lieutenant who questioned us yesterday. He was here for a long time, set up shop in the conference room, talking to people, asking a bunch of questions. Everyone is creeped out."

"Sorry I missed it. Tell Robert I'll be back soon." I was about to hang up, then thought about MN #3. "Edison, let me ask you a question."

"Uhm, hum."

"What, are you eating now?"

"Uhm. Donna brought in some donuts. The raspberry's delicious."

I could just picture Edison eating a jelly donut, the certain way he pursued his fetish. He would lick the sugar off the end opposite the little hole where the jelly is put in. Then he would nibble on the part of the donut that he had licked the sugar off, pucker his cheeks and suck out the filling. "Edison, when you found out that the truck was at the shop on Tuesday, why didn't you go there to get the body out?"

"I did, Ken. I went out there after work on Tuesday, hoping that I could get the—er—*it* moved once and for all. I borrowed my friend Chuck's '69 Cady and drove up to the shop."

"Cadillac?"

"DeVille. You know my truck doesn't have a bed cover, and the truck of that Cady is large enough to hold two, um, two of those things. Anyway, I went up there and it was locked up."

"The truck?"

"No, the shop. I could see the truck. They had it locked up inside the third bay. The doors are all window panes. It was sitting right there and I couldn't get to it."

After what I'd just seen that made sense.

"Thanks, Edison. I'll see you in a couple hours."

I turned off on Little Birch, and saw the school up ahead. I pulled into the parking lot and stopped but was unsure about what to do next. The parking lot was crammed full, including cars parked on the yellow caution stripes at the ends of the aisles.

It was 1:45. What time does elementary school get out? This was one experience I'd never had. Married and divorced before I was thirty. No kids. I spotted the Cruiser along the fence between the parking lot and the playground.

I didn't have to wait long.

A young couple headed for the car. The guy who I assumed was Joel was with a midget of a boy wearing a corduroy jacket and a brown knit cap, striding alongside a thin blonde, wearing a fur-trimmed leather jacket and blue jeans. I introduced myself.

"I'm sorry to bother you off work, but I've lost something and I wonder if you might possibly have found it."

Joel had a flat face. All of the features were there, but in the same plane. His forehead wide and tall, blond eyebrows so light they got lost in the expanse. Wide nose, receding chin. His cheeks were large planes that began just under the eyes and extended to his jawline.

His face was flat as a board.

I tried an elaborate lie. "I had a ceramic casting that I'd left in the bed of the truck, last week before Wally brought the truck in. The truck is a work truck, and everyone borrows it to go to different job sites. The casting is missing and I'm trying to track down what happened to it."

"I haven't seen anything like that. There wasn't much in the truck."

"This would have been in the bed. Did you happen to look under the bed cover?"

"Well, yeah, I did look in that truck bed."

My heart began a sprint.

"You did?"

"Yeah. We always wash the vehicles before the customer picks them up. With a truck like that, bed cover and all, we usually just wash the outside, but Wally and you-all were so patient with us, I took a peek into the bed. I figured if it was empty, I may just as well wash it too."

As cold as it was outside, a bead of sweat rolled down my neck. "And...."

"Ah, shoot. There wasn't a thing in it, so I unsnapped the cover, and gave it all a good cleaning."

"What did you do with the cardboard and plastic sheeting?"

He looked at me like I was stupid.

"There was nothing in the bed. Nothing."

Chapter 6
Confusing Conversations

"Let me get this straight," I said evenly. "You opened the bed cover and washed out the truck bed. There was nothing in there?"

"That's what I said." He glanced at his wife and son, who were sitting in the car peering out the window at him, the boy with ten fingers and his nose pushed up against the window.

Joel appeared anxious to go, and I couldn't think of anything else to ask. "Well, thank you for the information."

"I guess one of your work partners took it." Pools of darkness serving as eyes penetrated his flat face. As an afterthought he added, "Whatever it was you had in there."

I nodded slowly, and started toward my car. A sudden flash caused me to spin on my heels. "Joel, one more thing."

He looked back over his car door, which stood open.

"You washed the car Thursday?"

"Yeah, we got the transmission done in the morning, test drove it on the freeway for a bit, then I took it over to the wash bay after lunch."

"Had you looked in the bed prior to Thursday afternoon?"

I could see the puzzle encompassing his face. "No. Wasn't any reason to."

"So someone could have removed something from the bed earlier that week, before you went to clean it?"

"Well...." Joel said slowly. His bewildered face shook slowly side to side. "I suppose. But I doubt any of our crew would have done it. The truck was locked up every night. No one would have messed with it. Was it something valuable? We're not responsible for anything left—"

"—in the vehicle," I finished. "Yes, I know, it's just got...sentimental...value."

I hopped on eastbound I-96 and it was clear sailing. Hmm, nearly 2:30. I could make good time before rush hour. I reflected on Joel's commentary regarding the security of the truck bed. Edison had confirmed that the truck was in the repair bay—locked up at night. So when was the body taken? It bothered me that the truck was out of Edison's care for three days. During that time, someone could have reached the truck and removed the contents. But how did they get to it without being seen by the staff? And why would they take the plastic sheets and the cardboard too?

The nagging questions were interrupted by the phone just as I sailed onto Telegraph.

"Ken, I got the flowers," Mary said with a rather soft voice.

"Do you like them?" I smiled.

"You know how I love calla lilies!" Hope spread itself thick through her voice, and I pictured her brown eyes bright, full lips spread wide. "Remember the first time you bought me a bunch? We were out of town in Grand Rapids. We meandered around, exploring, and ended up in a flower shop, after we visited—"

"Meijer Gardens. Of course I remember! It was our first weekend alone. I'll never forget. Did we have fun! We went to that little Italian restaurant—Carlo Antoni's. Remember the old violin player, sauntering from one table to the next? He must have been eighty if he was a day."

"He played such beautiful melodies—Adagietto from *L'Arlesienne* brings tears to my eyes. How romantic! And the cigar room. Oh how I hate cigar smoke!" Mary laughed even as she expressed her annoyance. Perhaps this was going to work after all.

I pulled into the office parking lot, finding a spot near the back door. I left the car running and the heater on.

"Oh, Mary.... We've had such fun. Your—"

A knocking at my passenger window interrupted.

"My what? Ken, aren't you going to see who's at your window?"

Huh? I turned to see Mary stooped down, gloved hand on the door handle. I unlocked the door, and she slid into the seat next to me. Her open face—apple smiling cheeks, heavy Spanish eyelashes, rosy full lips showing just a hint of her pearly whites. I reached over and ungloved her hands, wrapping my fingers around hers. Sweet, warm gentle hands. "Oh Mary! This is a nice surprise!"

"Well you surprised me with flowers, beautiful delicate blooms—my very favorite—so it's only fair, I surprise you with...me!" She leaned in and gave me a full ninety seconds of sumptuous wet kiss. Pulling away and leaning back, she opened her coat suggestively, her eyes inviting me to peek inside. I looked down and caught a glimpse of fire-engine-red lace, interrupted by a knocking at the window behind me.

I turned to see Edison motioning me to open the window. Rolling my eyes, to Mary, I said, "Hold on a minute," while I turned around and lowered the window.

"Sorry to interrupt...uh," Edison looked sheepishly down to his shoes, "whatever...but Robert is waiting for you in the conference room. The meeting started half an hour ago. He saw you pull up and sitting here in the lot, and he's livid!"

"Tell Robert I'll be in shortly," I said. Edison shrugged, and turned on his heels. I closed the window, shifting my attention back to Mary, who'd tugged her coat shut, and now had her arms folded over her chest.

"Ken, we've got some things to figure out." Her voice was strained. "If this is going to work, there have to be some changes made."

The smile left my face, as if it didn't know me.

"Yes," I said, not entirely grasping her meaning.

"Ken, I need your attention. When we're having a conversation, you can't just go off every time your boss pulls your string."

I resented that last statement. "I don't like it either, Mary, but this is the man I work for. Yes he's unreasonable sometimes, but I find it hard to carry on a personal conversation—like yesterday on the phone, when Roberts's eyes were burning right through me while we talked."

"Let's have dinner tonight, and talk about it," she said, squeezing my hands. "I'll go home and get ready for you...while you finish up here, since it's so important for you."

Mentally, I cursed Robert Westin. "I can't tonight. I've got a business dinner."

She sighed heavily and flashed her eyes at me. "Get out of it. We've got to talk." Hardness edged into her voice, even as she spoke quietly.

I thought about the options. Robert would hang me if I dumped him for dinner at this late hour, especially after last night. "No, I really can't. How about tomorrow?"

Her eyes fired up to glare mode. "No, that's no good! Remember that St. Louis trip? I've only been telling you about it for the last two months. Don't you ever listen to me? I'll be gone until Friday, and I'd just as soon work this out before I leave...one way or another."

The last phrase shot through me like a lightning bolt. I'd hoped we could patch things up. Were we that close to finished?

Palmer was already in the office. We'd meet for an hour or so, then head out to Robert's favorite Italian restaurant, La Cortina. It was only thirty minutes away. Even with a leisurely meal, we could call it a night at 8:30. I could drive separately and—

"Ken...?" She shook my arm.

I turned to her and forced a smile. "Mary, yes. I was just thinking. I've got to go to this dinner tonight, but how about I come over about 9:00? We could talk while I help you pack."

"Well, that's kind of late. I've got an early flight." Her lips clenched as she spoke, her dark brown eyes cold as ice. "We have a problem here. Why can't you come over at 8:00? That should give you plenty of time to do your wining and dining, win the client, impress Robert and—"

The knocking on my window startled me. Edison shouted through the glass, "Ken, are you coming?" I looked back to see him shivering in his shirt sleeves.

"Mary, looks like I've got to get in there. How about if I call you after this meeting...in an hour? We can work this out then." Mary wrenched back her hands.

"No. Forget it." Erratically, she jerked on her gloves. "Forget me. Just get to your meeting and your dinner and your fix-it-up house." She balled up her fists and slugged me in the chest. "I'm tired of putting up with you and your crazy hours and living in disarray. Moldings and scraps of wood laying all around. Plaster dust. Nothing ever finished. And then when it is done, painted and clean, you give it away to someone else to live in. ARGHHHH!" She screamed, threw the door open, and stomped down the pavement.

Crap.

Edison, having gotten the gist of the conversation, offered his sympathies, then reminded me that people were waiting.

I went to the meeting and saved the day.

Later, I endured dinner with Robert Westin, Edmund Palmer and Donna Westgate, the other project manager under Gwen. The food was out of this world; the music was smooth and lively; I wasn't much good at conversation. Mentally numb, at 8:30 I excused myself and went home. Robert glowered at me as I departed. I didn't care. I had met my obligation to the firm and lost my girl in the process.

As I drove home in silence, I chewed myself out for losing Mary. Finally, I gave up, deciding that I'd be better off turning my energy to creative pursuits. I still had a couple of working hours. I could take the casings off the windows in the living room. The previous owner had put on this rather nice wood trim, but had cut the joints poorly, and then used caulk to fill in the cracks. The varnish was fading as well. It was horrid and needed replacing.

I arrived home, and changed into my repair jeans and Red Wings work shirt. I'd just pulled off the trim from around one of the windows facing the neighboring lot when the doorbell rang.

9:40 p.m. *Who could be calling at this hour?*

It was Gwen. Her deep blue eyes danced up at me creating a toasty feeling in my being. As I opened the door to let her in, she pressed a cold, gift-wrapped bottle into my hands.

"A little housewarming gift." She smiled and bounced into the room, her rich honey scent rousing my senses. "Champagne." I helped her shrug out of her coat, opened the closet door finding (thankfully!) one lonely hanger. Gwen wore a psychedelic peachy-pinky-yellowish outfit that wasn't exactly a dress and wasn't exactly a top and a skirt, but something in between. I'm no fashion expert. A wide strip of fabric matching her outfit adorned her hair. It crossed the top of her head to tie behind her neck. Her copper-colored hair seemed to dance with the pattern and the ensemble accentuated her cheekbones. I was smitten. Mary was forgotten.

"Sorry about the way I look," I said. "I'll just go change," I offered.

"Don't bother. The workman look aligns with me," she said, tilting her head and running her eyes down my body.

This didn't sound like boss talk.

"How did the proposal go?" I asked. "From the way it sounded, you were going to be at it all night."

Gwen slowly walked around the room, observing the room's details as she spoke. "I worked right on through. Just before eight, I finished up and went home. I warmed up some soup, made toast. Robert called to ask what was wrong with you." She stopped to face me. Her expression was one of curiosity, caring.

"What's wrong with me?" I puzzled. "What does that mean?"

"He said you seemed distracted at dinner. Staring off into space, skipping beats in the conversation, preoccupied. Then you left abruptly." Her blue eyes smiled into mine, as if explaining that Robert was amusing.

"It's been a rough couple of days, coming back to work...finding the—trouble—at the jobsite...and I think Mary and I broke up today," I said.

I sat down at one end of the couch, Gwen lowering herself onto the middle. The couch was one of my "garage sale specials." The cushions worn, permanent depressions in the center. The frame creaked. At that moment, I wished I had one of those "grand old places" Wally had mentioned. How amazing it would be to sit in a lavish living room with solid oak flooring and matching furniture with Gwen. We could drink that champagne in front of a roaring fireplace.

"There was a lot on my mind. I found it hard to focus on the conversation with Edmund Palmer. In the end, I decided to get out of there. Donna and Robert are better without my mood getting in the way. They can tell him everything that needs to be conveyed." I looked at the champagne. "I'll get some glasses." I lifted myself from the couch and moved across the room toward the kitchen as Gwen surveyed the space, brows relaxed and eyes wide.

"There's potential for an exceptional ambiance here," she said. "Opening up the wall at the stairway would allow rays of light coming in through the window up there," she pointed to the landing, "to reflect off the side wall of the stair onto the picture window in front. I'd use a satin finish, with a rag-roll pattern on the stair wall to diffuse the light a little. I expect the character of light bouncing off the front window at 4 p.m. would be regal. But I don't need to explain the mechanics of light diffusion. You certainly did a remarkable job on the house next door."

Finally! A woman who appreciated my work. "Thanks." I'd found a couple of appropriate glasses in a box on the counter, and was making room in the sink to wash them. "Would you like some crackers? That's about all I have."

"Crackers are fine."

I gathered up the glasses and crackers, and moved back into the living room. I re-took my seat and opened the champagne. Gwen poured and we toasted my new place. I admired her silky fingers daintily grasping the stem of her glass, the pink-beige polish accenting her narrow nails. I was still uncertain why she had come.

I didn't have to wait long to find out.

She turned to face me, kicked off her yellow pumps and slid her nylon-gilded legs underneath her. "Ken." She turned her blue eyes toward mine. "Ken, there's something I have to share with you."

I was ready to listen to anything! Perhaps this was the night we crossed over from co-workers to...something more....

She glanced down at her hands, running the fingers of her left hand against her right. "Ken, I had...there were...." Her satiny voice trailed off and she turned her face toward mine. Suddenly uncertain, eyes timid, searching. "I don't know if it makes a difference. Events took a turn.... I have to verbalize. Tell someone."

I reached my hand out to hers. "What is it Gwen?"

"Maybe I should inform the police. I don't know. If I do.... I just don't know what to do."

"Police?" Huh? What was this about?

Her eyes started to tear up. "It's Isa...." she stammered, "Isabelle."

I waited, bracing myself.

"The t-truck," she tripped over the words. "Isabelle had it last weekend. I didn't know it was...Monday morning, I went back and—"

I cut her off, trying to understand what she was saying. "Wait. Explain. Isabelle had the truck last weekend? The pick-up truck from work?"

Gwen nodded. Tears had filled up her eyes and were about to fall. She was looking around. I reached next to my end of the couch to the floor to a box of tissues and handed them to her.

She dabbed her eyes, blew her nose. "She was supposed to go visit her daughter last weekend—over

New Year's.... You know her sister is taking care of Trudy. I don't know how that arrangement works exactly, but a six year old wants to see her mother. Her car—that old Sentra she drives—had been having problems...." She reached for another tissue. "So she was afraid to drive it to Indiana. She thought she might get stuck on the road somewhere. I don't know how we came to the idea, but we were talking in the lunchroom, and it seemed like the perfect solution."

"What was?"

"I thought she could borrow the company truck. No one would be using it. It was reliable. She could get there safely."

I was puzzled. "I thought you'd borrowed the truck that weekend."

"I did. As a secretary, Isabelle didn't have the authority to sign the truck out. So I signed it out and, in effect, lent it to her to use."

I played it out in my head. "She drove the truck home on Friday?"

"No, she had her car at the office. I had left my car at home that morning, and caught a ride in with Donna. Then after work, I drove the truck to Isabelle's. She took me home."

Gwen must have seen the bewilderment on my face.

"I didn't want anyone to question the fact that I was taking the truck. If Robert found out I was borrowing it for Isy, he would have nixed the whole thing." She took a breath and reached for the champagne bottle. She refilled both our glasses.

After I took a sip, I asked, "Isabelle never made it to work on Monday. How did the truck get back to the office on Monday?"

Gwen looked at me with big, watering, red-rimmed eyes. "She lives—lived—in Berkley, so her house was on my way in. We had planned that I would stop by and pick up the truck, leaving my car in her drive. She would give me a ride home after work, and I'd pick up my car then. When I arrived at her door Monday morning, she didn't answer the doorbell. Then I saw that her car was gone, so I assumed that she'd already gone to work, forgetting that we were going to switch vehicles. I took the truck and left my car in the drive, as we'd planned. I was surprised that she wasn't at the office when I got in."

"Then later, we found out she was dead," I offered, "and your car was still at Isabelle's. Didn't the police ask you what it was doing in Isabelle's drive?"

Gwen shook her head. "Dwayne took it. He called me shortly after I arrived at work. School was canceled due to a water main break. He asked if he could borrow my car. You know teenagers. He had a sudden free day, and needed to be able to get around. I told him ok, if he found a ride to Isabelle's, and then picked me up from work later. I guess he talked one of his friends into dropping him off there."

The doorbell rang. *Now what?*

I got up off the couch, still holding my freshly filled champagne glass.

I opened the door to find Mary standing on my porch, beaming brightly and holding a bottle of wine adorned with a red ribbon.

"Ken, I decided to come over and—"

Her smile faded as her eyes settled on the glass in my hand, then past me into the living room.

"Mary, it's not—" I started.

Gwen jumped up. "Oh, Mary. I was just leaving." She looked around for her shoes.

"Don't bother," Mary screeched. To me she mumbled hoarsely. "You'll regret this, Ken. No one makes a fool of me." She turned and climbed down the three porch steps. As she reached the concrete walk, she spun back toward me. I was about to jump down after her, when she exclaimed, "Oh, I brought some wine." She stood back, held her arm out to the side, took aim and slung the bottle onto the porch. The glass hit the concrete slab and shattered, thin red liquid dripping out over the adjacent snow.

Mary dove into her car, and pulled out onto the street. She was three houses down before her headlights came on.

I stood, stunned for a moment, looking down the street after Mary's car. Slowly, I shut the door. When I turned back to the living room, Gwen had found her shoes and was preparing to leave.

"Gwen, I'm sorry about this," I said quietly.

"I'm the one who's sorry. It wasn't my intent to create a personal problem for you."

"You haven't. Mary and I have split up three times in the last two days, most recently this afternoon. As far as I knew, it was over."

Gwen smiled tentatively, her lower lip quivering. Precious.

I looked at the bottle on the coffee table. "There's just a little left. Why don't you help me finish this before you go?"

Gwen shook her head. "If I have one more, I won't be able to drive."

I gave her a playful smile and raised an eyebrow.

She sighed. "Why don't you have the last drink and I'll keep you company?" she offered.

We sat on the couch and she asked me about my remodeling plans for the house. We talked about nothing special. I was thoroughly enchanted with Gwen—and still feeling guilty about Mary. We said goodnight about thirty minutes later. We shared a short embrace and I ushered her out the side door to avoid encountering glass on the front porch.

I walked her to her car, and when we came around to the driver's side I noticed that the car was tilted.

Gwen groaned. Both the driver's side tires were flat.

Chapter 7
Edison's Explanation

Depressing. Two tires squashed flat, steel rims pinning the flaccid rubber. One spare tire. January wind howling at our backs and up our sleeves.

Gwen took a deep breath and leaned back to stretch, as if bracing herself for unpleasantness, the psychedelic band across her head striking an inappropriately positive chord. "Ok, let's review our options."

We stared at the ruptured tires. Gwen said, "We could call the auto club. While we're waiting for the wrecker, you could tell me more about your plans for the house." Her lovely blue eyes radiated strength.

I strained to make out the dial on my watch. 10:45. I considered inviting her to spend the night, but I didn't have any facilities to do that. Just the mattress on the floor in my bedroom, and the garage sale couch. Things would be less awkward—and less tempting—if I took her home. "It's late. It's going to take the service at least an hour to get here. And then what? They're going to take the car away, then you'll need a ride home. Why don't I drive you home now, and we can call the auto club in the morning?"

Gwen paused in thought, her index finger tapping her lower lip. "Ken, if you can drop me at home, I'll have Dwayne drop me off in the morning. I'll call the auto club at that time, and after they pick up the car, you can give me a lift into work. Once the tires are repaired, maybe at lunch, I'll get a ride from someone at work back to the shop."

"Sounds like a plan," I said.

The ride to Gwen's house was uneventful. Once I returned home, I turned in, too exhausted to think.

* * *

The noise was loud and irritating. Bang! Bang! Bang! *Someone shut that racket off!* Bang! Bang! Bang! *Someone please stop that clattering!*

"Ken! Ken! Are you in there?" The voice was familiar, female.

I worked my eyes open and turned to the alarm clock. It was 7:15. No! It couldn't be! I groaned. Did I forget to set the alarm? Or did I turn it off and go back to sleep? I fought to clear the fog in my head.

"Ken!" Bang. Bang. Bang. "Ken!" It was Gwen.

I grabbed my robe and went to open the door. Gwen's wool coat was the color of a shamrock. It extended to just above her knees, meeting the top of her black leather boots. She wore a black beret and a wide smile.

"You don't look ready for the drive to work," she said, reviewing my attire.

"The sandman beat me into submission, then took my alarm clock."

"Ken, it's seven-fifteen. You're lucky Dwayne had school today. He dropped me off and scooted out of here. What would he have thought if he'd seen you open the door for his mother dressed like that?"

"He would have thought the poor guy got to bed late last night."

Gwen took off her coat, laying it across the couch. "Why don't you take a shower and get ready for work? I'll fix some breakfast. But first I'll call the auto club. Perhaps by the time they arrive, we'll be ready to go to work."

I showered and shaved. The red crease on my

forehead was turning a deep purple. Why didn't it just go away? Explaining my accident to everyone was tiresome. There was nothing to be done about it; the damage would heal eventually. I padded across the hall to the bedroom. While I dressed, I began to pick up some delicious smells coming from the kitchen. Bacon. Eggs. Coffee. Yum.

I found that Gwen had prepared a feast on matching plates in quite an attractive arrangement. Where she'd found all of the coordinating elements, I was at a complete loss to explain.

"Where did you get the food?" I asked. "At last check, there was only mustard and pickle juice in the refrigerator."

"Yes, when I couldn't find anything worth fixing in here, I went outside, to see if I could find a market nearby."

I was puzzled. "And where did you find one?"

"Your next door neighbor, Earl, was just leaving for work. I introduced myself and he was kind enough to give you the food. Said he owed you anyway."

"You're going to give me a reputation," I said.

"One thing at a time," Gwen teased. "Let's just have breakfast right now."

I arrived at work refreshed and ready for the day. I found Edison sitting in my guest chair, nervously poking through my candy dish. That was a déjà vu I wasn't interested in experiencing. He looked somewhat agitated, leg crossed, foot tapping nervously.

"Good morning Edison. Find what you're looking for?"

He made a face, pulling his mouth to one side. "There isn't any chocolate in here. I'm not really a hard candy person. Don't you have some Rolos or Tootsie Rolls?"

I checked my candy drawer. "Fresh out of both. But I've got some Mary Janes."

Edison twisted his lips to the side, as if to say, *better than nothing.*

I poured some into the bowl. Time to go shopping.

"What's on your mind, Edison?"

His big puppy dog eyes looked pitiful. *What now?* "Edison, what's the story? Did you lose another—"

"Shhh!" he scolded. Then he took a sideways glance "I've got to tell you something."

"Well, I kind of got that, Edison. What's on your mind?"

"Listen, Ken."

I turned my face toward him, staring intently at his face. "I'm listening. Go ahead."

"Ken, last week—"

My phone rang, interrupting Edison. I picked it up.

"Cannoli, you stud, you." It was Wally.

Say huh?

"I saw you pulling in with Gwen this morning. Did the two of you have a good night?"

"Oh Wally, clam up. There's nothing to report."

"You say there isn't, I think there is. A person doesn't come in to work with a person of the opposite sex unless they had spent some time together in the morning."

"Wally, Gwen's car is in the shop, I picked her up. Not that I owe you any explanation." The conversation was over.

Edison had found his way to another piece of candy. He continued his story.

"Last week, when I found," he shifted his blue-jeaned body uneasily in his chair, "well, you know what I found—"

Rita poked her head around the partition. "Ken, I've got those papers for you to sign—for the permit submittal for Martina's Grape Arbor."

Edison's eyes grew as large as goose eggs.

I said, "I'll be over there in just a minute, Rita." I glanced at Edison, who was fidgeting like he was sitting on a hot plate.

She rounded the corner with a sheaf of papers. "I've got them right here, and I'll just thank you to put your John Hancock in this special place."

She pointed her blood red nail to a line on the paper. I signed and she flipped to a page further back, pointing to another location. There were several places to affix my signature.

Edison's squirming continued as he licked his lips and drummed all ten fingers on his legs. No doubt he was worried. I felt I should honor his feelings.

Rita left and I said, "Edison, let's go to the conference room where we won't be interrupted."

He sighed.

With the door shut, Edison lowered his massive frame into one of the stock roller chairs.

"You know, last week, when I found the body, and put it into the truck and then Wally took the truck and it had transmission trouble and Wally left it with the repair shop?"

"Yes, Edison, how could I forget?"

"I tried to call you. I tried your house phone, your cell phone. I tried everything. I called that Monday night. And I tried on Tuesday."

"So you couldn't reach me. What does that have to do with anything?"

"Yeah, I know. Well that's just it. I didn't know what to do. I needed your help. I just found the guy there. One minute he was in the truck, head twisted, laying there on the cardboard. The next minute I was showing Robert and Andrew around the project, and then I had to take Robert back to the office."

"Yeah, Edison. I know all that."

Edison had this intent look in his eyes. Like he was about to 'fess up to something.

"Edison. What's wrong? Just tell me."

He turned his big brown eyes on me. "I couldn't handle it alone. I wanted to talk to you, but you weren't.... I couldn't reach you."

"I'm sorry I was unavailable. I'm sorry I had my phone turned off. What did you do?"

"I told Isabelle." His eyes were studying me for a reaction. A nervous twitch started up in his right cheek.

Something dark and hot spread into my stomach. "You told Isabelle?"

Edison nodded. His stringy black curly hair jumbled in all directions around his head. "I had to tell someone. I finally couldn't keep it in any longer, so I started thinking about who could I talk to? She was at work and came over to talk to me about something and I suddenly had the idea to talk to her about it."

This is just like Edison—unpredictable! Do you move a body? No. You call the police. But imagine that you do move a body due to some misdirected impulse. Do you then tell people about it? Absolutely not! Edison is so...Edison.

"So, what did you tell Isabelle about the body?"

"I didn't tell her about the body. I asked her what should I do. I never would have talked to her about it if I'd have been able to reach you."

I was frustrated, and tired of him bringing up my state of unreachability. Frustrated with Edison for...this whole situation.

"So Isabelle knew about it? What exactly did you tell her? What did she say?"

"She didn't entirely know about it. I tried to ask her what I should do, without telling her what happened. I just needed someone to talk to."

"Did you tell her or not? What did you say?" I snapped.

"I told her that I found something—that's what I called it. That's exactly what I called it. I just said that it was at the jobsite and I didn't know what to do about it and I couldn't reach you and I didn't know what to do."

How can you tell someone you just found something and not explain to them what that something is? "How did you explain what it was?"

"I didn't. I just told her that I was doing the job inspection, and walking around I found something that you should be aware of and that I didn't know what to do about it."

"Didn't she ask you what it was?"

"Of course she did. I told her it was technical. Just that there was a problem on site and you needed to be informed I didn't know what to do."

"What did she say?"

"She was really supportive. She said that I shouldn't worry about it too much. That you would know what to do when you got back to the office."

I looked at the man in front of me. "Edison. Take a breath. This is really important."

"I knew it was, that's why I'm telling you."

"And I appreciate it. Listen, tell me exactly what you told Isabelle."

"I just did."

"No, tell me word for word. I need to know exactly what you said to her."

"Ok. She was at the folding table next to her desk, setting out the pages for a proposal on that Embassy project. She had all the colored printed pages set up and was organizing them into a certain order. I went over and I asked her how it was coming and then I said, 'Can I talk to you? I can't reach Ken and I need some advice.'"

"Go on."

"She said 'Sure.' I told her that I went out to the Flamingo Shores jobsite yesterday—the day before—to take some photos and notes for the job inspection. As I was looking around, I found something. I didn't know what to do about it and I had tried to reach you and couldn't. Now I didn't know what to do.

"She said, 'What was it?'

"I said, 'It's hard to explain. It's kind of technical. But it's something that Ken should be aware of.'

"She said 'if it's technical maybe Wally could help.'

"I said, 'No, I'd rather not bring it up to one of the other project managers,' and I told her to forget it. I'd just wait until I could reach you."

"What did she say to that?" I asked.

"She said, 'Don't worry, Edison. It will be ok.' Then she smiled and told me that you would know exactly what to do." Edison looked at me for approval.

I thought for a moment, then asked, "Why Isabelle?"

He paused. "I thought I could talk to her. That she'd know what to do. You know, Isabelle and I used to go out."

What? "You used to date Isabelle? When was that?"

"A couple years ago, before she came to work here. She was a waitress over at Hogan's. I used to stop by in the evenings for an apple pie and a large root beer. She got to recognize my 'usual,' and, well, we got to joking around. We dated for most of the summer and, well, it just didn't work out. Anyway—did you know that she's—she was—going out with one of the subcontractors at Crystals?"

"You mean recently? I had no idea."

"Yeah, she and Jay Stevens have been seeing each other—had been—for the last six weeks. Word is it was hot and heavy." Edison slouched back in his chair. The subject changed, relief spread across his face.

"The masonry contractor?" I said.

Edison nodded.

"No kidding," I said.

Edison went on babbling, apparently stimulated by getting this heavy burden off his chest. "Of all of the people I thought about talking to, she had to be the one. Jeanelle, she doesn't like me to bring work home. Isy and I—we didn't turn into best friends or anything after we split, but it was ok. Anyway, most of the office was gone, so it was on the quiet side, and it felt like a good time to talk to her without being overheard."

This got my attention. "Most of the office was gone?"

"Sure. A lot of people were out, due to the holidays. Most of the rest of the folks were down in Cleveland for that big meeting."

"Oh, the Raleigh Project," I said, remembering the big Six Forks Mall meeting was last week.

"Yeah that project gave me a grief attack. I had barely returned to the office on Monday when Cheryl snagged me to help with the presentation boards for Tuesday's meeting. They were running behind and needed someone to slam together some elevations and perspectives from the Skywing Center in Phoenix. I cued up the plots. I had to scam three computers to do it. Those files were so large that the plotter memory couldn't handle it."

"Oh," I said. "That was Monday, the day you gave Robert a ride back to the office after doing the job inspection?"

"Right, and by the time I got the presentation stuff underway, and went back to check on the truck—"

"Wally had checked it out."

"Right."

I replayed the information in my head, trying to

place it all in proper order. Did all of the pieces fit? "And then Tuesday, who all went to the meeting?"

"Let's see. Smartain came up from the Florida office to be there. Cheryl and Gwen went. Andrew and Robert. Those five. I guess that's why Andrew and Robert were out at Crystal's reviewing the job on Monday. They had the Tuesday Cleveland meeting. Wednesday they were going down to Dayton to meet with Foley's Angles."

"I can't believe those guys were working so much over the holidays."

"If you could call it work." Edison gave me a sly smile. "Andrew and Robert went down to Dayton to treat Jack and Bruce and their wives to a nice holiday dinner and dancing."

"Marketing." I said matter-of-factly. "A lot of it would get done at that time of year." I puzzled aloud, "Dinner and dancing? I wonder who Robert took." Robert and Gwen had ended their long relationship before Thanksgiving. As far as I knew, Robert wasn't seeing anyone currently.

Edison broadened his smile. Now we were in true Edison territory. "You want me to tell you?"

"You know? How did you find out?"

"I have my ways," he said with glee. "It was Charlotte Webster."

I got an uncomfortable feeling. "Charlotte Webster?" She was the wife of one of our more important clients. I had heard that she and her husband were separated. Still, it couldn't be right. "Are you sure?"

"I have it from the most reliable of sources."

It didn't make any sense.

I considered again what Edison had said to Isabelle. Edison hadn't actually told her anything. There was a problem. In so many words, that's what he said. I wondered how Isabelle had perceived the words Edison spoke. What information had she gleaned from the way that Edison had asked her? The fact that there was a problem at the jobsite wasn't really any alarming information.

So why was I unsettled?

Two days had already gone by since Edison had revealed finding the corpse. We had no identity on the body or how he was killed. Worse, the body had been missing for over a week. I was behind in a race where I didn't know the course, where it ended, or even where to search next. As much as I didn't want to be the one to get Edison in trouble, and for that matter, I didn't want to get in hot water myself, it was time to tell the police about the missing body.

What would I tell them? Someone told me about finding a body. He found it at the jobsite, and decided to move it. Well, after he put it in the truck, he lost it. No, I didn't see anything. No, I have no evidence. No, I don't know what happened to the corpse. No, I'm not certain there is a body.

What kind of story is that?

And what would they do to Edison? He found a body—a dead body, a real person who was killed, and proceeded to move it. Then he lost it. It's gone. No, we don't know where it is. It just disappeared. Tampering with evidence. Interfering with a crime scene. Misplacing a corpse. Those are serious crimes. Very serious. And yet—there was no body, no corpse, no solid evidence.

I changed my mind. The best thing was to find the body. Direct my full attention to finding out what happened to it. Who was it? Who took it? Where is it now?

And then figure out what to tell the police.

Chapter 8
It Happened to Hart

Vincent T. Lombardi, the greatest football coach who ever lived, who led the Green Bay Packers to five national championships, said: *The difference between a successful person and others is not a lack of strength, not a lack of knowledge, but rather a lack of will.*

Here's my secret: I don't know enough. Faced with a new challenge, endeavor, or undertaking, I'm staring with trepidation into the side of a mountain. How am I to conquer this fifty-foot high jagged piece of rock with my bare hands and tennis shoes? Where do I begin? Where is the point of beginning? I don't know. I didn't learn enough in school, missed the series on ESPN, skipped the chapter by Richard Feynman.

When this deficiency of confidence flares up, I remember Lombardi's quote and I plow ahead. I continue to read, study, soak up whatever bits of information are shoved in front of me. Time and again I'm learning to employ the power of will. Without a doubt, my intense attention to this murder problem would eventually bring it to resolution—by sheer act of will.

Immediately at hand, however, a project meeting at Crystals evoked my focus. Overall responsibility for the project was Gwen's, as the Associate in Charge. Day-to-day running of the job, however, was up to yours truly as project manager. I gathered up my planner and headed out. Edison was fiddling with several miniature wood dowels at his desk.

"Edison, how's that model for the Fenkel House coming? Can you join me at Crystals? I thought that you could retake those report photos that disappeared from the office, while I attend a meeting. Maggie Humes is all over me to get that report out."

Edison's curly black hair bounced in all directions as he looked up from his work. "Aye, aye Chief! This is not due till Monday. Just let me organize these columns."

It was almost 10:20 and the job meeting was set for 11:00. We had a few minutes to play with, so we agreed to meet five minutes later.

The phone rang as I returned to my cube. Serenity announcing that an overnight package had arrived.

I walked the aisle through the perimeter of the open office, landscaped with partitioned-off cubes. Full-height offices flanked the side and I switched to tiptoe mode as Robert's post loomed ahead. Just as I was sneaking by, he stepped into my path.

"Cannoli, I'm glad I caught you." His chiseled face appeared thoughtful. "At your job meeting today, pull Sharon Webster aside and remind her that we're still awaiting payment for the last billing."

I was not in a mood to get into an extended conversation with Robert, but I couldn't let this one pass. "Robert, that billing just went out on the 15th, so it's not late yet."

"Ask her about it anyway. You know we've had a lot of expenses in December. Our holiday party, gift books to clients, you know the situation. We have an urgent need to refill the coffers."

Robert's occasional bending of business protocol made me uneasy.

Robert wore one of his specialty tie-tacks. I gazed at a little scene of a mouse caught in a mousetrap, the metal spring-loaded bar pressing firmly on the mouse's neck as its little hands held the wedge of cheese. Today I felt like that mouse.

Reluctantly, I agreed to make an inquiry about the billing.

I stopped by the front desk and discovered the package from Milstone, containing the glass samples we had requested for the chocolate shop.

I picked up the box and collected Edison.

Traffic on Telegraph Road was medium heavy, the roads dry as the sun had first melted the ice, then evaporated the remains. I phoned Jester Cromwell to advise him that the samples had arrived. We agreed to meet at the jobsite after lunch.

"Sorry Edison, looks like I'm going to tie you up a little longer than anticipated. You can take the photos while I'm in the project meeting. After, I'll buy you lunch and then at one o'clock we've got to meet Jester Cromwell at the Truffle Shop."

Edison was happy to get a free lunch out of the deal.

We pulled into the Flamingo Shores parking lot from the Big Beaver Road side, encountering minimal delays as we wound our way through the surface lot, circling around toward the job trailer. I angled into an available space between a couple of heating and cooling company vans. I stepped out onto the slushy snow.

Edison grabbed the camera and clipboard and headed into the parking deck. I hoped he'd get some usable shots despite the police tape that was present in various locations throughout the project.

I climbed three wobbly wooden steps into the mobile job trailer. A raucous noise greeted my ears as I found twenty people already seated along the set of folding tables in the center. Attendees were predominately men, showing an overabundance of denim and flannel and at least a couple of overalls. Some wore "uniform" shirts with a company name stitched on the breast pocket. I recognized representatives from the various subtrades––mechanical, plumbing, carpentry, sheet metal, glass, concrete, steel, doors, ceilings.

Pontile Construction's project superintendent, Jason Tyler, sat near the business end of the table, as did their project manager, Mike D'Agastino, and two representatives from The Circle Group, owners of the mall. The room was out of control as people spoke to their neighbors in excited tones. Voices over voices echoed through the tin can office. Only the plumbing sub and one of the owner's reps were women, and 80 percent of the group was over the age of fifty. There goes my analytical mind, quantifying things again. Jason Pontile, in his early thirties, was one of the exceptions to the age situation. At forty-three, oddly enough, I was in the minority too. Sharon Webster, who worked for the Southfield office of The Circle Group, was in her mid-thirties.

Sharon exuded a polished appearance: expensive tailored suit, highly buffed nails, a soft smooth complexion, crisp eye make-up, short well-manicured hair that must have been a current style. No eyebrow rings or pierced nostrils. The only piercing I observed were her earrings, and there were only two of those— one in each ear, in the traditional location. As I squeezed past her to reach an open seat, I caught the delicate scent of her perfume: *Opium*. I only recognized the designer fragrance because it's my favorite perfume of all time.

Jason called the meeting to order, and began ticking off a prepared agenda. The weekly job meeting focused on the schedule—what needed to be done in the coming week to maintain the schedule's critical path and what problems needed resolution to preserve the completion date.

Two questions came my way: one was of a minor

nature, the other was relative to shop drawings for the glass railing that was to encircle the atrium at the upper floor.

"When are those shop drawings going to be released?" the specialty subcontractor asked. "The railings are a six-week ship time, and it's close to the time now when they could be installed."

I reviewed the situation mentally before answering. "We've asked for information twice regarding additional detailing at the juncture of the rail and the edge of the concrete deck. We are concerned about the visibility of exposed fasteners. As soon as we receive the additional information, we can finish processing the shop drawings."

Jason, perpetually seeking to keep the job moving, said, "Ken, can you release the glass portion? At least they could start fabricating those curved glazing sections."

"No, I'm reluctant to do that. The fastening detail at the bottom may affect the glass."

Jason instructed the subcontractor to get the additional details submitted posthaste.

We talked about the overall schedule and milestone dates required to reach the date of substantial completion. This brought about the hot topic of delays encountered due to the murder investigation.

"I can't get to the doors at the parking deck entry to make the adjustments to the closers," said the aluminum and glass contractor.

"Doors? How about this: I can't get to the vestibule ceiling to put in the diffuser. Without that piece, I can't balance that leg of ductwork," reported the heating and cooling contractor.

"What about that lot outside, how long is that going to be closed off?" complained the plumber. "What are they looking for there anyway? We've got a lot of material to carry in—and I mean carry, if we can't get the parking problem solved soon."

A man with a Clint Eastwood face—hard-lined and stern—spoke softly from near the opposite end of the table. "You do realize that these delays are going to cost the owner some money. Every additional day that labor is scheduled, every piece of equipment that is rented for a second time, every task done out of sequence consequently takes additional time to construct. All of it will be charged as additional work."

Jason looked at the subs, then said, "We understand all of your concerns with the restricted areas. We are working with the police in order to have these areas released for construction activity as soon as possible. Until then, I suggest you work in the areas that aren't restricted. Don't stop. Work around the area, get ahead on the other sections so that when these controlled areas come back on line, you'll be ready to focus on them.

"Daryl, as far as your comments about additional costs, write them up and get them to me as soon as possible so that I can advise the owner."

The trailer door opened and Lieutenant Coogan entered, as if on cue. I realized Jason must have invited him.

Jason continued. "And here to give us an update on the investigation is the person responsible, Lieutenant Coogan."

"Good afternoon, gentlemen." He looked up and paused as he realized that there were women present also, "and ladies. I'm sure that Jason has told you that we're going to be keeping the barriers on some of the areas that we are investigating. I hope this isn't causing you too much trouble. I've spoken to Chuck Hagar at Pontile Construction, and have been assured by him that it is a major problem. I do recognize that this is an inconvenience. We are working as diligently as humanly possible to bring this matter to a close and the Troy Police Department invites your cooperation."

The meeting ended with a crescendo of voices as twenty-some people prepared to return to work. My head throbbed, and I hoped to make a quick exit.

With an abrupt shove on my chair, I sprang to my feet, collecting my planner. Glancing around, planning my maneuver to the exit door, I found Sharon Webster looking in my direction. My course was set. I made my way behind the row of chairs, men still talking in animated tones about how they were going to solve a myriad of circumstances on-site.

"I thought you did a marvelous job of answering inquiries today," she said, showing off her pearly whites.

"All in a day's work," I smiled.

Sharon's emerald eyes glittered with flecks of gold, blue, brown and several shades of green. The array of glimmering fragments reflecting light gave the effect of looking into a kaleidoscope. I couldn't help thinking this inspired Elton John—or more correctly Bernie Taupin—to pen the expression "kaleidoscope eyes."

"Tell me, Ken, I have a question perhaps you can answer. There's a detail on the building I'm troubled about."

I helped her on with her wool coat, checkered in tiny black and while squares, and I escorted her out toward the building.

"It's here along the entrance." She pointed to the rear, glass skylight-covered entryway.

"The glass is pitched to each side, from a central gable. I'm assuming there are built-in gutters along the eave?"

I nodded.

"What about the problem of ice build-up? Once the gutters fill up with ice and snow, a sunny day will melt the surface while the flow is blocked down below in the gutter and downspouts. Water will drip off the sides onto the cars where they're lined up here for drop offs."

Those dynamic eyes held mine as I responded. "We've done three things to head off that situation. The gutters are extra wide—fourteen inches if I remember correctly—to hold as much of that snow and ice as possible. The outer edge is an inch higher than the inner side as an extra precaution against spill over. Last, the gutters drain into downspouts wrapped in heat tape. The downspouts run inside the columns to the storm sewer."

As I answered, I was acutely aware that lunchtime was upon us. The alluring woman before me, with the kaleidoscope eyes, registered 85 percent interested on my attraction meter. I didn't have any possibility of responding to that kind of relationship right now, and I would find it difficult to treat it as just business. I had also promised to treat Edison to lunch today.

"It sounds like you've got the bases covered!" she said, smiling broadly. Then abruptly, she looked at her watch, "Heavens! I'm late for an appointment. Ken, I'd love to have lunch some time. Would you call me?"

On impulse, I said, "That would be wonderful!" Then I remembered the invoices. "Sharon, Robert asked me confer with you about something. Have you had a chance to review our last invoice?"

"No, I haven't. It's sitting on my desk and I just haven't had a moment to study it. May I call you about it tomorrow?"

I agreed, and she hustled down the lot to her car. I wandered off into the parking deck to find Edison.

My hollow footsteps echoed through the structure. Yellow *Police Line* tape was still evident, barricading off certain areas. Cold emanating from the concrete floor shot through my shoes into my feet.

Edison was nowhere to be seen. I climbed the stairs

to the third floor and walked over to the side, looking out over the construction and the customer parking lot. I spied Edison, talking to a security guard next to one of the landscaped islands in the parking lot. It's a wonder my ice cube feet didn't shatter as I hurried down the two flights of stairs and across the lot to Edison.

"It was one of those judgment calls," the guard said. Deep vertical lines augmented his thin face, framing his mouth and pronounced beak. His short grey hair stood up in the wind. His shiny complexion reminded me of the cubes of wax my aunt used to make into candles. "It was sitting out there for several days before we towed it. The customers don't like us touching their vehicles. But after it didn't move for a few days, it was just an invitation for theft."

Edison turned to me. "They found Barry Hart's car in the lot. Apparently abandoned." I remembered Barry Hart, entrepreneur and one of the scheduled speakers at the Olson House groundbreaking, had turned out to be a no-show.

My bearings eluded me. "What do you mean, abandoned?"

The guard repeated himself. "It was left in the lot for several days, at least. I don't know how long it was before we noticed it. We had that snow last week and the plows came through here in the morning; they shoved snow around it and that's when it came to light."

"How did you know it was Barry's car?" I asked.

Edison took that one. "Black Land Rover, license plate 'WINNER'"

That was Barry's plate all right.

"What did Barry Hart say about the car? Why didn't he come for it?" I asked.

"We haven't been able to reach him. We called his office. No one has heard from him. He went on some sort of survival trip the latter part of December and he hasn't called. They say he's not back from his trip, hasn't left word, nothing. I guess he had a cell-phone with him. Can't reach him on that thing either. Don't know how the car got here. Maybe someone else was using it, no one at his office knows."

An uneasy feeling washed over me. I knew what happened to Barry Hart.

Chapter 9
Investigating Isabelle

It seemed a considerable coincidence that Barry Hart's car had turned up abandoned at Flamingo Shores the same time he didn't show at the Ground Breaking ceremony. In addition, he was unreachable during the past week, though he was supposed to be back from his survival trip.

"Edison," I probed as we walked over to the mall, "tell me again what the homeless man looked like."

Edison looked at me sideways, as if he were trying to read my mind. He shrugged and said, "He had on a brown coat and grey pants. Under the coat he wore a red flannel shirt and some thermal underwear. A week's growth of beard covered his face and his forehead had some smudges on it."

"Was he wearing any jewelry?"

"No rings or anything. Homeless people don't have jewelry, do they?"

I ignored the questions. "How about boots? What kind of footwear was he wearing?"

Edison scrunched his face up in thought. "They were brown, chocolate brown. Still had some good tread on them. Why? What are you thinking?"

I had reservations about whether to tell Edison my suspicions. I felt if he knew, he was likely to blab to someone. Depending on whom he told, this could influence some of the people I wanted to talk to. In the end, I decided against it. "Just trying to get a clear understanding of the facts."

Edison and I approached the main entrance to the existing Flamingo Shores. Shoppers entered through glass doors in brushed steel frames. An artist's ornamental abstract of the mall's floor plan comprised the door handles, with a bright blue dot indicating the entry point. I wondered how many of the bustling patrons understood the reference.

Polished marble flooring greeted our cold feet, while columns simulating pineapple trees formed a colonnade leading to the two story center court. An elaborate water fountain consisted of perhaps a hundred leaf-shaped copper dishes creating a focal point. Water cascaded from one leaf into the next, splashing into a rugged stone basin. A couple dozen pink flamingos pranced around on a copper island. Three bundled up children with a young mother *ooed* and *ahhed* at the display. The images moved my child-like heart as well.

Twenty past twelve. We'd have to hustle if we were going to eat before meeting Jester at one o'clock. The food court had been inserted into shopping space four years ago. Sections of mall, originally dry goods stores on opposite sides of the center mall aisle-way, were renovated into a dozen individual food counters. Depressed two steps, the dining area was smartly fitted-out with seating for 200 on ornamental metal tables and chairs.

A couple of notches above the fare at your average food court, options included no fast food hamburgers, subs, pizza or tacos. Our choices consisted of Designer Deli, with sandwiches all named after—I supposed—famous designers, although I hadn't heard of most of them; Francois's Bistro, offering fancy French-sounding fare; Souper Energy, where each of ten daily soups came with a suggested juice drink that would address your specific energy depletion and nutritional needs; and Mother Earth, whose quiches, casseroles, and vegetable dishes were all made from natural ingredients with no preservatives, chemicals, or saturated fats. Food for the fashionable tastes.

Edison did not hide his disappointment.

"Where are the coney dogs? I need some chili fries." He affected his puppy dog face.

"This is a designer mall." I said, "They have designer food."

"Ken, look at me. Does this look like a designer body?"

His face was round. His belly was round.

He continued. "Let's go somewhere else. There's a coney island over at Crooks and Maple."

"Sorry, Edison. There isn't time to head out. Let's just find something here. It'll be an adventure."

Grumbling, he settled for the 'Fendi turkey and Swiss on seven grain bread with romaine lettuce and honey-mustard dressing,' and I went for the 'Mother Earth sweet potato casserole with fresh snow peas, corn, and broccoli.' It actually was quite tasty. However, the salad that came with it included about six different colors and textures of leaves. Alas, a little too adventuresome, even for me.

Just as we pushed back our chairs after hastily devouring our gourmet lunch, Rita and Serenity walked by.

Serenity, our receptionist, was a dark-skinned young woman of twenty-three, with long straight black hair down to the center of her back. The dark mysterious eyes and high cheekbones alluded to Native American ancestry. She said, "Hey guys, what are you doing here?"

Edison spoke, "Ken had a meeting and I had to take some pictures. What about you?"

"We just decided to come out here for lunch. It's a little drive, but I like the atmosphere."

Rita piped up, "And the chicken salad on croissant at Francois' is excellent. There are peanuts in it."

They offered Edison a ride back to the office, which he heartily accepted. I hustled off to meet with Jester.

The connection from the existing mall to the expansion area had not yet been constructed, requiring me to exit from the mall and circle around the outside. I gathered the glass samples from my car on the way.

From the rear service corridor, I slipped through the metal door into the storage room of the chocolate shop.

Jester was in his office, directly opposite, working on his books. Attired in a brown western-style shirt and string tie, he was absorbed by the large format ledger before him: green pages with a dozen columns and closely spaced lines. He looked up with a friendly smile when I entered.

"Oh, Ken. Is it time already? I've just got a couple more entries to make here. Ted is out front. I believe he has questions for you. I'll be right there."

I exited his office, and walked out on the plain concrete floor. Two workmen actively screwed black anodized U-shaped channels along the floor that would create the seat for the glass storefront. The 5/8" thick glass panels sat on a cart along the wall, awaiting installation. Four foot wide, the clear panels were to run floor to ceiling, with a spacing of 3/4" between the glass segments. The concrete floor had been marked to indicate the location of the bottom channel and the pivot hinges for the glass doors.

Ted reviewed plans over a saw horse table, one hand on the plans, apparently searching for an answer. He looked up when I entered. Ted always had questions for me and today wasn't any different. After we cleared up his concerns over millwork detailing, I brought out the box of glass samples.

"Ted, I received these from Milstone this morning.

Let's see what we have here."

Jester came out of his office, and we examined the options.

Three pieces of etched glass sat in the package. One was almost completely obscure, providing a frosted center with a pattern of clear leaves around the perimeter. The second was reversed, with a pattern of frosted vines and leaves around the edges of clear glass. This made a nice presentation. The third was a pattern of frosted stripes.

Jester spoke excitedly, picking up the second pattern. "I love this. It will frame the chocolates. The vines look elegant, don't they?"

Ted looked at the glass, touching the etchings. "This must be some kind of sandblasting process. Very rich."

It was settled. I made the call to Milstone and put the issue to bed.

As I left the meeting, I began thinking about the facts and what I thought I knew about the murder investigations. Even though everything had transpired within the last three days, details were already a blur in my head.

I decided to pursue the investigation by doing what two of my favorite detectives did. Kinsey Millhone and Archie McNally have very different personalities and different styles, but they both write down all the clues and information. Archie, playboy detective, writes down in his journal the events that occur during his "discreet investigations." From time to time, he reviews his notations. Kinsey, on the other hand, regularly puts her information on 3" x 5" index cards and sorts through them to organize and reorganize them into some pattern that makes sense.

I found a paper goods store—Archives&Chronicles––and purchased some index cards. These must have been quite special, because they cost me almost four bucks.

I set up a work space in the food court. Lunchtime had passed, shoppers had returned to shopping, and no one would mind if I spread out. The first table I sat down to was wobbly, even though on inspection, someone had already stuffed a folded paper under one of the legs. The next was not unsteady, but it contained wet circles where drinks had stood. Once that was wiped off, I began my analysis.

I wrote down all of the facts that I was aware of, listing on each card the name of the person involved and the fact, such as:

Edison—found a body on 12/27
Wally—took truck with body into shop on 12/27
Joel—had possession of the truck with the body
        12/27 - 12/30

I decided it would be helpful to identify dead body facts as well:

Body—second floor of parking deck 12/27
Body—in truck 12/27 until?
Body—not in truck on 12/30

The process proved tedious and time consuming. To save on space, I used a shorthand, abbreviating FS for Flamingo Shores, PD for parking deck, TK for truck, and Isy for Isabelle. I returned to the paper store to buy a second package of 50 cards. When I finished, I'd gone through almost half of the second stack, and eight dollars. Did Kinsey Millhone encounter this much grief? I gave her a lot of credit.

I shuffled the cards and worked them back and forth, discovering something interesting. Here is what four of the cards said:

Edison—told Isy he found something at FS PD on
    12/27
Isabelle—Gwen borrowed the TK for Isy 12/31 - 1/3
Isabelle—found murdered on 1/3
Isabelle—dating the masonry contractor at FS

I wondered if there was any kind of connection between Isabelle and the murdered man Edison had found. It seemed kind of thin, but it was something that would be good to rule out. Edison had revealed the relationship between Isabelle and the masonry contractor. Perhaps a cautious discussion with him—after all he could have done Isabelle in—would shed some light on the subject. I gathered up the index cards.

Light snow had begun to fall, blowing gently across the parking lot. Tiny flakes bounced across my skin, as I made my way through the lot again, past the parking deck and into the job trailer. Jason Pontile was on the telephone when I arrived.

"Ken, what can I do for you?" he asked when he had finished his conversation.

"Do you know where I can find Jay Stevens?"

"Sure, he's in there." He pointed to Crystals.

"I didn't know if he'd taken some time off, after what happened to Isabelle day before yesterday. I understand that they were seeing each other."

"Yes. Jay is really busted up about it. But he just keeps working. Tough guy. He's pushing toward that deadline and doesn't want to let the team down. Masonry is one area that's not being held up by the police investigation. He doesn't have a whole lot to finish either."

"Well, it takes a lot to keep going under the circumstances," I said. Truth was, people respond to death in different ways and on alternate time lines. I imagined the realization would hit Jay at some point.

At any rate, he was on the premises.

Jason said, "He's working on the chimney structure in the middle of the building."

"Thanks, Jason."

I found Jay on the second floor. We had designed a rather elaborate maze of fireplaces throughout the building. The connecting chimney consisted of not one, but rather a series of connected shafts that threaded through the building's interior. Jay was preparing a section of stone banding for inclusion in the shaft structure.

"Jay, can I talk to you a minute?" I asked.

He looked up. He was in his early thirties, fair hair cut short in a traditional no-nonsense style. Gold chain, tight to his muscular neck. Brown and white plaid flannel shirt. Muscular arms punctuated by bulging veins. His skin was tan and smooth. "Sure."

"I'm sorry about Isabelle. I've heard you two were close."

He waved his hand, "Yeah, thanks. It's over for her. Not for the bastard who killed her. She was such a sweet thing. Loved life. She really looked toward making something of herself. She was always in the moment, living each minute as if it was precious. Isy taught me a lot about taking the day as it comes, standing in the here-and-now, looking around you and enjoying every ray of sun, and every cool breeze that's present. You know what I mean? She was your secretary, wasn't she?"

"Well, technically. She worked at the office and helped all of us out." He looked at me, apparently anticipating more from me. "She was something," I murmured. "How long had you known her?"

"We dated for about six weeks, that's all. We met, strangely enough, at the fruit and vegetable market in town. In the exotic fruit section. I asked her if she knew about mangos. She told me about some recipe: chicken, mangoes and goat cheese in a flour tortilla. Once we started talking, we discovered that we had the Flamingo Shores project in common. After we'd been going out for three weeks, I learned that Isy hadn't seen the project yet. I suggested showing her around, but it wasn't until two days after Christmas that we finally had a chance to visit the project."

My alarm bells went off. "You showed her around here?"

"Oh, yes."

"Two days after Christmas, on Monday?"

"Yeah, Isabelle had taken the day off, and I knew the place would be deserted so it was a good time. We drove out here after breakfast. I showed her the highlights."

My heart was racing now. "Did anything happen? Did you see anything unusual?"

He looked at me quizzically. "No, what do you mean? We just walked around. I wanted to show her some of that special brickwork we did on the inside, on the second floor. A little later, Isy wasn't feeling well. Did you know there's no place in this mall to buy any aspirin? Anyway, I took her home a little while after that."

Chapter 10
Family Fiddlings

The pivotal ingredient to a delicious Portobello sandwich is the provolone cheese. It must be sliced paper thin and blanket the mushroom completely. It is essential to melt the cheese sufficiently to broadcast the indentations of the surface of the mushroom, but not to the point of rendering the cheese sticky. I had crowned the cheese with green onion and was about to cap it all with a grilled slice of rye when the phone rang.

"Ken, I've got some news." Gwen spoke fast, the timbre of her voice higher than usual. "Greene's called. You know, the shop where I left those tires for repair."

I must have guzzled the last of the ginger ale the night before. The refrigerator held only root beer and coke. Neither would do to accompany this sandwich. "What's the news, Gwen? Were they able to make the repairs?"

"That's just it. It turned out to be more complicated than we thought."

Tea would have to be the order of the day. The noble Portobello demands to be accompanied with ginger. The flavors complement each other. And the hot tea would go down well on a frigid night like this one. "How complicated can a flat tire be?"

"Four punctures. Each tire."

I stopped in my tracks and stared at the phone. "Four?"

"Uh-hun. Made with an ice pick—or something similar."

Pondering the ramifications, I said, "This wasn't an ordinary slasher. This action is one of vengeance or anger. Who's got you on their list?"

"No one. I swear. I live a pristine life." I could hear a vague laugh in Gwen's voice now.

Extracting a cup from the cabinet, I filled it with water, and positioned it in the microwave. I set the timer for two minutes. When the hum began, I distanced myself from the noise. "Well, someone's got it out for you. Maybe one of your clients? Contractors?"

"No."

"A new client? Someone at the office?"

"Certainly not."

"Someone from the meeting last week?"

There was a pause.

"What meeting last week?" The puzzle in Gwen's voice was overt.

"Didn't you go down to Cleveland last Tuesday to meet with the Medici Partnership about the Raleigh project?"

Gwen was suddenly unfocused, tipped off balance. "Yes....Tuesday. Right, I forgot."

"I heard Smartain came to town and everything."

"Yes, that's right." She was back in the conversation, like a switch had been placed into the socket. "I picked him up at the airport Monday. Then Cheryl, Andrew, Robert, Smartain and I all went to Cleveland Tuesday morning; of course, I remember."

"How did the meeting go?"

"Fine...fine. We explained our approach to the project, trying to distinguish ourselves from the competition as exceedingly qualified for the project. Edison's stack of boards made a slick graphic show. It went fine." Gwen sounded distracted again. Her words had become mechanical.

The microwave *dinged*.

"Ken, you must be having dinner. I've got to go too. I just wanted to let you know about the tires."

I said good-bye, and fixed my tea. Something had just gone oddly wrong, and I didn't have a clue what it was.

After consuming my feast with relish, I resolved to place a call to Isabelle's sister, Genevieve. Edison had filled me in on Isabelle's background. She was raised by an indigent inner city family, living in the tenements along Jefferson Avenue in Detroit. Two sisters and a brother. Her alcoholic mother lived on the cheap wine that she hid in the linen closet. Her father spent days at a time playing the horses at Hazel Park Raceway.

Following her senior year in high school, Isabelle had a daughter, Truancy. What a ghastly name! What parent in their right mind would invite disaster by naming their child that? No sign of the father. Isabelle had cast her off to her sister Genevieve in Indiana to raise.

Yes, Sunshine was Isabelle's real middle name. Isabelle Sunshine Fix. Gwen had borrowed the truck over New Year's for Isabelle, so that Isabelle would have reliable transportation on her way to visit her daughter in Indiana.

After a couple of false starts, I was able to get the correct phone number from the operator.

I dialed.

"Hello?" The voice was female. Earthy.

"Is Genevieve there, please?"

"This is." The voice was wary. "What's your business?"

"My name is Ken. Ken Knoll. I worked with your sister, with Isabelle. I'm calling to express my condolences. I'm very sorry."

Sniffles. "Thank you. It's a darn shame, woman working so hard and then somebody kills her cold.

Leaving her poor child without a mama. How could anybody be so cold-hearted?" Sobbing. "You say you worked with Isy?"

"Yes, we worked together at BPW Architects. Isabelle was a real asset to the office. Always working hard, staying late."

"I'm sorry...your name was...Karl?"

"No, Ken."

"Ken. Thank you. Thank you for thinking of me. I've been taking care of this child for going on three years. She just started first grade this year. What a wonderful little girl. Great big eyes and soft blonde hair, just like her mama's. And sharp as a tack, that little one. Do you have any children, Ken?"

"No, I never had the...no I don't."

"Well, I've got three. Two of my own, boys. They're eight and eleven. Trudy is six. Each one is different. And each one needs his mama. I don't care how independent they think they are, they all need their mama every now and again." Her voice broke with emotion. I've never met Genevieve, but I could picture her eyes filling with tears, overflowing and slowly rolling down her cheeks.

"I don't know what your business is at that office, Ken, but I have to tell you something." Her voice was stronger now, with an edge to it. "I think it's just pitiful that y'all didn't give Isabelle no time off for New Year's. Whoever heard of working on New Year's Eve? Y'all are just pitiful. Didn't you know Isy was planning on coming down here and seeing her daughter? How can you keep a mama from her little girl at the holidays? Trudy was so upset that her mama couldn't come, she cried and cried. The only way she could stand having Christmas, was me reminding her that her mama was coming down for New Year's. I reminded her and reminded her. Now somebody done killed her cold, and Trudy will never see her mama again." Genevieve broke down and started sobbing.

"Isabelle didn't come down over New Year's?"

"Not with all that work y'all give her to do. How can you expect somebody to work so hard, and then have them working all the holidays, too? A person's got to have some time to rest and visit with the family. 'Specially at holiday time.

"Only blessing she got from that job is all the money she sends—sent—down here for Trudy. Lordy! That money did make things better. Trudy got herself some nice things from her mama. But, a girl wants her mama to hold her and love her and be with her, not just send the dollar."

"Isabelle took care of Trudy financially?"

"Oh, yes. Sent money for living. Sent money to buy things. And sent money to put away for the college. She wasn't going to have Trudy have to live hand-to-mouth like her and I grew up. I don't know what it was, but Isy was working on some special project. She said she only needed one more big project and she'd be able to come on down here and get Trudy for good. Take her away and buy a big house. She had her some dreams. My little sister did. She had her some major dreams. But that's all over now." Genevieve wailed into the phone. "I just don't know what I am gonna do now."

I mumbled something I hoped was comforting.

"I'm sorry, Ken. I have to go. We-all are fixing to make the trip up there tomorrow morning to finalize arrangements...for Friday. The police are finally finished with Isabelle and we're gonna be able to get on with it and lay her to rest."

"Genevieve, Trudy is lucky to have you taking care of her."

"Thank you. Thank you. Good bye."

Our conversation was brief, but I couldn't help

thinking that Trudy was going to be in good hands with her aunt.

I played the conversation over again in my head. I kept coming back to two nagging questions.

What had caused Isabelle to change her plans? She had apparently gone through some lengths to have Gwen borrow the truck for her. Trudy was counting on her mother coming to see her. No matter what kind of mother she'd been, I couldn't believe that Isabelle would cancel that trip without a very good reason.

And what "big job" had she been up to?

Chapter 11
Alarming Action

Brilliant rays of sunshine poked through the crack between the shade and the window frame, stabbing through my eyelids to announce the day. Toes poking out from under the comforter found the air temperature less than friendly. My body refused to ascend to a vertical position, though my mind raced feverishly.

I had further questions for Joel the mechanic and I sought to carve out a two-hour time slot in my schedule to make the trip. The morning would be spent addressing a host of issues that had arrived on my desk during my time off: 1.) studying the site plan for a new union hall to reconcile it with the City of Palmer Hills's zoning ordinance (not enough parking or landscaping to meet the requirements); 2.) reviewing the contractor's pricing for a legion of changes at a new three story Federal Credit Union facility in Madison Heights (cost figures were too high); and 3.) writing proposals for three new projects in Indianapolis, Indiana, (due Monday).

A public relations meeting for the Six Forks Mall project was scheduled for 2 p.m. A typical affair—owners coming in to meet the staff, check out the office, etc.

If I could pry myself away from the morning activities at eleven, I could make Brighton before noon, take Joel to lunch, and return in time for the two o'clock meeting.

After convincing my body that it had enough

sedentary comfort for a while, I moved into the shower, dressed and had a breakfast of instant coffee and oatmeal with bananas. I pulled out the number to Valley Auto Repair and Parts, and dialed. It was only 7:15, but the phone was answered and I asked for Joel. He came on the line. I arranged to meet him for lunch. Noon was a little late for him, but he couldn't leave the building anyway. When I offered to bring food in, he jumped at the offer. He liked Chinese.

My cube screamed *deadlines!* when I entered my office forty-five minutes later. Site planning in Palmer Hills is a frustrating process of balancing the requirements of the city's esteemed leaders with the needs of the building users. The city planners have legislated social responsibility, invoking developers with the task of providing an abundance of parking, landscaping, bike paths, sidewalks, and "suitable" building treatments. The case at hand was an eight-thousand square foot union meeting hall. Sixty-five parking spaces would assuredly meet the needs of the users. The city required ninety-eight. The city required landscaping in a thirty-foot wide strip along Spectral Road, with an additional 2,500 square feet of landscaping within the parking lot. Another hunk of land along the rear of the property would be eaten up by an eight-foot wide bike path.

I was reeling from examining the options for site layout, when I looked up to see Rita poking her head around my partition. She must have been fresh off a break, harsh cigarette smell emanating from her waxy, crimson lips.

"Mr. Knoll, Robert requests the pleasure of your company for lunch," Rita announced.

I looked up. Rita's hair, tinted a deep burgundy, was arranged in a well-manicured stack on top of her head, little ringlets patterned around the circumference of her crown. "Sorry, Rita, I've got plans for lunch." I looked at my watch. 10:58. "And I've got to be going."

"Maybe you didn't understand me. Robert and Gwen require your attendance at lunch to review the agenda for the meeting this afternoon."

"Robert *and* Gwen?" I posed.

"Yes. I've made reservations at Jack Butler's."

Fancy place. What in the world could this mean? I made a fast decision. "Tell Mr. Westin that I heartily accept."

"Sure," she said, stomping away on black four-inch spike heels.

I called Joel and postponed our meeting to the dinner hour.

Jack Butler's was built in the European half-timber style, stucco planes dissected by deep brown timbers, steep slate-covered roof, small steel-framed windows. The disappointing reality? The stucco was synthetic, the wood timbers were straight boards, not half sawn logs, and the slate was a man-made reproduction.

Energetic valets jumped in and out of vehicles, moving them a couple hundred feet into a rectangular array, and then retrieving them a couple hours later. They must have been cold in their smart little red vests and white shirts. All part of the job.

My eyes struggled to adjust to the dim light as we entered through heavy wooden doors with mammoth wrought iron handles. The deep red carpet felt cushy under my feet, a short-lived pleasure, as my tootsies encountered uneven rustic ceramic tile not far into the room. I couldn't help notice the grout lines extended diagonally to the far corners of the room.

The roof structure was exposed, as rough-hewn, unfinished timbers supported 3x10 planks to make up the planes of the roof. Those real wood timbers supported large, wrought iron chandeliers a full ten feet in diameter, fitted with small electric bulbs simulating candles. A roaring fire warmed the cozy room we were ushered into. Real wood logs burning in an actual stone fireplace with accompanying chimney proceeded up through the roof. Nice. I half expected to see the valets sitting with their backs to the fire getting warmed up. Cloth doily-style place mats, crystal glasses and ornate silverware sat on highly polished black walnut tables with matching high-back chairs. Their laundry bill must have been enormous.

Gwen wore a pleated white blouse with pearl-like buttons beneath an electric blue double-breasted jacket. Her analogous blue eyes fairly danced out at me and the firelight glow bouncing off her hair gave her a sort of halo.

We ordered drinks and Robert began. "I'm glad you decided to have lunch with us. It occurred to me recently, perhaps you don't like to eat."

I took that to suggest he was alluding to the two dinner invitations he recently offered—one which I'd declined, the other where I'd skipped out early. "You've got to know better than that," I joked, patting my belly.

Gwen gave Robert a questioning glance and picked up the menu. It was one of those *get with the program* looks that husbands shrink from. Though their romantic relationship had been over for a couple of months, it appeared as though portions of the male/female rituals remained. Out loud she said, "Oh, just look at these appetizers."

I studied the menu. It was a debate between the roasted pepper sandwich with melted Swiss cheese and chives, and the spinach salad with raspberry chevre dressing. Or the black bean soup, served with grilled eggplant with roasted corn pudding.

I decided on the sandwich before asking, "What are

we doing at this afternoon's meeting?"

Robert looked dapper in his charcoal suit, white shirt ensconced with light gray threads, and his art tie of fifteen gray shades. Serious rectilinear gray shapes played against black vertical and horizontal lines in the tie. One of his specialty tie-tacks, a tiny milky-white light bulb pierced by a little black screw, completed the black and white ensemble. His left pinky finger sported a gold ring with a square onyx stone bisected by a line of small diamonds. The same hand had a gold bracelet, large links encircling his heavy wrist.

Robert took a sip of his iced tea. He closed his eyes briefly, as if steeling himself for the moment. "We have decided to make a change. The Raleigh project is one of the larger projects in the office. A million square feet. Raleigh is the hot spot of East Coast development. The site lays out beautifully. The situation is ripe for an architectural coup. The developer is eager for the project to make a splash. This will take a few dollars to accomplish. The design money is secure. This is the hottest project in the office right now." He paused, letting the comment sink in.

"Gwen has had her hands full with overseeing the Flamingo Shores project, and, as you are aware, many of those tenant improvement commissions are still going strong, not to mention the complications created by the murder investigation. With the daily work on Brighton Mall and the Olsen House, she's booked up. And it looks like Crispy Greek is in the bag too. She'll be going to Denver every two weeks."

Gwen shifted uneasily in her chair. She looked at Robert, then at me, cleared her throat and started, "Ken, I think...."

Robert considered me with cold eyes, then turned his attention to Gwen.

Gwen looked down at her highly polished coral-rose

nails. She glance up to me faintheartedly, then averted her eyes. Whatever intimacy we'd shared the day before had evaporated.

She turned her head up to Robert. Their eyes locked, then she glanced away. Robert continued, "Gwen, tell Ken what a wonderful opportunity this is for him."

Who's got a wonderful opportunity? What did I miss?

Gwen took a deep breath, raised her eyes to meet mine. I held them deeply, with only a detached stare in return. "Ken, Robert wants you to handle Raleigh. It'll require an enormous investment in time and energy. The team will combine two designers and three or four technical people to start, then ramp up to twelve. Coordination with the usual disciplines, plus civil, landscape and signage. Handling the city-county approvals will fall under your direction as well. You'll have to employ all your project management skills. You can certainly shine, show the firm what you can do." She swung her delicate eyes to Robert as if to say, *Satisfied?*

I understood that the Robert-Gwen break up had left scars, but the interaction before me certainly suggested that the damage went deep. Robert appeared to be looking for a response.

"I'm flattered, honored," I said. "The scale of the project is larger than anything I've done, but I'd love to get involved. What exactly would be my position in this?"

Robert cleared his throat. "Overall responsibility. I'd like to introduce you this afternoon as the project manager in charge of the project. You report to me, Principal in Charge, and you're next in line. Direct responsibility."

The food arrived.

The implications rattled around in my mind. I had

hoped and dreamed to be in charge of a project of this magnitude. A million square feet would take thousands of hours to develop. This project would keep me in the fray for the next three years. As I was savoring the moment, I couldn't help wondering what was behind removing Gwen from this assignment.

"Well, are you interested?" Robert asked, breaking into his shark medallions.

"Yes," I smiled. "Yes, I'd welcome the challenge."

I pulled up to the repair shop at ten minutes to five o'clock. I grabbed the plastic bag containing two Styrofoam containers: one Number 5 Combination and one Number 11. Several years ago I worked with someone who ordered Chinese food by picking numbers at random. It was always a guess, resulting in a surprise meal.

Joel waved to me as I entered the blue door. I suppose the bag in my hand reminded him who I was. I nearly walked straight into a guy on a bright yellow ladder. He was feeding wire up to the inside face of the door.

Once I laid my eyes on Joel, I remembered his uniquely flat face. His extended forehead was pasty white, contrasted by black grease, and his wide nose had somewhat more color. His receding chin had a day's worth of stubble on it. His face was flat as yesterday's pizza.

"This sure is a nice surprise," Joel said after he had disappeared to the rear of the shop and returned with (mostly) clean hands. "There's a room in back. We can sit and chat for a while."

"Great," I said, following.

A narrow white corridor led to a small room with block walls painted aquamarine. A minuscule metal table with two folding metal chairs sat in the center of the room. Just as I began to sit, Joel called out, "Hold on!"

I froze my rump in midair. He ripped three sheets of paper towel from the roll at the sink, and reached over to wipe my chair, which was littered with sticky crumbs.

We sat down and I unpacked the dinner containers. Joel offered me a Cherry Coke. I'd forgotten to get drinks. Once we were through the set-up, Joel asked, "So, what's on your mind? It sure must be important for you to buy me dinner."

"I'm still trying to locate the things I had in the truck bed last week. The ceramic casting is still missing, and everyone at work denies having seen it. Here's what I know. It was in the truck last Monday morning and gone last Thursday when you washed the truck. Since the truck was here most of that time, I'm thinking that the piece disappeared from here."

"Well, I don't know how. I trust the people here. I don't like what you're implying."

"I'm not implying anything. I'm just trying to figure it all out. Was there anyone here? Did anyone stop by to ask about the truck?"

"That skinny fellow from your office dropped the truck off on Monday."

"That would have been Wally."

"Then there was the girl from your office, who came to check how the repairs were coming."

"Girl?" I asked. My ears perked up. "What girl?"

"She said she was from your office. She just wanted a time frame when the truck was going to be done. I told her, and she got impatient on me. Couldn't wait. Well, I told her that it takes what it takes."

"Can you describe her?"

"Sure. Prettiest blonde I've laid my eyes on. Long straight hair, delicate skin, just like the fancy dolls my wife collects. About twenty-five. Isn't that someone from your office?"

That description certainly rang a bell. "Do you remember what kind of car she was driving?"

"Sure, '87 Sentra. I remember thinking, that car's not going to make it through the winter. I sure hope she got home."

"What was her reaction when you told her it was going to take a couple more days?"

"She grew indignant on me. As if it was life and death. I suppose there were people waiting to check that truck out."

"Oh, yes," I said.

We finished our meal, and as I was leaving, I had to go around the man on the yellow ladder, fixing wires to the wall. I asked the man what he was doing.

"Oh," Joel offered. "He's putting in an alarm system. We were broken into last week."

Chapter 12
Secret Search

"Broken into?" I said. "What were they after? Do you keep a lot of cash here?"

"No. The cash is taken out of the register and Larry drops it off at the bank on his way home every night. Kind of stupid if you ask me. All the tools in here. Must be thousands of dollars worth. They didn't take a darn thing."

I said good-bye and walked to my car, reflecting on this development. "Oh Joel," I said, turning back, "What day was the break-in?"

Joel scratched his chin stubble. "It was Wednesday night," he said. "I had breakfast with Loretta at 5 a.m. Thursday. She fixed me up some of them crêpes with strawberries and cream cheese. I was running late on account of she burnt the first batch. No fault of hers. She only makes them special for me a couple of times a year. It was my birthday. Anyway I didn't get in here until seven and by then everyone was jabbering about it."

I mulled this new information in traffic. It was going on 6:15, and I-96 moved at a snail's pace under a dark sky. I've gone through this season forty-three times now and it still surprises me when darkness falls at 5:30.

What prompted Isabelle to check the status of the truck? I doubt that anyone sent her out there. And why did she make the inquiry in person rather than by telephone? Wally, Gwen, or whoever, would have asked Rita to call, as she was in charge of the truck. If Rita recruited Isabelle to do some follow up, she certainly wouldn't send her on a ninety-minute round trip to Brighton when she could make a telephone call to gather the same information.

Something transpired to make Isabelle take a personal interest in the truck, where it was, and when it would be returned. But what?

Isabelle began to figure prominently in my 3x5 card deck. Gwen borrowed the truck for Isabelle for New Year's Eve, and then Isabelle failed to make the trip to Indiana. Isabelle toured the jobsite on Monday, the day that Edison discovered the body. Did she see something...and later was killed for it?

I called Edison from the car. He was just leaving the office to get some dinner. I asked him to meet me at the office at 7:30 p.m.

I pulled into the office parking lot, observing that the pole-mounted light over the entrance drive was out again. I'd have to tell Rita in the morning. Edison's blue Chevy pick-up was nowhere in sight.

Sliding off my coat on the way, I traversed the office to my cube. I laid my coat across the guest chair, and out of habit, checked voice mail. Nothing of note. I headed to Isabelle's desk. As I approached, I noticed that her supplies were gone: scissors, tape dispenser, stapler. Even her pencil holder. The vultures don't take long. Every time someone quits, their stuff is gone, divvied up among the staff before the seat is cold. Speaking of a seat, her chair was gone too, replaced by a rickety orange number with roller wheels that doesn't roll, at least not in the direction you want it to. I thought we'd gotten rid of that piece of junk a long time ago.

Sitting in the orange chair, I went through Isabelle's drawers. It felt a little creepy. Ok, it was *really* creepy. I shouldn't have been rifling through someone else's desk. Even if they were dead. Or maybe a person's privacy should be respected especially if they were dead. I proceeded, however, on the basis that I might gain some understanding of what she may have seen that day...something that might have gotten her killed.

The top left drawer contained a pile of coins, a collection of old timesheets, yellow sticky notes, paper clips, staples, and rubber bands. The top middle drawer held copies of memos that had come from Robert or Andrew: memos to the staff on everything from filling in timesheets to making print orders. The top right-hand drawer was stuffed to the brim with coupons: shampoo, cereal, dish washing liquid, candy bars, coffee. There didn't seem to be a rhyme or reason to it. They were all simply crammed in there. I poked through them, and felt something hard and plastic in the back. I pulled out a rubber lunch container.

I had a feeling in my gut that Isabelle would have left some small clue—a note to herself or maybe a photo. Did her boyfriend Jay mention whether or not Isabelle had taken a camera to the jobsite? It also crossed my mind she may have kept a diary. I almost hoped she hadn't, as I didn't know if I would be able to bring myself to read it.

The second drawer on the left contained pretzels: a box of hard pretzels and a bag of thin twists. The second drawer on the right held an assortment of scarves, pins, and other hair holding devices: clips, combs, bands.

Both right and left bottom drawers held job files: Skywing Center, Olsen House, Brighton Mall, Boxing Dorrey Center, Martina's Grape Arbor, King's Crossing.

Nothing out of the ordinary. No notes, no personal notebooks, folders, or diary.

As I was fingering through the last of the folders, I

became aware of heavy breathing. I jumped when I saw Edison looking over the desk at me.

After a calming breath, I said, "Edison, don't sneak up on a person like that!"

"Sorry," he bristled, as if to say *oh well*. "What are we looking for?" He picked up her black phone, held it up to his face, turning it to explore all sides.

"We're looking," I said, pushing the phone and his hand back down on the desk, "for something that indicates what Isabelle may have seen at Crystals last Monday. There doesn't seem to be anything here."

"Last Monday? The day she died?" His eyes grew worried.

"No, last week Monday. Apparently she was there the day you found...him."

Edison's features developed a sickly pallor. "She was there? She saw me....?"

"I don't know what she saw, Edison. Jay Stevens told me the two of them went to the jobsite. He showed her around. She got sick and he took her home. Something seems odd. I can't quite make it out. I feel like she must have known something. If she did, maybe she made a note of it."

"I could check her computer." Edison said, reaching under the desk beside my leg and pushing the button on Isabelle's CPU tower.

"I'm surprised the scavengers didn't take that thing too," I noted.

"No point." Edison said.

I raised my eyebrows in question.

"This machine is one of the dinosaurs in the office. No one wants a downgrade."

The login screen came up, requesting a password. I watched as Edison tried a number of letter/number combinations before breaking the code. "Edison, how?"

His Hershey-colored eyeballs turned up at me.

"Hmpf," he began, "Isabelle had a habit of using boys' names for the alphabet portion, and dates or weight for the numerical portion of the code. I just took a few combinations to arrive at *Jay118*. Her boyfriend, and the weight she was trying to get down to."

I shook my head in awe.

Edison punched keys and zoomed in and out of files on-screen while I continued checking though the paper files. Completing my tossing of the desk contents, I turned to the shelves and file cabinets behind her desk. These were more public than her desk, so I didn't expect to find anything, but I kept looking. I dug intently through the third file drawer, while Edison read Isabelle's personal correspondence.

We turned up nothing of relevance.

"Edison, this is hopeless. Let's get out of here," I urged.

"Sure," he said, turning off the computer. "Do you have the munchies?"

"Edison, let's just go."

He grumbled his reluctant agreement. We grabbed our coats, and headed back through the office.

"Edison," I asked, "Do you know where she lived?"

"Who? Isabelle?" Edison questioned.

"Yes. I think we should see what might be hiding in her house."

"Cool. You drive."

As we headed for the office back door, Edison excused himself and disappeared. While I waited, I went over to the utility closet and grabbed a couple of flashlights. What else would we need? I had a tool box in the car. Nothing else came to mind.

Edison came back like a man on a mission, a bag of Ruffles in his fist, and led me out the door.

We took Telegraph to I-696 East, exiting at Southfield Road and continuing east on the service drive into the heart of Berkley. Edison munched on the chips, getting greasy chip dust in my car. We pulled down a small street, arriving only fifteen minutes after leaving the office. A single light on a wood utility pole cast a pool of light at the street entrance. I could see flurries floating down, little spots of shimmering movement across the dim light. The wind picked up, and the snowflakes grew in size. Only a dusting of the white powder lie on the ground currently, but the weather service had predicted a winter storm. That could be anything from three inches to a foot. Or the storm could be blown off course, and dump its load on Cleveland.

In Detroit, one never knows.

Just before I pushed into the drive, I thought the better of it, and parked on the street, three houses down. The house was a bungalow—steeply pitched roof covering one and a half stories of house. In the forties during the war these houses were built by the hundreds. Basement. First floor with kitchen, living room and two bedrooms. Upstairs in the peak of the gable, sometimes one room, sometimes split into a couple of bedrooms. A few of the houses in this neighborhood were rentals, and I expected Isabelle's was, too.

Just as we were about to exit the vehicle, the startling realization hit me. How were we going to get in? I didn't have any burglary experience. I was hoping that Edison didn't either. It was a detail that I'd blatantly overlooked. Edison, his fingers clutching the door handle, said, "Are you ready?"

I thought about what information might be inside. I also thought about a charge of breaking and entering that would be on my record, in addition to the withholding evidence and obstructing justice charges that were already in the column marked *Ken's shameless violation of the law*. We could break a window, or bust in a door. This is not what architecture is about. Why hadn't I thought this through?

"Ken?" Edison prodded. "Let's go."

"With what? Edison, we shouldn't be breaking in. It didn't even occur to me how we were going to get into the house. I'm sorry I dragged you along, but—"

Edison scooted his butt forward in the seat, slouched down, and dug his hand into his jeans pocket. He pulled out a key, dangling from a large plastic pink daisy. "We're not breaking in. We're just going in the back door."

"Huh?"

Edison smiled triumphantly. "Isabelle kept a spare key at the office. Just in case. She was always misplacing her keys. She told me I was welcome anytime."

My sense of right reared its stubborn head. It wasn't proper. Isabelle was dead. We couldn't just walk into her house. "Edison, this isn't acceptable. Just because we have a key, doesn't mean we can barge into a dead person's house." I felt hot.

"No, Ken. It's ok. Isabelle was always telling me: 'Just stop by anytime. Walk in. Help yourself to a Coke. Take a break, stop in, watch some TV.'"

I was wary. "Really?"

"Ken. Listen. Isabelle and I used to go out. Sure it was over, but we still got along. She told me to make myself at home. Sometimes, when she went away for a long weekend, I'd stop by, water her plants, take out the trash, watch a football game, whatever."

Sometimes Edison surprises me. And I like it.

We grabbed the flashlights, exited the car and walked quickly across the street. The front yard was a scant forty feet wide, and the house was set back only about fifty feet from the road. We made our way carefully up the driveway to the rear door. As we entered, I quietly cautioned Edison about turning on the lights. We didn't want to alert the neighbors to someone being in the house of their deceased neighbor. The kitchen was before us. I turned my flashlight on. Dingy yellow floor tile, plywood cupboard doors, yellowed counter top with metal edging. I poked my head into one of the cabinet doors: two glasses. The cupboard was bare.

From the kitchen, we entered the living room, which sported shag carpeting in a shade of puke green, a leather-like sofa and an overstuffed chair of a nondescript beige flower pattern. Off the living room, a tiny hallway led to a bathroom, stairway to an unfinished attic, and two bedrooms—one of which had been fixed up for a computer room. When we got there, Edison let out an exclamation of awe. "Look at this. State of the art. This baby has more speed, RAM and memory than anything we have the office. Top of the line."

He looked around the room. "Laser printer. Paper supply."

While Edison marveled at the computer, I checked the shelves. DVDs, video tapes, arranged alphabetically, and neatly labeled, smaller format mini-cassettes, square format zip tapes, CD's, apparently divided into music and software. She had country, rock, blues, classical. Well-rounded tastes. Every surface in the room—the desk next to the computer, a small corner table, an extra chair, and the top of a small bookshelf—was piled with DVDs, tapes, cassettes and CDs as well as software instructional manuals and pages printed from Internet download.

We looked around for a while. Edison turned on the computer and checked a few things. Nothing seemed to be what we were looking for.

At 11:00, I got the willies so bad, I told Edison we'd

better wrap it up.

We left the computer room and went through the hallway. Moving into the living room, my flashlight came upon something glimmering in the carpet. Curious, I bent down to pick it up. A tie tack. A miniature scene of a horse pulling a carriage with a pumpkin inside.

Chapter 13
Midnight Mysteries

Ray's Coney was a hole in the wall—a narrow storefront on Twelve Mile, sandwiched in between a classic comic book store and a science fiction memorabilia shop. Situated only a sidewalk away from traffic, parking was in the rear with lights on utility poles illuminating a marginal number of spaces on uneven concrete slabs. The snow came down heavily, with three inches on the ground already. In spite of the accumulating snow and the lateness of the hour, I invited Edison to one of his favorite meals: coney dogs and chili fries. I thought we might gain some insight by kicking around what had transpired during the day. Plus, I felt guilty that Edison had been cheated out of his requested meal at lunch the day before.

The tables consisted of varnished plywood, edged in dark half-round molding attached with nails that were rusting in place, seeping brown smudges into the varnish. Chairs must have been garage sale specials, because few of them matched. It was a motley conglomeration: wooden chairs with spindle backs in various designs; kitchen chairs covered in faded vinyl--some green, some dingy white; a couple of white Eames molded plastic side chairs, the kind that were molded to fit one person's posterior, but were under—or over-sized for the rest of us. Those little molded-plastic numbers were low enough to leave a person's chin on the table.

An occasional strip fluorescent served as lighting, screwed to a 12" x 12" stick-on acoustical tile ceiling that was in need of replacement. Walls were dark paneling with marks where cellophane tape had previously attached posters or holiday decorations. The black and red checkered vinyl tile floor stuck to my shoes in places. Though the pattern is back in fashion, worn spots in the red tiles indicated this was a hold-over from when it was last in style.

We didn't come for the decor.

Their chili is marvelous, thick and flavorful. They make a terrific spinach pie, too, warmed up in the oven leaving crisp edges, unlike the sad microwave versions offered by most restaurants these days. Nuking the pie just makes the phyllo dough tough and leathery. I ordered the spinach pie with a vanilla shake. Edison got his usual fare. One day, Ray will name it "the Edison combo": two coney dogs with extra mustard, chili cheese fries, and a large root beer.

When we'd settled in, I asked, "What do you make of finding Robert's tie-tack at Isabelle's?"

"Beats me. You really think it *was* Robert's?" Edison was playing with the metal napkin dispenser, separating the halves, hinged at the bottom, and peeking inside.

"Of course it was Robert's. How many people have a tie-tack of a carriage with a pumpkin inside? Have you ever seen anything like that on anyone else?"

"No. I did know a guy once, he had cuff links that were mirrors. Different shapes and sizes. Some had silver rims. Some were black." Edison chuckled at the thought. "He even had one set, shaped like the side mirrors on a car, you know, round with a convex surface. Those things must have been an inch across. Printed on them were the words 'Objects in mirror are closer than they appear.'"

I was shaking my head in disbelief when the food arrived.

"I'm not talking about cuff links," I said. "Tie-tacks are the subject. No one else wears them like Robert." I took a sip of my shake. The cold made the back of my throat ache.

"So, if it *was* Robert's, what was he doing at Isabelle's?" Edison said with a mouth stuffed full of gooey fries. Even as he chewed, he picked up his messy coney dog.

"That, Edison, is a big question. But a larger puzzle is this: what did Isabelle see at the site last Monday?"

Edison dropped his coney dog, splashing coney sauce across the table. "Sorry," he said, wiping up the mess with itsy-bitsy napkins. "That one worries me. If she saw me—" Edison looked around at the sparse number of patrons, then lowered his voice "—then she saw what I did." His hairy left hand began to shake, and he put it under the table.

"I'm wondering more what she saw before you got there. She was in the office last week, right?" I said.

"Yeah, except for the Monday she was off." He rocked back and forth in his chair.

"And she didn't say anything? Didn't mention anything about being at the jobsite on Monday and seeing anything weird?"

Edison shook his head, apparently calmed down enough to gently pick up his coney dog with both hands and shove it in his mouth.

"She didn't mention being ill the day she was off?" I said.

"No. She didn't even tell me she was at the jobsite when I talked to her about...finding something unusual. You know, when I couldn't get hold of you."

"I remember," I said, poking in the last bite of my spinach pie.

"Maybe she saw nothing," Edison said hopefully.

I had to agree. "That is one possibility."

I paid for the midnight snack, and we headed to the back exit. Snow blew into the room when we opened the door. Another inch of snow had hit the ground. Four inches and the white fluffy stuff was still coming down. With warm, satisfied bellies, we trudged back to my vehicle. I started the car, revved up the heat, then reached behind my seat to grab the brush. Back out in the cold, I cleaned off the windows, using the scraper to remove chunks of ice that had formed on the rear window, beneath the fresh powdery snow.

Driving through four inches of snow is like propelling a vehicle through Jell-O. Motion is sluggish and the car may glide sideways a bit, especially when it meets an obstacle like a curb. Turns are slow, and the car may slide out of the curve as it passes through the arc.

After making our way through the parking lot and the side street, we pulled onto Twelve Mile. None of those driving surfaces were plowed at this point, but the snow on the street was crushed down and rutted, providing vehicles some advantage from the traffic that had gone before. Cars were sparse at this hour, but with the heavy snow, the ride back to the office took about twenty-five minutes. I dropped Edison at his pick-up truck, waited until he'd successfully started the vehicle and cleaned off the windows, then drove home.

It was pushing 1:00 a.m. when I pulled onto my street. The night was eerie. Fresh snow made the ground uniformly white, reflecting the glow of lights into the sky. It was nearly as light outside as some cloud-covered days. I opened my side window a tad, and listened to the night: the stillness had a certain crisp quality to it. Sounds were sharp and definite. The night felt alive in silence.

I pulled into my driveway, parking up close to the side of the house to minimize the drifting that would occur around my car overnight.

Sleeping did not appeal to me. Perhaps it was the stillness of the night. Maybe the food. 6:30 a.m. would come quickly, yet the thought of shutting my eyes and laying still did not invite me. I pulled off my shirt and shoes, and sat down at the kitchen table.

Facts of the murder investigation had not yet formed themselves into any kind of order. Maybe if I played the facts back and forth, upside down and backwards, I could force a revelation. I pulled out my detective pack: the seventy-five cards or so that held my accumulated facts. I added some new cards to cover today's unfoldings. It seemed much like a game of solitaire: arranging the cards in various arrays, changing their respective positions in search of a new insight.

After thirty minutes without any fresh realizations, a thought came to me to assemble a picture of where everyone was last week during the days subsequent to Edison's discovery of the body.

A time line.

I went down to the basement and rummaged through my things until I found my old portable parallel bar, given to me a decade earlier by a former mentor when he retired. Used before the computer age, this drawing board is fit with a bar that slides up and down on a pair of side cables. Every line drawn along the straight edge will be parallel to every other line. Used in conjunction with a plastic 30/60 degree or 45 degree triangle, horizontal and vertical lines can be drawn at right angles to one another.

I found some paper and made a crude chart, listing days across the top, each day divided into two-hour blocks of time. Monday, December 27, the day Edison found the body, through Monday, January 3, the day Isabelle's body was found. Down the left side of the paper, I listed all the people I knew were somehow connected. If I located every person during each two-hour time period, something would surely reveal itself. I listed Edison. He found the body at—? What time did he find the body? I didn't know. Did he tell me that? He was out there doing the job inspection, found the body and moved it, and then Robert and Andrew showed up. I added lines for Robert and Andrew. What time did they arrive? I didn't know that either.

I wasn't as good at this detective business as I thought.

I continued. Once the thing was blocked out, the spaces could be filled in as I went along. So far, the only thing it revealed was what I didn't know. That's ok, I decided, just don't stop now. I remembered Vince Lombardi. *Strength of will.*

Andrew went to the airport to pick up Smartain, who was out of town when the whole thing started, so I did not add him to the chart. But what time did Andrew head for the airport? Edison took Robert back to the office, with the body in the truck. I made a line for the truck—to indicate its movements, and I added a space to indicate when and where the body was.

I distinctly remember Edison saying it was 4:00 p.m. when he went back out to check on the truck, and Wally had driven off with it. Wally would have to be added and his movements graphed too. That would be a short one, because he only had the truck long enough to get it to the repair shop.

Then Gwen borrowed the truck for Isabelle later in the week, so I added her to the list. I also made a line for Isabelle. She was at the jobsite with her boyfriend the Monday that Edison found the body. What time were they there? I only remembered Jay saying they went after breakfast. I really would have to sharpen my detecting skills! I added Jay too.

The list of people to keep track of was getting long,

but reducing the facts to paper relieved my mind of carrying the details.

I racked my brain, including everything I could remember, then pulled out the detective pack. Methodically, I logged everything that had a time associated with it, and made a note of items requiring double-checking. The list of things to follow up on was quite lengthy. I sighed.

During this process, an interesting contradiction came to light. Gwen had told me in passing that she had gone to the airport to pick up Smartain on Monday, the 27th. Edison had told me the reason he was compelled to return to the office with Robert, was that Andrew was heading to the airport to pick up Smartain.

What had really happened?

There was no reason for Gwen to have made this up, and if Edison had been untruthful, what was he trying to hide? Andrew was the straightest shooter I'd ever met. He certainly wouldn't have lied to Robert and Edison about where he was going. Is it possible Gwen and Andrew got their wires crossed, and both went to pick up Smartain? This was a nagging little question.

The other mystery was this: who had erased the photographs of the jobsite inspection that Edison had taken on Monday? I added another line to the chart to indicate when the photos had been at the office the time they had disappeared.

This graph was going to be telling. I would be useless tomorrow if I didn't get some sleep soon.

It was almost 3:00 a.m. when I shut my eyes, wondering who had, in fact, met Smartain at the airport.

Chapter 14
Funeral Friday

The phone rang, the shrill sound sending a shock-wave through me as I slowly worked my eyes open. Sunshine spread through the lids to my irises, and there was a sticky, crusty mess along the lashes on my left eye temporarily gluing it shut. The phone continued its desperate cry.

What day was it? How long had I been asleep? I reached my hand out toward the noise, felt along the floor to the phone, and picked up the receiver. It was cold against my skin.

"Hello?" I managed to mumble.

"Ken, it's Rita. Am I ever glad I caught you before you left home. I wanted to remind you that the funeral is today."

The fog had claimed a large section of my brain, refusing to lift. "Funeral?"

"Ken, are you up? It's 8:15."

"Sure I'm up," I said, swinging my legs around to the side of the mattress. "I've been up ever since the phone rang."

"Ken, shame on you. What are you doing sleeping in, on a wonderful day like this? I suppose I should warn you the roads are a mess. Last night's storm system left us with about six inches on the ground."

"Well, thanks for letting me know." I was puzzled, and grateful, for the heads up.

"The funeral. Don't forget to dress for it. I thought I should remind you, seeing as it's Friday."

Right she was. The last day of the week typically meant jeans and a polo shirt. Rita and I don't always see eye to eye, but she tends to keep me out of trouble for things like this.

"Thanks, Rita. Hey, listen, that light at the parking lot entrance is out again," I said and hung up the phone.

I waddled to the bathroom, startling myself when I looked in the mirror. The large red crease in the middle of my forehead was turning blue and purple on either side. This gave my face a grim look.

Rhythmic streams of steamy water engulfed me in a massaging shower, hot water seeping into my pores. After a time, guilty feelings stirred, overshadowing my cozy indulgence. I was probably going to be late for something. Terminating the blissful spray, I completed my morning routine, and pulled on a t-shirt. My dark suit would be appropriate, but I didn't have a clean shirt. The dark grey turtle neck would have to do.

I checked to verify that my black shoes were sufficiently clean, slid into them, and then yanked on thin rubber overshoes and found my topcoat.

Snow was piled five inches deep over the car. First I brushed the white powder from the edges of the door to prevent an avalanche onto the seat. I started the engine, turned on the rear defroster and the flow of air to the front windshield.

Snatching the shovel from beside the house, I removed just enough snow from behind the rear wheels to guarantee a running start down the driveway. The snow was deep, but relatively dry. If it had been wet snow, it would have been twice as heavy. The remainder of the driveway and the sidewalk would have to wait until evening. Leaning the shovel back against the house, I began to feel sorry for school kids who'd have to shuffle along the depth of snow. Grabbing the shovel, I hustled to the sidewalk, and gingerly cleared a single scoop width across the length of the walk. Lifting a shovel-full, then twisting my torso to chuck the snow sideward was an operation that would not be approved by my chiropractor.

By the time I finished that little bit, the car was heated and so was I. Obtaining a house with a garage suddenly moved up on my priority list.

Rita was right, traffic was slow and heavy. When I pulled onto Ten Mile, I called Jeff Smartain. Jeff is one of the company's four Associates, and one of the firm's more experienced architects. He runs the Florida office, a group of five professionals who've worked together the last seven or eight years. We jokingly call them the "hit team." Given a project, they will turn it out in record time. Each knows the other so well, they anticipate each other's moves and tag team the project to completion.

"Jeff, it's Ken Knoll up in Detroit," I said cheerily.

"Cannoli! How are you? It's a shame we couldn't get together last week when I was in town. How was your holiday?"

It sounded like he hadn't heard. "Fine, fine. It was a good Christmas. Hey, listen, Jeff. I've got a bet going here with Edison. Last week when you flew into Detroit, who picked you up at the airport? Edison says it was Andrew. I say Andrew was too busy with other things and Gwen picked you up."

"A bet? Don't you guys have anything better to do than make ridiculous bets?"

"Jeff, you know what an idiot Edison is. He'll lose a buck over anything."

He laughed. "Well, Cannoli, this time you lose. Andrew picked me up on Monday. I had talked to Gwen the week prior. She had planned to meet me at the airport, but I guess she was tied up on Monday, so Andrew picked me up."

That settled it. Gwen had out and out lied to me. But why?

I arrived at the office twenty-five minutes past nine o'clock, as a mass exodus of employees headed toward their cars. After weaving through the nearly deserted office to my desk, I quickly checked messages. Edison poked his head into the cubicle as I was making a note to call Jester Cromwell.

"Can I catch a ride with you, Boss?" Edison said.

"Sure," I replied. "Just let me check with Gwen to see if she'd like to go with us."

I walked over and leaned into Gwen's office. She was wearing a beaded necklace, inch-long balls swirled in white and green. Each ear was adorned with a dangling piece of the same design. A teal suit and crisp white blouse completed the ensemble.

"Gwen, would you care to ride with Edison and me?"

Gwen glance up, copper frosted lips pursed in thought. "Oh, I didn't know whether or not you were going. I've already arranged a ride with Wally and Rita." Her face was noncommittal, eyes unfocused as she looked down at the papers on her desk and arranged them in piles.

Wally squeezed by me into the office. His outdated *old man* cologne choked me in the process. "Gwen, are you ready?" He said, then cheerfully to me he said, "Cannoli, how's your Friday?"

I murmured a good morning.

They plodded past me and I heard Gwen say to Wally, "I'm so glad you're going with me. I'm a little uneasy about going to funerals and this one's got me spooked."

Did I just get the brush-off? What was going on?

Edison knew the way to the funeral home, so I was glad he was driving with me. If he was feeling the least bit slow from the previous night's clandestine search and midnight coney snack, he didn't exhibit any signs of it. My body, on the other hand, felt like it was ensconced in molasses.

Robert J. Robertson Funeral Home was on Southfield Road, a few miles east of the office, just north of Eleven Mile Road. This stretch was five lanes wide, bordered on either side by office buildings set back by an expanse of parking lots aligned from one block to the next. The two-story structures bore distinct characteristics of the nineteen fifties: brick with strong horizontal stone banding and flat steel entrance canopies. Fenestration was accomplished in narrow bands of linear steel windows with occasional sections of glass block thrown in for good measure.

The funeral home was a break in the pattern. Tall, colonial and stately, the home welcomed visitors with a two-story porch fronted by four white columns. A large copper and glass lamp dangled two stories from a decorative copper chain, intertwined with cinnamon-colored vines and leaves. White double-hung windows flanked by dark green shutters contrasted against a buff-tone brick wall.

I wheeled into the lot.

A proper looking gentleman in a black coat was directing traffic, steering vehicles to the procession line if they were going to the cemetery. We opted for self parking. We'd arrived just before 10:00 a.m., which left us with roughly an hour to extend our sympathies to the family before the funeral services at 11:00.

Entering from the rear, we approached a pair of white stile-and-rail doors with gilt panel edges and elaborate hardware, pull handles decorated with renaissance cherubs. Another pair of black-suited men greeted us a few steps inside the doors. A central hallway ran front to back, parlors on each side sporting plaques announcing the name of the dearly departed. In theory, you could have six groups of mourners concurrently. One of the somber gentlemen who greeted us at the door gave us a mini-tour. Between the second and third parlors on the right were the men's and women's rooms. Across the hall was a gathering room which used to be the smoking parlor. With Michigan's ban on smoking in public buildings, this became a place where grieving could be a little less restrained.

Edison wore his customary hiking boots, but had upgraded his blue jeans to black ones, and he wore a navy button-up shirt.

We entered the room designated for Isabelle Sunshine Fix. A small group had gathered already. Wally, Gwen, Rita and Serenity were standing near the windows. Wally must have been telling quite a story, for two of the women appeared spellbound. Gwen, on the other hand, appeared ready to jump out of her skin. Her eyes darted around the room with a nervous twitch, fixing momentarily on something, skipping about, resettling to focus elsewhere. Slender fingers adorned with a French manicure played erratically with her necklace.

Two other groups stood in the back of the room: a cluster of three men and a group of four men and a woman. I didn't recognize any of those people.

Soft background music was interrupted by riotous laughter erupting from the "smoking room" across the hall.

Edison and I slowly made our way over to the office group standing off to the side. We passed a setting of two wing chairs and a sofa. The beige upholstery was embroidered with large red roses, appropriate for the Queen Anne legs. Silently we took in the atmosphere. I let my eyes wander around the room until they came to rest on the coffin. A simple box in a red mahogany finish. The lid was open, white crepe fabric lining the inner surface. Not wanting to face my fears, I turned my head. There would be plenty of time to pay my respects later.

We joined Wally's group and conversation stopped. Wally looked at us and said, "Kind of a stuffy place, isn't it? I was just telling the ladies how it needs a good face lift."

"It's somewhat on the conservative side," I said.

"Conservative?" Wally said. "It's downright stifling. Bring in a wedge of natural light, substitute cardinal curtains and indigo carpet and you'd affect a dramatic change in this somber room."

"Wally, it's supposed to be somber," I said.

Rita was following Wally's every word, her head bobbing up and down. Serenity, her thin model's frame attired in a flattering—but unusually conservative— simple black dress, appeared mildly interested, tilting her head with an expression of amusement. Gwen gazed at the floor to her side. She didn't look up at me when I spoke.

Edison changed the subject. "Is Robert coming?"

Gwen turned her head in Edison's direction. "No," she said with a frog in her throat. "Huh-em. No, Robert was called out of town yesterday. Wilson Tractors summoned him to a planning meeting in Roanoke."

Edison whispered an expletive and kicked the carpet, causing Serenity to shriek and step back. Edison ignored her. "Out of town? I've been working on the boards he needed for this afternoon's Crispy Greek meeting."

"Oh," said Gwen. "That meeting's been moved to next week. Thursday, I believe. Didn't you get a team update? I'm certain I copied you," she said, her voice unsteady, looking away.

"Oh," said Edison, trying to catch Gwen's eye. "No, I didn't see it. I'll have to check." He glanced at me quizzically.

Gwen tightened up, arms at her sides, both hands balled up into fists.

Wally either was ignoring her, or oblivious. "Crispy Greek? How do they get him crispy?" he said. "Put him in the deep fryer? Roll him in phyllo dough and bake him?"

Rita giggled, her crimson lips widened, pulling tight the wrinkles on her smoker's face. "Hey, I'm impressed you know your Greek cooking."

Without looking up, Gwen mumbled something to herself, turned on her heels and walked off. The talking stopped. Serenity looked after her, following her with her eyes, as if deciding whether to follow.

As soon as Gwen was out of earshot, Wally asked me, "What's up with her, Cannoli? Did you two have a spat? Of course, I'm not ungrateful. She came to me this morning looking for a strong man. You know what I mean," he shrugged his shoulders and chuckled.

"She's really taken Isabelle's death hard," I observed slowly, ignoring his crudeness. "Seems like this funeral has thrown her off balance."

"Oh, I think there's more going on than Isabelle's death," Rita said, bringing up her hands to talk. "I mean, that's plenty by itself, but Gwen hasn't been herself since last week." She spread her hands apart, gesturing with an up-and-down motion to emphasize her words. "She's missed appointments and made careless mistakes. Ever since they all came back from that Cleveland meeting, she's been a brick short of a load. She can't focus. Not all of the time, but she slips in and out of...oh, like depression. Something in her head has got her rattled."

"I heard she made a critical blunder at the meeting

down there," Edison said, putting in to the gossip mill. "She was supposed to present our techniques for project management and cost control. She got lost halfway through and missed a whole section in the middle. Robert had to come forward and smooth things out."

Wally jumped in to the fray. "Well, all of that business with Barry Hart has had her shaken up for the past couple of months. With him trying to buy the firm, and forcing his business practices on our little company, her nerves have been on edge, that's for sure."

"A shame too," Rita said. "All those arguments she and Robert had over Barry. I could hear them through the walls of his office. She'd be screaming at him so hard the glass would shake. Of course he wouldn't listen. They *never* argued so much before. I think that's what finally did them in. If Barry hadn't come along, they'd still be together."

"What?" I said, trying to catch up. "Gwen and Robert? They broke up over Barry Hart?"

Wally looked at me like I was from another planet. "Have you been under a rock, Cannoli?"

I was dumbfounded. "What does Barry Hart have to do with it?"

Serenity, who'd been silent until now, took pity on me. She touched my arm with her slender fingers, tossed her head to the side—à la Cher—to get her long black hair out of the way. She turned her dark eyes to mine. "Ken, are you aware Robert is trying to sell the firm to Barry Hart?" I nodded. "From what I know, Robert has been desperately trying to make the deal. He and Hart are in the final stages of negotiations. Gwen was diametrically opposed to it. I haven't been privy to the details, but I gather there are several specific points she is dead set against. Of course, it's not her decision, yet she was compelled to bend Robert's ear about it.

And she sure bent it—loudly! They fought almost constantly the last couple of weeks before they decided to end it. From what I know, it was the root cause of their break up." I was shaken. Gwen hadn't mentioned anything to me about Barry Hart. Why was I held in the dark? Not that Gwen owed me anything.

I excused myself from the group.

Turning away, my eyes fell upon a matronly woman sitting in one of the large wing chairs. I placed her in her early thirties, but her frizzled brown hair pulled back into a bun, and in-expertly applied make-up made her look older. Her round, full face looked soft and puffy, eyeliner smudged and blue eyes glassy. Barely audible, she spoke softly to a young girl perhaps six years old wearing a dark blue dress with black tights. Curiosity pulled me momentarily out of my Gwen-stupor, as I suspected that this might be Isabelle's daughter and sister. My thoughts were confirmed when she called the child Trudy.

On the furniture nearby, two boys slightly older than the little girl played, arranging tiny plastic figures and giggling quietly.

As I approached Genevieve, I was bathed in scents of roses and perfume from the room. Introducing myself and offering condolences came easily.

"Thank you, Ken. Thank you for coming. It's heartening to see that my dear sister was so well considered." Her eyes were tearing up, and she lifted a crumpled tissue up to her face.

I turned my gaze to the girl. "And this must be Trudy. What a lovely little girl," I said.

Trudy turned her big brown eyes up to look at me. She shrugged back, snuggling into the crook of her aunt's arm. Genevieve patted the girl's head and stroked her hair with her large, plain hands.

Remembering my forehead, I said, "Oh, I ran into a

door the other day." I put my hand over the mark on my head. "I'm sorry it's scary looking." With her head turned away, the girl's eyes snuck a peek back at me.

"Trudy is just trying to make sense of it all," Genevieve said, oblivious to my comment. "And that's a particular hard thing to do when there's no sense to be found."

"You're a very caring person, Genevieve," I said. "I can see you have a great deal of concern for Trudy." I winked at the girl and she turned her back into her aunt's shoulder.

Genevieve continued to caress the child as I turned away.

Movement at the door caught my eye. Jay Stevens entered the room alone, dressed in an ill-fitting brown wool suit, with wide lapels and rounded corners. He scanned from one side to the other, apparently looking for someone. Our eyes locked briefly, before he was approached by a young man, perhaps eighteen. The teenager was tall and thin, with straight blonde hair worn short and a lean, bony build reminiscent of a tennis player. He was dressed in a lavender shirt with no tie and black pants. He said a few words to Jay, then led him out the door. Jay made a sideward hand motion in my direction, as if to say "see you later." A few moments passed and I heard loud cackles coming from the "smoking parlor" across the hall.

I exited the room to get a drink of water and take a peek at who was making all the commotion. Jay Stevens was sitting on a couch between two women who were probably in their fifties. The one to the left was made up in the working poor version of Hollywood glamour: bleached blonde hair, puffed out to twice its normal size, heavy makeup, a shimmering grey tunic, black leather pants and three inch red heels which matched the one-inch red nails on her fingertips. She used her hands to talk. The one to the right was dressed in dime store black stretch pants and a white sweater. Her mousy brown hair was streaked with grey, cut in a simple no-nonsense style. She drank coffee from a paper cup.

On adjacent wing chairs sat the young man in the lavender shirt who had summoned Jay from the parlor, and a second male, in his late teens also. The second teen was attired in a white shirt, red tie and black dress pants.

Jay Stevens motioned me inside.

"Ken, I'd like to introduce you to Isabelle's family."

'Hollywood chic' turned out to be Isabelle's mother, Susie, who spoke with a raspy voice that probably was a sexy asset at one time, but with the drinking problem I'd been made aware of by Edison, it was plainly depressing. The way she held herself in exaggerated calmness led me to think she'd indulged in her affliction that morning. The plain woman was Isabelle's Aunt Darcy and the mother of the two young men in the room.

"How do you do, Hun," said Susie, studying me briefly. Standing within six feet of her, I became acutely aware of an alluring charm that enveloped my sensibilities, causing me to immediately find her desirable despite her obvious faults. Giving me an exaggerated wink, she said, "Have yourself a sit down, sweetie." Then she turned to her sister, winked, and continued her conversation. "Well, I think it's just dreadful, Ginny showing her ass like that. What got into that girl? I remember Mike and me were over to Uncle George's. You know he had that fish fry on the lake?"

I pulled up an upholstered chair from across the room.

Darcy nodded. "Just like he does every year. I don't know what happened at the last one. Those babies were vile. I got a stomachache so bad, I was doubled over for three days."

"Oh, Darcy, you're such a hypochondriac. There wasn't nothin' wrong with those fish. Bob kept getting up and going for more. He must have ate fifteen of 'em."

"Well, that man will eat anything. Look at the gut on him. And he didn't get up, he kept making Flo go back and fix him another plate. Why that woman puts up with that crap I'll never know."

"Anyway, Ginny got up there, and when she saw the food she threw such a fit, you wouldn't believe it. 'Is this all there is?' she says. 'Where's the ribs? Mama, you told me there'd be ribs. And I don't see no green beans and ham either.' She walked up and back at that food table, putting everything down, stamping her feet. If she was so damn picky, she should have stayed home."

I noticed that none of the men joined in the conversation.

"That food *was* awfully greasy. Did he roll those fish in lard? And those fried potatoes were drenched in it! And cold to boot. I don't blame Ginny one bit. Uncle George does make some mouth-watering ribs."

"Oh, with that sauce he makes up? Yeah, well, the fish fry is the fish fry. You don't have no ribs at a fish fry," she flashed her raccoon eyes at Darcy. "What really fried my ass was when she went over to the fruit salad and started picking out the marshmallows with her fingers! Stickin' her fingers in her mouth and then putting them back into the fruit salad. Disgusting!"

"That salad was good though. I like the coconut in it."

Susie murmured her agreement.

Sitting there listening to that drivel, I longed to make my exit, but didn't want to appear rude. Heavens! I'd be the subject of next year's story.

A somber fellow began to make his way around the room announcing that the service was about to begin. The welcome news enabled me to make my exit. I went back to the main parlor, found Edison and settled into some folding chairs that had been arranged at one end of the room.

The service was uncomplicated. A soloist sang *Amazing Grace*. The minister said his piece about life being merely a transition between birth and death, with death being a passage to the next dimension. Genevieve said a few words about Isabelle's lust for life.

Many cried.

Six men in dark suits walked to the front and took charge of the casket, which they carried laboriously down the aisle and out the side door to the waiting hearse.

Funerals always end in an anticlimactic manner. Everyone gets up and doesn't know exactly what to do next. There's no definite point in time when it's over. People just start leaving, or talking to each other, or reminding each other where the food is. There seemed to be plans for everyone to meet at Darcy's house for a family lunch.

Wally walked out with Gwen, Rita and Serenity in tow.

They obviously didn't want us tagging along, so Edison and I went to Ray's Coney, where we drowned our woes in chili cheese fries and chocolate milk shakes.

Chapter 15
Pizza Pie

Events of the day rolled around in my head. New information I had gleaned at the funeral found itself stirred in with established data. Facts and impressions pushed, shoved, cajoled, and generally made my head swim. The fact that I was hungry did not help the matter.

I needed a break.

It was going on 5:30 and nearly everyone in the office had made their flight to the beckoning weekend. Leaving a mess of papers scattered at my desk, I hurried toward Edison's workspace.

Cubicles on my side of the office were outwardly focused—set up running along a central spine, four cubicles on each side facing opposite directions. This gave us immediate access to the aisle way.

I made my way along the partitions—steel-rimmed, fabric-covered panels that came to five and a half feet above the floor—to the intern area, the "swamp," as it was lovingly called. This area was walled off, with each cubicle facing inward to the graphics and model building tables. The interns, Edison, Derik Sun and Kelly Dustre each had a corner. I found Edison working at the center table, an area set up for model building and preparing presentation boards.

Edison methodically scored the rhythm of window mullions on a piece of Plexiglas with a steel knife for the Fenkel House model.

Long tables on either side were fitted out with

cutting boards, metal straight edges, and a scroll saw. Stacks of art board, cardboard and foam-core board sat along one wall, some in odd-shaped pieces where the guts had been cut out. An open shelf contained aerosol spray cans: fixatives to keep pencil drawings from smearing, spray glue—both permanent and removable, and twelve or more colors of paint. An assortment of spring clamps, knives, rolls of tape, and push pins were crammed onto another shelf. Everything needed to build a world-class model was at hand.

"Are you going to see Jeanelle tonight, or do you want to get some dinner?" I asked.

"Jeanelle's gone to Vancouver for a couple of days on a fashion shoot," Edison said while he continued his work.

How Edison managed to charm celebrities and models was beyond my comprehension. Maybe if I spent more time with him, some of it would rub off on me.

Early in his adulthood, Edison was what you might call a kept man. At the tender age of 18 he'd caught the eye of Motown hip hop queen QDevine. Hot stuff, her "Pop the Top" single crashed into the Billboard Top 10 and stayed there for 12 weeks. Follow-up hits made her a household name and earned her enough money to build a recording studio in her Detroit mansion, an 8,000-square foot affair in Detroit's grand Palmer Park district. She met Edison at Pontiac's annual Labor Day "Arts Beats and Eats" Festival, where she welcomed the public in a "meet and greet event" prior to performing on the main stage. They began hanging out and soon she invited him to live with her.

QDevine introduced him to half the world of celebrity. They turned the city upside down throwing lavish parties and attending all of the premier social events, until Q—as she was known to her friends—

kicked him out for some unexplained reason (unexplained to me, at any rate). Rumor has it that QDevine's hit "Hurt Nobody" recounts the story of their breakup.

It's also my understanding that it was Edison's time in that part of town, with its richly detailed homes, that turned him on to architecture.

"Feel like a pizza?" I said.

The magic word had been spoken, and Edison went into a food trance. He put down his steel blade and metal straight edge. Looking up, conflict rippled across the surface of his face, his cheeks puffing out and his eyes widening. "Oh man. This needs to be done for Monday. Robert'll have a fit if it's not on his desk!" He wavered perceptibly as his eyes shifted back and forth, the fingers of his two hands aligning tip to tip, hands pushing in and out. Slowly, relaxation dissolved his facial stress lines, signifying a decision. He pushed his chair back. "Well, I have all weekend to finish."

Only one question remained. "Shield's or Buddy's?"

Detroit's deep dish pizza rivals both offered thick, gooey pizza with sauce that hinted of garlic. They are amazingly similar in content, yet anyone asked will surely have their personal favorite.

"Buddy's, of course." Thankfully, Edison and I shared a passion for the same pizza composition.

Grabbing our coats, we headed the car up Telegraph Road toward Northwestern Highway. We passed Shield's Pizza on the way, but a true pizza connoisseur won't take convenience over taste. In addition to the extra distance to reach Buddy's, we also had to transverse the 15 minute mile: Northwestern Highway between 12 Mile Road and 13 Mile Road. Guaranteed on any work day to eat up a fourth of an hour. On a Friday, it could take longer.

The parking lot was jammed, as was the lobby. We

settled in for the wait, amusing ourselves by commenting on baseball memorabilia affixed to the wall. There was a photograph of Sparky Anderson sitting in the dugout at the old Tiger Stadium, before they built the new ballpark named after some bank. Doesn't tradition mean anything? Why not retain the name Tiger Stadium? There was a bat autographed by Kirk Gibson, before he was traded to Los Angeles. The real treasure was a photograph of the 1968 World Series Champion Tigers sitting in their dugout. Staring out at me were Al Kaline, Mickey Lolich, and Denny McLain in all their glory. That was a summer my father would always reminisce about. What a team. Detroit was on top of the world.

Rows of long picnic tables filled the center of the dining room, with booths lining the walls on both sides. We were lucky enough to be afforded a booth, and left to study the menus. Pizza decisions are based on the "how hungry" rule. Deep dish pizza comes in a small size, sold as six pieces, but it's really only the size of four slices cut into six. That would hardly do, unless we ordered soup and salad. We opted for the large pizza, eight nice-size slices. We decided to split a small antipasto salad as well. That would give us something to munch on while we waited.

"Make any progress on the investigation today?" Edison asked. "I noticed you talking to people at the funeral."

"Yes, it was a good chance to chit chat a little and dig around. I felt a little funny, though, considering the occasion."

The salad arrived and Edison extracted a big scoop, a real challenge due to the height of the pile of lettuce, salami, cheese and tomatoes. The wedges of tomato were arranged so evenly, they must have been measured. Edison grabbed two bread sticks from the basket.

"I talked to some people myself," Edison offered.

I looked up as encouragement for him to continue.

"Isabelle's sister."

"Oh, Genevieve."

"You know her?"

"I talked to her a couple of days ago. I found out that Isy didn't go down to visit her and Trudy like she was going to over New Year's."

"Yeah, she told me that too. Genevieve seems like a real mom type. The way she quieted down her boys, while also keeping Trudy occupied took patience and caring. I can't imagine Isabelle managing her daughter the way Genevieve handles the three children she's got now." Edison had taken one of those little containers of butter—the little square package with the foil top that peels off—spread the whole thing on a bread stick, and was opening another package, presumably to do the same.

"Edison, you're going to clog up your arteries, eating like that." Two packages of butter on a bread stick? I always felt guilty when I used one.

He leaned across the table, whispering, "Ken, we're having salad with oil and vinegar dressing, Swiss cheese and salami, then we're going to eat a pizza loaded with pepperoni and about two pounds of cheese––that's a pound for each of us. This teeny weenie packet of butter is not going to kill me."

That made too much sense. I reached for a bread stick and my own two packets of butter. Edison was one of the few people I could have dinner with, eat what I wanted, and not feel guilty about it.

"Edison, I've been working on a timeline of the events of last week and I need you to fill in some blanks for me," I said.

"Ok, shoot."

I pulled some crumpled notes out of my pocket. "The day you were at the jobsite and you found...*it,* what time was it?"

Edison scrunched up his face. "Let's see. I was a little slow getting into the office. It was the Monday after Christmas. I ate so much the day before that I overslept. I think I arrived about 9:30. I stopped by Rita's desk and chatted with her and Serenity about how our holidays went. Then I went to gather up the reports. I couldn't find batteries for the camera.

"I must have left the office about 10:00 o'clock. Then I stopped at the drugstore to get some batteries. Oh, and I stopped at McDonald's to get a sack lunch. I planned to eat while I was walking around. There was a long line in the drive-thru at Mickey D.

"I pulled in to Flamingo Shores a little after 12:00, but the parking lot was crazy. People were backed out onto Big Beaver Road. I considered parking in the office building next door, but then I remembered that the contractors had the day off, so there had to be plenty of parking in the construction area. Maybe it was 12:15 or 12:20 when I parked. It was freezing cold, so I ate my lunch in the car, and then started looking around at the construction. I kicked off the review on the mall side. I suppose it was a half hour later when I actually found...*him.*"

"That would have been, what, about 1:15?" I was scribbling notes as Edison was talking.

"Maybe. Around there."

"Then you put it in the truck. What time did Robert and Andrew show up?"

"By the time I found some cardboard and plastic sheets, moved the truck, and maneuvered the b—" He stopped and took a breath. "—*it* into the truck, it must have been close to 1:30. Robert and Andrew appeared out of nowhere. I'm just glad I had lunch before they arrived. We spent about an hour touring the building."

I continued, "What time was it when Andrew left for the airport and you headed back to the office?"

"It must have been about 2:30 when we all left, because I got back to the office at 3:00. The moment I walked in the door, Cheryl recruited me to help with the boards for Tuesday's meeting. She must have had me on radar."

I thought for a moment. "During the time you were at the jobsite, did you see anything unusual? Anything appear out of place? Was anyone there at the site other than Robert and Andrew?"

Edison had a blank look on his face. "No. Not that I can think of."

I consulted my notes. "Edison, you said that you dated Isabelle for a while. What was she like?"

He closed his eyes for a good forty-five seconds. I thought I'd lost him to a cat nap when he responded. "Deals, Ken. She was always looking for deals. Every place we went to, she always wanted to meet people. She would ask me if I knew this person or that person. What those people did. How I knew them. The wheels in her head were always turning, looking for an angle, looking to put a spin on something."

"What do you mean looking for an angle?"

"I'll give you a for instance. I hang with the Pistons sometimes."

"I'm aware of your social circles," I said. "Speaking of someone who is always meeting people."

He gave me a dirty look. "I'm trying to fill you in here. So Isy and I are in the sports bar, over on M-59 and Williams Lake Road, and in walks Joe Dumars. Well, he spots me, gives me a high five, and I introduce Isy. Within five minutes, she's all over him. Can he show her this and can he show her that? Where did he get that jacket? It was as if someone had turned on a switch. One moment she's a nice normal human being. The next, she's Chatty Cathy, asking personal questions and going on about herself. Joe leaves and now Isy's pumping me for information. Where did Joe go to school, where does he live, what kind of car does he drive. What are his social habits. Stuff like that."

"Go on."

"Well, I tell her to pay attention to me. So she makes like she's interested in me, and starts asking all kinds of questions about how do I think he's financing his new Porsche, and how much do I think his mortgage payment is."

"She asked you those questions?"

"Yeah."

"Do you even know the answers?"

"Some of them."

"Ever figure out what her angle was?"

"Nope. I just finally told her, she's lovely, but I can't take all of the deal making. Like she was in the business of looking for a meal ticket every minute."

"Any of her inquiries ever pan out?" I asked as the pizza arrived. The waiter placed a silver stand between us, setting the pizza on top, a good five inches above the table.

"Not that I know of. But she sure was intent to make a change in her life."

"Yeah, Genevieve told me. It seems she was driven to work hard, save a bunch of money, and buy a nice house to make a nice home and get her kid back."

Edison's jaw dropped to the floor and he looked at me with a gaping stare. "Have Trudy live with her? Not likely! Isabelle wanted to move to Hollywood."

Chapter 16
Dangerous Discussions

Edison's truck stood alone in the office parking lot. I dropped him off and headed home. The snow had turned to a brown-grey mush on the street. Municipal trucks had dumped tons of salt, melting the virgin snow, the resulting paste sullied by the continuous stream of traffic. The frozen slurry stood erect in ridges marking traffic patterns and turning radii. Little hunks of the re-composed mixture dappled the street. Stalled-out cars were nearly hidden in center turn lanes, buried in banks of snow.

My neighborhood did not appear quite so dingy. Plows had cleared the street, pushing up mounds of snow to each side. A heap, triangular in cross section, pushed up into the front yards and filled the space where the driveways met the street. Across the edge of my drive, the pile was more than two feet high, and almost three feet across. I was forced to park on the street, climb the snow pile and trudge across my snow-covered driveway to retrieve my shovel. When I reached the house, I decided to warm my stiff fingers and change clothes first, before tackling the snow removal process.

The message light on my answering machine blinked up a storm. It was Robert. He was back in town, and no less ornery than when he'd left. "Cannoli! What's the status on your review of the contractor's extras at Federal Credit Union? I need that information first thing in the morning!" The message showed it was left at 8:17 p.m.

I changed into sweat clothes, and went back out into the cold night air for some heavy-duty shoveling. The mound of snow across my driveway was hard and chunky. A small shovelful was all I could lift at one time. Heave it, throw it to the side, and then shovel another. Slow going. Thirty minutes later, I started shoveling the driveway and the sidewalk. Retrieving an old paint can filled with rock salt from inside my door, I tossed handfuls onto icy patches along the sidewalk.

When I finished, I drug weary feet to the mailbox and claimed the day's offerings. Ignoring my aching back, I fixed a pot of coffee to brew while I changed wet socks and pulled on a sweater. At the kitchen table, I sorted the mail and discovered a handwritten letter postmarked St. Louis. I opened the pink envelope from Mary with trepidation. It said:

Dear Ken,

I'm not used to being scorned and I won't stand for it. When you come to your senses and realize the mistake you've made, your heart will bleed for me and I won't be there.

My wishes for you are pure and deep: that the rats and roaches that live in the project you call home, mutate and multiply; that the sewer pipe fills with debris and backs into your tub; and that the snow on your roof collapses the structure while you sleep.

With joy in your discontent,
Mary

Folding the letter, I slid it back into the envelope, and pitched it in the trash.

The detective pack called to me. I pulled out the rubber-banded cards and added today's conversations and notes, a tedious process. Next I updated the timeline. Quite a few facts were useful in filling in some blanks. Nothing struck me as being of major significance.

Suddenly, I was beyond fatigue, and with Robert's call nagging at me, I decided I'd better pull a Saturday morning at the office. I collapsed onto the mattress. My ancient bones were so stiff, it was awkward to crawl into the low bed. I would have to put up the frame soon. The alarm was set for 7:00 a.m.

The last thing I remember is my head touching the pillow.

I awoke to a loud static-filled racket, wondering first and foremost who was responsible for the commotion. In short order, realization hit and I flipped over to turn off the clock radio alarm. Somehow, the station had gone off channel. It wasn't a pleasant way to begin the day. I wrestled with the question of adding a few more minutes to my sleep time, but decided against it. More than likely, I'd fall asleep again and not rise until noon.

At some point during the night it had become clear to me: Robert must be confronted about the tie-tack I found at Isabelle's. It wasn't normal behavior for Robert to visit a secretary. What had been his purpose in being there?

A deep-seated concern compelled me to find out, but the process necessary to get the information was not something I wanted to go through. How do you confront your boss with the knowledge that he was at a dead employee's house? How do you ask him his purpose for being there? Images of our possible conversation filled my mind. I could follow several possible scenarios to their logical conclusions. It made me sick to think about it, but it could not be avoided.

Saturday the office would be quiet. I could have a discourse with the boss in private. Just a quiet chat with someone who held my livelihood in his hand, asking him what he was doing at the dead girl's house. Telling him I knew he was there because I found his tie-pin in the living room. Asking him if she was still alive when he left.

Perhaps being alone with him in the building was not going to be a plus.

I showered, dressed in blue jeans and a turtle neck and sat down to a quick and easy bowl of cold cereal.

When I arrived, the office was noiseless, but a row of lights were turned on, and half a pot of coffee sat warming on the burner. It was only about 9:30 and I didn't expect to find many people at work. Robert was the only one present. Wouldn't you know it? I expected Wally, Gwen, and Edison would be in at some point during the weekend. Would it be better to have the confrontation while Robert and I were still alone? Or a bit later when there was someone else in the office to back me up in an emergency?

I opted to jump in.

Robert occupied one of three private offices, enclosed floor-to-ceiling. Full height glass faced the rest of us, a number of horizontal mullions breaking up the expanse into visually manageable pieces. Window mullions and the solid door were colored a muted oxblood.

Robert was reading one of his favorite papers, the *Wall Street Journal,* sitting there in his black shirt, elbows on the desk. Newspaper flat, covering up whatever piles were on the desk to begin with. The face of the desk was red oak, a book-matched veneer that gave the desk an old style character.

Robert spoke without looking up from his paper, a habit that frustrated me to no end. "Have you reviewed those extras on Federal Credit Union?"

"I was going to work on that today."

Eyes still glued to the paper. "Look at that. Canvas

Royal is down seven points. Does me absolutely no good."

"No, Robert. Maybe not. Robert, I've got to talk to you." I fingered the tie-tack in my pocket.

He looked up over the top of his black framed reading glasses. "Well, here I am."

No offer to sit. Truthfully, I was more comfortable standing. Closing the door, I began with trepidation, "I was thinking about Isabelle. I was wondering how you felt about her."

"How I felt about her?" he looked up and spoke with a gravelly voice. "What the hell does that mean? One of my staff was murdered. A shame. It's a damn shame. That's what I think about it. The poor thing was only—what—twenty-three? She hadn't even seen anything of the world yet. Murdered on our project, that's what hurts. It's a grave circumstance that she was killed at Crystals. I was talking to Henry Tisk at The Circle Group. They're beside themselves. Not only is the project further behind, but they're worried about the downside of the murder transpiring at the store entrance. You know that customers will take that as a bad sign. Some people may boycott the store altogether. No one wants to shop for a designer wardrobe in a space where someone was killed."

In between his babbling, Robert turned back to the paper. Why won't the man look at me! "Robert, what I was wondering, is what kind of relationship did you have with Isabelle?"

"Relationship?" He slammed the paper down and snatched the glasses off his head, tossing them on top of the paper. He glared at me for a full ten seconds, then put his elbows on the desk, and raised his hands to rub his eyes with the palms of his hands. Sighing, he said slowly, "We didn't have a relationship. She worked here. What are you getting at? Why the questions?"

I stood momentarily wondering which question to answer first, when the phone rang.

"Westin.... No, goddamn it, we're not going to roll over on that...I know...I know...yes...I know.... It was supposed to have been done on the sixteenth.... I know it.... Listen, you can tell George what's-his-name that I don't care if the product is blue or pink. I want that fire proofing out to the jobsite pronto." Robert turned in his swivel chair, putting his feet on the wall behind his desk. I could see the black half-moons on the wall where he'd done this many times before.

While he talked out this situation with whoever was on the other side of the phone call, I played the various options through in my head, deciding which to pursue when Robert got off the phone.

"And tell George that I want seats to the sky box on the 28th. I know it.... I know. Just tell him...he'd better make it happen.... Listen, give Janice my love. Talk to you on Monday." He hung up the phone and looked in my direction without talking.

"Robert, I just want to know if you had any personal dealings with Isabelle. Did you call her? Did you see her outside the office? Do you know anything about her personal life?"

A flash of—something—crossed Robert's face. Recognition. Anger. Fear. As if he'd been punched by someone from behind. He settled on anger. "Hell, no. I didn't call her. I didn't see her. Cannoli, you're out of line. What is this about?"

An uneasy male voice came over the intercom. *Ken, you have a call on line 1. Jester Cromwell's on the phone.* It sounded like Edison, who must have arrived not long after me, using the system to notify me of the call because he couldn't find me.

Robert looked at the telephone with disgust. "You'd better take that call. And see if you can resolve Jester

Cromwell's fixture delivery concern. He keeps calling to cry on my shoulder. Just get it solved."

Out of habit, I reached for the phone to pick up the page. Robert put out his hand. "Cannoli!"

I left the office and went to my cubicle, picking up the phone.

"Ken, I'm glad I caught you."

"Good morning Jester. What can I do for you?" I said with my pleasant voice.

"I was thinking about those glass samples we looked at a couple of days ago. I know we talked about the one with the vine around the outside. But I was thinking, maybe the glass sections at the ends of the counter could be the solid frosted. Maybe with a pattern. I just don't know if it's going to be too much of the same thing to have all the glass pieces in one pattern."

I took a deep breath. "Jester, it's going to be beautiful. What are you worried about?"

Here we go again! "Do you think so? I just don't know. I wouldn't want it to be too much."

"Jester, think like a customer. You're standing at the front of the counter, looking in the glass. You're looking at all of the chocolate choices, and something in a tray to the rear catches your eye, but you just can't make it out. What are you going to do?"

"Well, I move over a bit, and try to look sideways at the display, maybe peek around the corner, through the side—" He laughed. "Ok, got the picture. Leave it as it is."

"Ok, Jester. I'll talk to you beginning of the week."

"Wait, Ken, there's another matter. Some of the ceiling tiles are wet. There seems to be a leak. You can see the moisture, there's a darker area on the white tiles...it shouldn't be like this."

"Jester, can you talk to Ted about that one? He can check it out."

"I already did that, Ken. Ted doesn't have a clue. It isn't too bad right now, but some of the tiles in my office are wet. Some others just outside my office, in front of the bathroom, drip occasionally."

It couldn't be a roof leak; there was a floor above. Probably the piping. "I'll check it out next time I'm out there, Jester." I hung up the phone and walked back over to Robert's office.

The nerves in my stomach were taking over. My knees weakened with the feeling. I was, in effect, accusing Robert of some improper behavior. But what? When all of the circumstances were set aside, I only wanted to know one thing: why had he been at Isabelle's?

He still had the phone at his ear, so I waited as unobtrusively as possible near his office.

Of course, it was none of my business. It just seemed odd. I had thought that Robert had no particular feeling one way or the other about the people in the office. Isabelle was just clerical staff. No one of any significance. Isn't that why Gwen had to borrow the truck for Isabelle—because as clerical staff she was not allowed to borrow the truck? Gwen had said something to the effect that if Robert found out, he wouldn't have approved.

I glanced around the corner, and saw Robert placing the receiver in the cradle. He waved me in.

"Now you've been talking in circles about my relationship with Isabelle. She was an employee. She handled paperwork. What more is there to say? Tell me, Ken, exactly what you're talking about." He folded his arms across his chest.

"Well, I found something. I'm just trying to figure this thing out."

"What thing? Isabelle's murder? Is that what this is about?" His neck changed color, a deep red bleeding around his collar. Blood vessels popped in his eyes. "I heard that you were poking around. Why don't you leave these questions and the investigation to the police? Who do you think you are, Spencer for Hire?" A smirk across his chiseled features gave him an ugly look.

Calm. Keep it calm. "No I just thought I'd help out. I'm just trying to find some answers."

"By asking me what I was doing with Isabelle? What kind of a question is that?"

Time to put it all on the line. I reached into my pocket. *Let's just get this done!* To my dismay, as I was extracting the tie-tack from my pocket, I saw Edison through the glass, hustling toward us with a full head of steam. His face set with urgency. I hoped it was for someone else.

He stopped at the door and knocked. I dropped the pin back into the pocket, extracted my hand and opened the door.

"This better be important." I said when I opened the door.

Edison looked at me, wordlessly, then at Robert.

"Robert, you have a visitor. A Mr. Hall?"

Robert looked up with satisfaction. "Tell Mr. Hall that I'll be right with him. Ken and I were just finishing."

Edison said, "Yes, sir."

I closed the door behind him. Robert glared at me disapprovingly and began to open his mouth. Before he could get anything out, I reached into my pocket, pulled out the little horse and carriage tie-pin, and placed it on Robert's desk in front of him.

He looked down at it with recognition. Another emotion crossed his face, something parallel to disdain? He hesitated, then smiled. "Oh, my tie-tack. I wondered what happened to it. You know I found this one in a little jewelry shop on Van Dorn Street in Lincoln. Nebraska. Not too far from Guitars and Cadillacs." He smiled. "I've had some tasty Margaritas there...tasty women too. Where on earth did you find it?"

"It was at Isabelle's. I found it on the floor."

Robert looked up with suspicion. "At Isabelle's?"

"I wondered what had prompted you to be at her house. I thought perhaps there was some sort of reason. Maybe you'd gotten to know her outside the office. Maybe you went to her house to talk. Maybe you— well, maybe you could tell me why you were at her house."

He narrowed his eyes, placing the tips of his fingers together in a thoughtful position. Several seconds passed. "Well," he said, "I don't want to speak ill of the dead. But since you asked and won't let the subject go, I'll tell you. It was a week or so ago. We had a meeting here at the office with the Fenkels—you know the ones. The couple with the little yippie dog that they bring to all of the meetings. I had worn this horse and carriage tack in the morning. Then, when I realized the Fenkels were coming in, I took it off, trading it for the sad puppy bird tack—you know the one."

Another of Robert's stupid scenes. A terrier puppy with a dead bird in his mouth.

"After I made the switch, I placed the carriage tack on my desk. Later, when I went to look for it, it was gone. Just gone. I never saw it again until just now."

"So how did it get—"

"To Isabelle's?" Robert grinned wickedly. "I won't speculate, Ken. It's not good to speak ill of the dead."

I didn't buy his story for a minute. It was shocking. That Robert would pull a big lie like that, to cover up— what? What had he been doing at Isabelle's? And why the secrecy? What was he hiding?

Robert stood up. "Now, I've got to meet with a new

client."

Stunned, my feet refused to move. Robert started out from behind his desk when the phone rang.

He grabbed the receiver. "Hello?" He listened. "But what?....Where are you?....What!" He sat down. As he spoke, the healthy tan on his face turned pinkish white, making his skin appear sickly. "Just hang tight.... No, I'll call Mark Weintraub. We'll be down as soon as I can get him.... Don't say a word until we get there."

He hung up the phone and stared at it. To me, he said, "Gwen's been arrested for Isabelle's murder."

Chapter 17
Anxious Arrest

Gwen arrested? My head spun, a thousand thoughts competing for attention at once. Arrested, why? Where was Gwen right now? How was she? My last memory of her, at the funeral home, had her numb and shaking. How would she handle arrest, incarceration?

It puzzled me also that the police would conclude Gwen killed Isabelle. Shot her, no less. What motive did they assume?

I needed to see Gwen and get some answers. "Are you going down there?" I asked Robert. He had picked up the phone and was in the process of dialing. "Where are they holding her? Let me go with you."

Robert's lips formed a stone grimace. Without looking up, he said, "Are you crazy? I wouldn't let you near her with your wild innuendoes. She needs help right now, not your melodramatic allegations." His voice un-edged as someone at the other end picked up. "Yes, it's Robert Westin; is Mark Weintraub there? Yes, I'll hold." Robert scowled at me. Reluctantly, I left the room.

The rest of the day blurred out, as I stumbled dazed through motions and activities. I shoveled some papers, wrote a few reports and worked ineffectively to resolve code issues. I found myself calling Jack Hout and begging to postpone the completion of proposals for three new strip shopping centers that were due Monday. I'd be hard pressed to give a detailed explanation of what I did that Saturday. Papers on my desk were straightened. I read the same paragraph three or four times, without comprehension. I went through my in-box. Twice. Edison came over to ask me something about the Fenkel House. My answer was unintelligible, even to me at the time. I do remember that I told him what had happened. He ran out of my cubicle to make some phone calls and get some answers. Mentally I was with Gwen. I've never been arrested. Never even saw the inside of a police station. What on earth was she going through now?

I attempted to imagine steps that she was taken through—what I learned from TV—fingerprinting, stripped of personal possessions, given some green or orange prison outfit to wear. Do they do that at this point in the process, or does that come later? There's an arraignment—to file charges and set bail. That comes real fast. It was Saturday afternoon, however. I wouldn't imagine they could get that together before Monday sometime. But isn't there a "Night Court"? Or is that just on television? She must have been arrested in Troy, as that was the jurisdiction leading the investigation.

Robert was in the process of contacting our company attorney. Would Mark be able to do anything? Don't lawyers specialize: contract law, civil law, criminal law? Isn't it odd that a regular person accused of a crime is defended by a criminal lawyer? Aren't those just for criminals? I'd only met Mark a couple of times. He was around whenever the firm needed some practical advice on contracts, business dealings, and the like. I wondered if *he* had seen the inside of a police station.

Nonetheless, certainly Mark would have connections to an excellent criminal attorney.

"Ken," Edison said quietly.

I looked up from the paper I'd been staring at

without cognizance. "Yes?"

He lowered his frame into my guest chair. He spoke slowly, quietly. "Here's what I found out. Gwen was arrested and booked at Troy police headquarters. She's being held there until her arraignment on Monday. No time has been set yet."

I got up. "Ok, Edison; let's go." I began to move out of the cubicle when Edison put up a hand to stop me.

"Ken, sit down."

I looked down at him. He didn't move. Reluctantly, I sat back down. "What?"

"Ken, we can't see her."

"What do you mean we can't see her?"

"They don't allow visitors."

"That's ridiculous. How can they have someone in jail and not let them see the people who care about them?"

Edison's big puppy-dog eyes seemed sad. "Apparently, they don't have the facilities. They aren't set up for handling a visiting situation."

The frustration and disappointment advanced through me like a hot flood.

Edison must have seen it on my face as he continued, "The Sargent I talked to said she'd be allowed to make as many phone calls as she'd like to."

"That's some substitute for being able to sit face to face with your friends," I commented.

"She's going to be held there just until the arraignment. On Monday, she'll be transferred to the lock-up at the court next door. After they establish bail, she'll be released when the money is posted."

"And if we can't post bail?"

Edison looked down at the floor. "She'll be transferred to Oakland County Jail in Pontiac."

Gwen didn't call me on Saturday.

Sunday morning took a long time to arrive.

The night was restless, no position comfortable. I felt lumps in the mattress, I was cold, my arms hurt, my neck was stiff. I kept waking. When I did float into sleep, my dreams were about walking through the office. The floor was uneven. Repeatedly, I nearly fell over. My footing was lopsided, my shoes slipping on the surface. The carpeting was darker than I remembered it. Upon closer examination, I discovered that the floor was not a carpet at all, but a mass of thousands of bugs, beetles, ants, earthworms, slugs. Crawling, slithering, slimy little disgusting creatures. The motion of the tiny beasts was unnerving. I was dizzy. They were crawling up the furniture. I awoke with my stomach in knots and my hair damp.

Hauling myself out of bed, I showered, dragged the razor across my face and dressed. On a normal Sunday, I'd have enjoyed fixing myself a farmer's breakfast of fried potatoes, eggs, onions, and ham. But I still hadn't gone shopping, so I settled for cold cereal again. The first bite was sour milk; I spit out the unpleasant surprise with dismay.

I poured the milk down the disposal, turning my head away in disgust from the smell. I took the last two paper towels from the roll and wiped my mess off the table. When would I get to the grocery store?

The living room couch was uncomfortable. I lay staring at the ceiling, pouting, thoughts parading through my mind. My body distressed, my mind jumbled. *Ken—get a grip!*

Gwen was in lock-up. Mary had dumped me. I thought about the letter I'd received from Mary the day before. It was finally over between us, a concept I held with acceptance. Her instant anger had always troubled me. Now my life could go on in another direction.

Gwen's face was sallow, eyes glazed over and seemed deeper in the sockets than I remembered them.

The surface of her cheeks was coarser, more real than I was used to seeing at the office. Hair was combed and presentable, but not the same somehow. She ordinarily wore her copper hair in a tousled look, but seeing her before me, I realized that the look must have taken some daily work to achieve. Presently it was disorganized, spikes of hair pointing out in all directions. Her eyes appeared smaller, duller, and less alive without mascara or eyeliner. The eyes themselves seemed lifeless, shimmerless blue irises centered in milky white pools of despair.

It was going to take some effort on my part to present an upbeat front. While I stood mute, searching for the right words, Gwen said, "Hey, thanks for coming. I've had a hell of a night. Why don't you come here and—"

The shrill ringing of the phone rattled me. My arms flew out in front of me, and I nearly fell off the couch reaching for the receiver.

"Hello," I said, eyes adjusting to the light, the scene in my dream still floating through my consciousness.

"It's Gwen." The volume of her voice was soft, the tone clipped.

I suddenly was wide awake. "Gwen, you've been in my prayers. How are you? What's going on?"

"The night's been excruciating. I hate the world being like this. I have so many things to do. They won't let me see my kids. Why does this always happen to me? So many forces asking me to lose myself. I've got to get out of here. Take a deep breath, Kathryn."

She called herself by her middle name when the going was tough. My heart wrenches when she talks that way.

"I feel confined in this room. The walls are enshrouding me, stealing my breath, closing the drapes on my life. I struggle to suck air. There's this 30-pound weight on my chest. I'm compressed, confined, oppressed. How can they do this to me? Don't they know how debilitating it is to be in here? I go round and round with this stuff in my head, and come to a conclusion that it will be better this afternoon when I can stop by Starbucks to have a coffee—then realize I can't go to Starbucks. I can't go anywhere. I'm stuck in this room, on these stitched-together lumps they call a mattress. Yikes!

"I feel strung out. There's no rest. I can't relax on this who-knows-where-it's-been cot. No peace of mind here. People walking by the glass front of my cage. Mostly they don't look at me, just walk by doing their business. What's worse? Ignoring me, or staring at me like a caged animal? My nerves are raw, shattered. I think about work and the dozens of things I should be doing. Pieces that will fall through the crack like marbles down the stairs. I've been so stressed-out lately anyway, with the Robert deal and I've got to prepare a presentation for my Tuesday meeting with Crispy Greek. Where am *I* in all this?"

She stopped talking for a minute.

"Oh, Gwen," I said. Where do I begin? "Listen, you are going to get through this. You are one of the strongest people I know. I've seen you in many difficult situations. Time and again you find the strength to compose yourself and work through, even when the madness has taken everyone else. I know you can find your center now. It's inside you. I know it. I've seen it."

She seemed to relax. "I take it Robert told you what happened?"

"I was in his office when he got your call. I wanted to come down with him yesterday, but he nixed it. Edison found out where you were, and told me something strange. They aren't letting you have any visitors?"

"No. That part is really rough. After some negotiations yesterday, they finally let Mark Weintraub in, and he laid out the plan for the arraignment Monday." She sighed deeply. "Edison found out? That guy, he's got his connections, doesn't he?" The words were forced as she struggled to make it friendlier.

"Yes. Gwen, what's happening?"

She hesitated. I pictured her looking like she did in the dream I just had. No makeup. Hair a mess. Looking down at the floor, her mouth tense. "It won't be today. Mark says they're trying to get the arraignment set for tomorrow. They'll set bail. I just hope," she got a cry caught in her throat, "just hope I can get out of here soon. I can't relax, can't let my guard down. I'm out in the open. And all those people walking by—who...who the hell are they?

"Dwayne and Patrick want to come down here, of course. My mom's trying to keep them calmed down, but she's got issues herself." She gasped a breath, silent for a moment. "And I would really love to see my kids, but I don't want them to see me like this either."

"Do you need anything? Is there something I can do for you?"

She paused. "Yes, Ken, I could use your help. Mark says they've got a body of evidence; different pieces and disjointed parts that they're building a case around. It's all circumstantial. It's all—I don't know. You've got to help me, please." Her voice cracked. I pictured her tearing up and I couldn't help responding in kind.

"What can I do?"

"Find out what happened. Uncover what happened to Isabelle. I don't understand. Someone's trying to frame me, and I can't fathom why they would." Her voice broke, and my uncomfortable feeling grew deeper.

"What do you mean, frame you?"

"The gun. I lost the gun last week. It was there one day and gone the next." Her voice rasped out, raw. Bare, fragile emotions spilled without restraint.

"Gun, what gun? You had a gun?" I tried to follow what she was telling me.

"Yes, a .38. For protection. You just never know these days. I bought one after Craig died. A woman living alone with her kids. I was scared."

"And you lost the gun? What do you mean?"

Some guttural sounds came over the wire. "It was...I...had...I don't know...." her voice trailed off, "...when. It just disappeared.... Vanished.... The police say it's the gun that killed Isabelle."

I tried to focus on what Gwen was telling me. She had a gun. She lost it. What did she mean, lost? It killed Isabelle. What were the chances of someone losing a gun which later killed someone that worked in the same office?

How could I understand? "You said there were more...things? Circumstantial evidence?"

Her voice shook. I felt invasive, prying into her wound, putting her through the pain again. "One of the neighbors saw me pull up to her house on Monday, leave my car and take the truck. They thought it was odd. So they kept an eye on the BMW. They saw it sitting there all morning. Later in the day, after the body was discovered, the police went to the house and poked around the neighborhood. When they asked the neighbors if they'd seen anything suspicious, the cops were told about it." She stopped. "Umm, ok," she said to someone at her end. "I've got to go now."

"You keep your head held high, Gwen. I'll check into things and see what I can find out. Call me when you can. Meanwhile, you're in my prayers."

"Thanks, Ken. Thanks for helping me." Her voice held a small bit of relief.

I hung up wondering how I could help her. There were nagging questions. I found myself wanting to believe her, desiring to help her. But portions of her story didn't make sense. A few nights before, she'd come to me, to my house, sharing that she had borrowed the truck for Isabelle, and had made the vehicle exchange that Monday morning.

Had she told me the story merely so I could validate her tale now?

How cynical was I? I kicked myself for not believing her.

And where did she get a gun? I don't know anybody who owns a gun. For protection—is she crazy? People get killed with guns. And where did she lose it? How do you lose a gun? I realized, too late, that she said she "lost" the gun. She didn't say that it was stolen. Does a gun just fall out of a dresser and get lost?

I longed to help her, to believe her, but questions niggled at me—not about her innocence exactly, but the trappings surrounding her account didn't fit. I didn't believe that she'd killed Isabelle, but the narrative had holes large enough to drive a Mack truck through.

It was after noon and suddenly I was famished. I decided to head to the office and make up for yesterday's miserable work attempt. I stopped at a greasy spoon on Telegraph Road. Momma's Moonlight Café sounds like a delightful place, but it's just a simple lunch counter, offering the coney island Greek menu that's typical in a lot of Detroit area establishments. In addition, they've got a 24-hour breakfast menu. I was hankering for the usual big Sunday breakfast that I'd missed that morning.

I walked in and looked for a seat. The building was narrow, with just one center aisle. A row of booths lined one wall, while the grill and waitresses' pickup area was arranged on the other. Midday Sunday, it was a full house. As my eyes made a second pass through the seats, I spotted Wally in one of the back booths. He caught sight of me and waved me over.

He was sitting with Rita Bankstahl from the office. I was surprised to see the two of them together outside the office.

"Cannoli, have a seat," Wally spouted. "It must be old home week; I walk in here, and there's Rita, and now here you are."

"Hey, Ken." Rita slid over to make room for me.

"Rita, what a nice surprise."

She formed her red lipstick-covered mouth into a smile. "Ken, what are you doing out? On the way to work?"

"Yeah, I thought I'd try to get that code study wrapped up for the UAW hall."

Rita explained, "Wally's going there too. Me, I'm not working, I just thought I'd come in for an omelet. Take a break from the cooking."

"Guess you're just lost without a man to take care of," Wally offered.

Rita swatted him with her menu. "George is just gone for a couple of days. It's nice to have some time to myself." When I gave her a questioning glance, she continued. "He's gone down to Dayton. They've got a convention for hardware suppliers."

Wally said, "My goodness. Thousands of square feet of nothing but hardware? George must be in his glory."

"Don't you know it," Rita put in. "That man can get excited over a new line of hinges with non-removable pins. All I have to do if I'm in the mood for sex is wear my Schlage t-shirt and he's all over me."

I had to chuckle. Did George know she talked like that?

The waitress came and took our order. Wally surprised me by ordering diet food: a plain baked potato, no butter or sour cream and a village salad with no feta cheese. Rita ordered the western omelet. I went with the farmer's omelet. I like it because there are potatoes inside.

The conversation turned serious as we discussed Gwen's state. I filled them in on my conversation with her that morning.

"That poor thing," Rita put in. "What a trauma to go through. What on earth makes them think a wonderful young woman like that would murder somebody? I just don't get it."

"Apparently," I answered, "it was Gwen's gun that killed Isabelle."

"Heavens!" Rita looked truly shocked. "Gwen's gun? Oh my goodness. I just can't believe that Gwen killed someone."

"She didn't kill her," I said. "Gwen lost her gun, someone else got it and used it to murder Isabelle."

They both looked at me. It sounded far-fetched to me too. I said, "I didn't even know Gwen had a gun. She says she got it for protection."

"That's right," Wally said, realization registering across his face. "This explains some of the questions the police asked me about."

Rita and I looked at Wally. I said, "The police asked you about the gun?"

"Yes, they were aware that I'd helped her purchase the firearm, and asked me about the details. Last month, she asked my opinion about what to get. We went shopping together and I gave her some pointers. That place on the east side—Nick's Guns and Ammo—they don't have anything worthwhile. I took her over to Nestor's Gun Shop in Southfield, and helped her pick one out."

"Last month?" I said. "I had the impression that she'd bought the gun after her husband died."

"Oh, no. We just went shopping for it after Thanksgiving. That was, what, six weeks ago? She said there'd been some burglaries in the neighborhood and she feared for her kids. I told her the best thing was to get a .38 special. Those little 22's aren't the thing for protection at home. What you want is a reliable gun with enough stopping power to make it count. Of course, I didn't go into that much detail with Lieutenant Coogan.

"After she bought the gun, I took her over to Mike's Target Hut in Royal Oak, and helped her with some target practice. After a few visits she got so she wasn't afraid of it anymore."

I was sure that Gwen had told me she had the gun for years. If she just bought the firearm a few weeks before it was used to kill Isabelle, this was not in her favor. And why did she deliberately mislead me by telling me she'd had it for a long time?

Rita was intrigued. "I didn't know you were a gun expert, Wally."

"Oh, it's just a hobby. For a while I was going to Mike's Target so often, I started making my own bullets to save a few bucks."

I left lunch that day wondering if everyone I'd ever met had another side to their lives that I knew nothing about.

What you don't know about someone, I thought, *really could kill you.*

Chapter 18
Body Blind

The phone rang persistently as I reached the door, leaving for work. It was 8:00 a.m. Monday morning.

Gwen's voice was steady and sharp. "Ken, I'm so glad I caught you. The arraignment is set for 11:00 o'clock and I wanted to discuss a few things before the procedure." Her tone expressed resolution.

"Sure, Gwen. How are you? You sound more connected today."

"I feel better right now. I'm going to take this one minute at a time—or maybe even one *instant* at a time. I'm overjoyed to hear your voice across the line, though I'd much rather be sitting next to you."

Smile. "What do you need right now?" *I have to take care of the girl.*

"Two things, Ken. One, don't come down here today."

"To the arraignment? I thought you'd feel supported to see some friends." Her comment confused me.

"It's going to be a zoo, Ken. My intention is to focus on getting through it. I'll be ok." I heard the rush of air as she sighed. "Stay away. Rather, employ the time investigating what really happened. As we discussed yesterday. The most support you could offer me is to solve the mystery."

Questions sprouted inside me like fizz in a Vernors. Was I supporting her? I had an overabundance of doubts. Inconsistences in her words needed to be discussed; her details didn't make sense. I resolved to push through the uncomfortableness and ask for her honesty.

"Gwen. I'm focused on helping you through this, and I'm working to unearth the truth."

Silence, then, "I sense a 'but' there."

I choose my words with care, the heavy stillness hanging between us. "I'm prosecuting this search with as much creativity and intensity as I can muster. I need you to be candid with me, Gwen. I've been going over my notes about the events of the last two weeks and there's a bit of confusion on my part."

"What is it?" she asked guardedly.

"Tell me about the gun. When did you buy it?"

"The gun? Like I said—"

"From what you explained to me yesterday, I got the impression that you acquired the gun for protection when Craig died. Now I...I understand from Wally that he took you to buy the gun, just a few weeks ago."

The crackle on the line accentuated her silence. "It was just after Thanksgiving," she swallowed hard, "I thought it would look bad if you thought I'd just bought the gun. Ken, I need your help so badly. I wanted you on my side, and I didn't know if you'd believe me. The facts.... I bought a gun, lost it, and then it's used to kill someone I work with. All within five weeks? It sounds bad even to me. So much has happened." The sobbing began slowly. "*When* I bought the gun wasn't as important as that it was lost. It seemed like a small detail. I just need a friend—and your help."

"I want to see you through this, Gwen, truly. You know I value our friendship. But I wonder about some of the details you've told me. Details that have turned out not to be completely true."

"I explained about the gun. I'm sorry."

"Gwen, there's something else; I'm uneasy bringing up these inconsistences. I want to help you. I want to see you here, next to me. But I needed to find out what was really happening."

"What is it? Ken, I need your help. Please, I can handle it, I want you to have everything you need. Ask me."

I swallowed hard. "Last week you told me that you picked up Smartain at the airport, when Andrew had actually picked him up. Maybe you miss-remembered?"

She didn't speak. I heard her breath become short, more rapid. She started to speak, stopped, and started again. A rustling came over the line—something against the receiver—and she blew her nose. There was some sort of internal struggle going on, and I felt she was about to explode.

"Gwen," I said steadily. I was concerned about her mental stability. "Gwen," I said quietly, "I'll do what I can to help you, but you've got to level with me."

"He was going to ruin Robert," she spoke so softly that I could barely hear her. I strained to listen. "Robert had been managing the books ever since Andrew had gone into semi-retirement, and he wasn't handling it so well. Robert had taken the profits, investing them in some projects that should have made us a nice sum, but one after the other they failed. The firm lost a ton of money. Robert didn't know what to do. We were going to fold if something didn't happen soon."

She paused.

I didn't say anything.

"He started talking to Robert. Talking about investing in the company, buying a major share of the stock. At first he was like a godsend, a relief. He was our way out. But then he started asking Robert to do things. Robert went along in order to please him."

"Him? Who?"

"Barry Hart," she said. "What a mess. The further he went, the deeper trouble we got into. Like, we were supposed to do a job in Mesa, Arizona. Well, he told the client that I was operating out of the Phoenix office. You know, we don't even have an office on the west side of the country. Barry set up a phone on a desk somewhere in Phoenix, and had the calls forwarded to me here. It rang on my desk. When that phone rang, I knew it was a call to the Phoenix office. I had to answer it as if I was there. I was always scared to death someone would call and want to drop by. Or ask me about the weather. I didn't know if it was raining or sunny. Robert wanted an 'in' with this guy, and put me in the middle to do it."

"Is that what lead to your break up with Robert?"

"Essentially, yes. I couldn't stand it anymore. I told Robert that we didn't need Barry's money that bad. I asked Robert to tell Barry 'no,' to quit doing those questionable dealings. Robert refused and we called it quits." She took a breath.

"But it didn't end there, did it?"

"No. I took it upon myself to talk to Barry directly, to try to get him to stop making Robert do things. Leave us alone. But he just yelled at me, swearing in all kinds of nasty language. It did no good. But I kept after him. Then he started threatening me. He told me to lay off him and keep quiet to Robert or I'd find myself or one of my kids hurt, laying in an alley somewhere. Just the thought of it—"

I whistled softly. "That's when you bought the gun."

"I was scared. I didn't know what to do. I was afraid of him. I couldn't stop asking Robert to do the right thing, I just couldn't back off. Wouldn't let go. So I got the gun to protect myself if things went bad."

I wondered where this was leading, but I didn't want to stop the train of information now that it was coming. I waited for her to continue.

"Barry called me the day after Christmas. I was

home. I don't know how he got the number. I suppose Robert gave it to him."

"I heard Barry was out of town on a survival trip."

"Yeah, I guess he thought dealing with me was more important that doing his survival thing. He told me that we—he and I—needed to resolve this thing once and for all. He wanted to meet me. I wanted him on my turf. I thought the parking deck at Crystals would be perfect, knowing that it would be deserted two days after Christmas. I arranged to meet him on the third floor of the deck. I could situate myself early, and observe the parking lot from the roof of the parking deck. I could watch for his arrival so he wouldn't sneak up on me.

"Due to the construction staging, the ramps to the parking deck were not yet complete. I had to park on the surface lot. I assumed he'd park next to the deck like I did, but he appeared out of nowhere.

"At first he spoke normally, like a person. Then he started yelling at me, waving his hands in the air; I thought he was going to hurt me. I just wanted to slow him down, and show him that I had something going for me too.

"I pulled the gun out of my purse. That got his attention. I yelled at him, motioning with the gun. He took a couple of steps back, lost his balance and fell backward down the concrete stairwell.

"It took me by surprise. I couldn't believe that he stumbled back like that. I thought he'd be livid, falling onto the concrete. I ran down the stairs, dropping my gun along the way. I thought I might run into a raging bull. But, he just lay still. I propped him up against the elevator wall. He wasn't breathing. When I realized he was dead, I was in shock. I remember crawling into the car to think. What should I do? I was freezing cold. I started up the car and turned on the heater. I just stared into space for the longest time. I was numb. The entire scenario played and replayed in my head. I didn't know what to do. When I looked up—I don't know how much later—Edison was walking around the deck with a clipboard and a camera. All I could think then was not getting caught. Of course, Barry was still up there, but I just drove away. I don't know how I thought that would get me out of any trouble. You're always responsible for what you do. Momentary blindness, I guess. Well, I just drove a short distance, a couple of miles, I guess, and pulled over. I was too nervous to drive. I was shaking so badly. Between the cold and what I'd done. I completely lost it. I just cried for a good twenty minutes. Finally, I pulled myself together enough to go back. I wanted to see what I'd done. I went back to the jobsite, parked next to the company truck that I guess Edison had checked out, and walked slowly up the stairs. He was gone. Vanished. It was odd. Could I have been wrong about Barry being dead? Then I got this creepy feeling that he wasn't dead, and that he'd be coming after me for sure. I went back downstairs to see if his vehicle was still there. I didn't see it on either side of the parking deck, but I did see Andrew's car. I guess he was there to check the job. I certainly didn't want to run into him, feeling like I was, so I left. Looking over my shoulder all the way."

I felt like I'd been run over by a semi-truck. This explained why Gwen had tried to make something up about being somewhere Monday—picking up Smartain.

"Gwen," I was shaking. "Why didn't you tell me this before?"

Chapter 19
Rocking Revelations

"That I killed a man?" She sniffled, then blew her nose. "I wanted to. Really I did. I'd planned to tell you that morning, when I came over to take care of my car, but Robert made me promise to keep it to myself. He thought if this got out, it would hurt the firm. I just don't know what to do. My life is at stake now."

"You told Robert?" I said in disbelief.

"I was lost, Ken. The world began to close in on me. I was so angry with Barry, and then he fell backward, and I thought I'd killed him. Everything in my life— everything I knew to be true—was in question. Then he disappeared. I didn't know which way was up any more. I couldn't withstand these events alone. I was desperate for help. I turned to Robert for...for...I don't know...to bolster my courage, for help in knowing which way to turn, how to proceed. I shared with him what happened. Robert has an inner strength and sometimes has insights that transcend apparent circumstances."

"And he told you not to tell anyone?"

"Well, at that point, we didn't know for sure that Barry was dead. When I got back to the parking deck, Barry was gone. For the next two days, I didn't go anywhere without looking over my shoulder. I kept thinking he'd show up and hurt me or do something to the boys. The day after, on Tuesday, when we went down to Cleveland for the Six Forks Mall meeting, I dropped the boys off at my mother's so that they wouldn't be alone in that house."

I asked, "What do you mean, at that point you didn't know he was dead? His body was gone. What makes you think now that he is dead?"

Gwen's nose was running. She made some sniffling noises and continued. "On Thursday, I found a note on my desk. A blackmail note. It said that they'd seen me kill Barry." Gwen started sobbing out loud. "And they wanted two thousand dollars to keep quiet."

I sat back in my chair. Blackmail! "What did you do?"

"I went to Robert. He said to pay it."

The next question had to be asked, though I didn't want to know the answer. "Did you find out who the blackmailer was?"

She was silent.

"Gwen?"

"It was Isabelle."

I no longer knew what to believe. I hadn't thought Gwen capable of murder. She'd just confessed to killing—albeit accidently—Barry Hart. And she kept that a secret from the police, as well as from the person who was trying to help her—namely me.

This bombshell added an unwelcome factor to the mix. It gave Gwen a prime motive in Isabelle's murder. That motive in combination with the timing of the gun purchase would make her innocence difficult to prove.

At the same time, this revelation also provided a motive for someone else. Someone whose tie-tack I'd found on the murder victim's floor.

What was I to do now?

"Gwen, remember when you came over to visit me on Tuesday night, to tell me that you'd lent the truck to Isabelle for the weekend?"

"Uh-hun."

"Why did you stop by? What prompted you to come

over and tell me about that?"

"Ken, it was Robert's idea."

"Robert?"

She cleared her throat. "Ahem. Robert told me that you'd been poking around, asking questions. He was concerned that you had found out about...about what had happened to Barry. He called me when you left his dinner meeting early, and urged me to talk to you to see if you knew anything about that."

One final question had to be asked. The day before I had not thought it possible, but given the new information....

"Gwen?"

She was silent.

"Did you kill her?"

"No, Ken, I swear I didn't."

Without any real reason, deep within myself I believed her.

A glimmer of what had transpired in the last two weeks was beginning to appear in the fog, but there were still some missing pieces. Gwen's disclosure about what happened to Barry Hart shocked me personally, but fit into the puzzle. Other nuggets of information she revealed added to the picture.

The meeting to discuss the extras on the Federal Credit Union was positioned for the afternoon, so I headed into the office.

The moment I entered the building I knew something was off. Half the office was still. Desks were empty, computers turned off. People who were present were sitting at their desks, working quietly. Everyone was stone faced. There was no talking, no chit chat. What on earth had happened?

I sat down in my cubicle and phoned Edison at his desk.

"Hey," he answered.

"Edison, what's going on? What is the matter with everyone?"

"Didn't you see the papers?"

"Papers? No, I didn't see the newspapers."

"It was on the front page today. *Architect arrested for murder*. Photos of the project. Picture of Gwen. Speculation on what is happening at our firm."

"What's happening at our firm? What does that mean? How does the firm tie into it?"

"Ken, the accused murderer and the victim both worked here."

I put my hands on my face and sighed deeply. My nervous system couldn't take much more. So that's what Gwen meant when she said it would be a zoo at the courthouse. That's why she wanted me to stay away. Rita came around the corner, so I signed off with Edison.

"You heard?" she said, crimson mouth set in a hard line.

"Edison was just filling me in. How's Robert taking it?"

She rolled her raccoon eyes. "He's stomping around. It's bad. He's fending off calls from reporters. The newspapers want to know all about Gwen, asking about her work record, her mental stability, her projects. If that wasn't enough, Robert is having to answer calls from clients, tell them everything's okay, and their projects won't be affected. Some clients are quitting us. Crispy Greek is gone. The Fenkels have decided to go elsewhere. Robert's on the phone with Howard Birch right now trying to calm him down. Trying to convince him Olson House won't be tainted. Robert's in a rage. He's going to talk to you about taking full responsibility for some of the projects—notably Flamingo Shores and Olsen House."

"So that's what's happening. Why are we at half-staff?"

"Some of the guys went home, under the assumption they could get more work done there, than with clients calling and wanting explanations. Maybe you should go home too."

"No, Rita. I think I'll stick it out here for a while. I've got a lot to do. And, as you said, Robert may want to talk to me anyway."

"Well, keep your guard up," she said and walked off.

My thoughts went to the previous week when Robert and Gwen had taken me to lunch, and asked me to handle Six Forks Mall. Gwen had seemed so disturbed by the change in players. Was that Robert's idea, changing project managers in anticipation of Gwen's unavailability? Did he think Barry's death would trigger some charges that would result in Gwen's arrest? Or did he believe that, due to the potential hew and cry from clients as a result of her actions, it would be better to dissociate her from the project?

With meetings canceled, I made use of the time, forcing myself through the turmoil of feelings lurching and rocking inside me. Reluctantly, I worked on the proposals that had been put off, although with everything that was happening, there was a question of whether or not Hout Development group was interested in proceeding with any work by our firm. I went in circles finishing the code study for the UAW hall, as answers to fire ratings and handicap accessibility requirements repeatedly slipped through my awareness.

I reviewed some of the answers to RFI's that Edison had put together. I went through my in-box, and delayed some of my correspondence.

Just after lunch, we heard that the judge had denied bail, and Gwen was being transferred to the jurisdiction of the County Sheriff. She'd be moved to the Oakland County Jail to await the preliminary hearing set for ten days out.

I felt so bad for her. How would this polished, delicate woman withstand the unpleasant prison environment? Trauma shuddered through the nerves and sinew of my body, the tattered remains weak and disoriented. Hot, flu-like symptoms erupted in my chest with intent to consume me. I struggled to maintain my strength and my wits, steeling myself against the pressure. I wrestled to endure, to forge on. Focus. My charge was to concentrate on the mission, and discover what had really happened to Isabelle.

For Gwen.

Shortly before 5:00 p.m., I headed for the swamp looking for Edison. Derik Sun directed me to the server room.

The office file server was located in one of the rooms which had full-height walls. The office computer network was tied together into a file server—a central box that served as storage for the electronic files in the office. All computer-created documents on any project––correspondence files, drawing files, electronic photo files—were stored in this central retrieval system. Anyone from any computer could access all of the project files. Periodically, a back-up tape was made of all of the files in the server. This was done as a precaution in case a file was accidently deleted or became corrupt. Back-up tapes were done on a daily basis. Once a week, the back-up tapes were relocated off-site. If the place burned down, we would have a record of the work that was done.

Back-up tapes served another vital function: sometimes we revise construction drawings to implement a change. Later we decide—or receive direction from the owner—that we want to do it the original way.

Edison was searching through last week's back-up

tapes to find the floor plan on a project where the owner had changed his mind on the location of the toilet rooms.

"Edison, feel like Mexican tonight?" I asked.

"Yeah. That sounds good. I was supposed to go to a wallyball party but they canceled on me."

"How much longer do you have?" I said, pointing to the back-up machinery.

"This should be it." He placed a mini-cassette tape into the front of an electronic box about four inches wide and fourteen inches deep. The tape started whirring around, making a high-pitched grinding noise.

"It's amazing, isn't it?" Edison said. "Thousands and thousands of pieces of information on that little tape."

We stared in awe at the machine, running through its motions, searching through the information on the tape to find the precise location of the electronic file that held the floor plan in question.

"There must be hundreds of letters, memos, drawings, and photos in the files that are backed-up every night," I said.

It was a minor miracle.

And it made me think of another useful application. "Edison, not only is it extraordinary that we can easily retrieve this information, but look at all the file space these documents would take up if they were in hard copy format."

"Yeah, a real space saver." Edison looked up at me. "How did it go today?"

"Oh, you mean with the clients?"

Edison nodded.

"Okay, as far as the phone calls I received. Robert took the brunt of the fallout. I just had a couple of calls, including Jester Cromwell who didn't even mention it. He's intently focused on getting his store open. He complained again about the leaking through his ceiling tile. I don't understand—the contractor should be handling that."

"His ceiling is leaking?"

"Yeah, apparently the tiles in and around his office have been wet. I told him I'd check it out next time I was there."

Edison looked thoughtful as the tape machine found the file that he was after. With a couple of keystrokes, he copied the file into the project folder.

"Ok, Ken, I'm all set. Shall we go have some Mexican?"

I nodded.

"Don Carlos?" he asked.

"Sounds good to me. And after that, if you're up for it, we're going to do some serious detective work."

Edison looked at me with wonder. "What are we going to do?"

"You'll see. Let's eat first."

Before we left the office, I packed a couple of flashlights, a pen knife, some plastic zip-lock bags and rubber bands.

Two hours later we were sitting in my car outside Isabelle's house. I was a little wary of going into Isabelle's house again. Even though Edison had a key, Isabelle was dead and it seemed too much like breaking and entering for my tastes, but it was the only way.

We sat and surveyed the area for a few minutes, observing the houses, cars, and sidewalks. When we were satisfied that no one was watching, we stepped out of the car, down Isabelle's driveway and around to the back of her house.

The snow in the driveway had a tangle of footprints that weren't there a few days before. This worried me for two reasons: one, I thought it possible that Isabelle's relatives—Genevieve, Susie, and Darcy—would have come to the house to divide up her things. If they had, I hoped they hadn't taken what we were looking for. Two, perhaps one of them may have decided to stay here. I would not like to enter this house, only to find the barrel of a gun in my face. The lights in the house were off. It was only 8:00 p.m. so I doubted that anyone was inside with the lights off. The next fear was that someone would show up while we were inside.

"Edison," I said. "Let's be quick about this. And don't touch anything. I know you have a kind of permission to be here, but we don't want to find ourselves in the same position Gwen is in."

He nodded and we went inside. I turned on my flashlight and took off my gloves, stuffing them into my coat pocket. We went through the back of the house from the kitchen to the dining room. The dining table and cabinet were gone. We walked around to the front living room. We ran the flashlights around the room and found that everything was gone. Couch, chairs, end tables. All had evaporated. Isabelle's family had done a quick job of cleaning things out.

Strewn about all corners of the room were drinking straws, paper plates, paper cups. I took a look around the corner into the office. The computer and printer were gone, as were the computer desk and chair. The room was empty except for scraps of paper, rubber bands, and a couple of cheap paperback romances. I looked in the closet. Empty too. Considering what they had taken, I was surprised that the curtains remained in place.

I sat on the empty floor. Everything was gone. If there had been a tape here with something on it, it was not here now.

Edison gave me a questioning glance. "This narrows down the places where we can look."

"Yes, that's true, but is there anywhere else?"

Edison shrugged. "Taped underneath something, like

one of the drawers in the kitchen, taped onto the ceiling of the lower cabinets. Attached underneath the toe-kick at the front of the cabinets."

We checked them all and found nothing.

"Do you remember a movie where they stole some diamonds?" Edison said suddenly. "It was in the sixties. I don't remember exactly, but all through the movie they were looking for these diamonds, and all the time they were someplace simple. Remember where they hid them?"

"Ice cube tray!"

The appliances must have come with the rental because they were still there. We looked inside the freezer compartment. There were two ice cube trays, both full, and there was a rectangular white plastic bin, filled to the brim with ice cubes. I cautioned Edison not to touch anything in the freezer. I put on the winter gloves I'd taken off when we came in. There was a set of tongs to use for the cubes. I used those to remove the ice cubes, placing them on the floor of the freezer compartment one at a time. Buried underneath the stack of cubes was a little package wrapped in plastic. I could see through the layers of clear plastic. At its heart was a mini tape.

"Do you have a way to see what's on that?" I asked as I held up the package with the tongs.

"No sweat. The equipment we have at the office will work this tape."

I pulled a zip-lock bag out of my pocket and dropped the little package inside. Then, I used the tongs to place the ice cubes back into the bin in the freezer.

We took a last look around to make sure we hadn't disturbed anything, and exited via the back door. We went down the driveway, crunching across the snow. There was no one on the street.

We crossed to my car, got in and pulled away from

the curb. The car reacted slowly to the acceleration, bumping along the road. I stopped the car, got out and walked around the vehicle. The rear passenger side tire was flat.

Chapter 20
Saucy Snapshots

"What's the problem?" Edison asked from his open window.

"Come and look for yourself," I said softly.

Edison stepped out of the vehicle and studied the flat tire. He ran his hand across the surface. "Puncture wound," he whispered.

I looked around us, up and down the street. There was no movement. Houses were dark, street quiet. Whoever had done this was long gone...I could only hope.

After pulling the car toward the curb, we hastily changed the tire. To our advantage, there was only one tire flat, and we had a ready replacement. My finger froze as I worked to unscrew the nuts. Edison crouched down, watching silently as my toes turned to ice. He hauled the spare out of the trunk, and switched the tires when I had the nuts off. I was quiet, nervous from what we'd just done. I looked back down the street anxiously, terrified someone would come along and bash our heads in.

We completed the change and were on our way again shortly.

"Ken?" Edison broke the silence as he scooted back into the passenger seat. "What now?"

"We go back to the office, and find out what's on that tape. How long will that take?"

"There's usually a directory. That only tells you the names of the files. In order to see what's actually in them, you've got to copy the file from the tape to the hard drive, then open the file using the application it was created in."

"Let's open it through Isabelle's computer. Chances are, she was using the same software at work that she had at home."

We entered the I-696 on-ramp, which was cris-crossed with patches of ice. We slid onto the freeway, nearly side-swiping a white stretch limo before our tires caught on an area of dry pavement.

I released the breath I had not consciously held. "Edison, I'm worried about keeping that tape for any length of time. Is there a way we can make a copy, so that we can restore the original to its hiding place?"

Edison paused before he answered. "Well, it's not like having one of those double cassette boom boxes, where you can copy one tape from the other. But we could dump the entire contents of the tape onto the 'C' drive, pull the tape, and then back-up the files onto another tape."

"Let's do that. But remember, we don't want to leave any finger prints on anything—the plastic bags or the tape."

"I remember."

We arrived at the office. The parking lot was devoid of vehicles except for Edison's pick-up truck. Quiet prevailed at the office, with no left-over reminders of the hectic day. No one was working late. The quiet hum of the equipment and lighting ballasts gave the office an eerie quality.

We made our way to the model building area and cleared off a surface to work on, moving the Fenkel House model Edison had spent the weekend completing. Had someone told him that the job had been pulled from the office by an anxious client? If he was aware of it, he didn't let on. If he didn't know, I didn't want to tell him right now. I pulled the zip-lock bag out of my pocket. Edison grabbed a box from the supply shelf.

"Surgical gloves?"

"Yeah, the un-powdered kind. I use them for the fussy model building stuff—like working with polished metals, where I don't want to leave any finger prints."

He put on the gloves and opened the bag, extracting the freezer package. It had an outer wrapping of plastic food wrap, which he carefully removed. Inside, the tape was enclosed in two smaller bags, one inside the other, with the closures at opposite ends. Opening one package and then the next, Edison pulled out the inner tape with a flourish.

"Let's see what's on this puppy."

When we reached Isabelle's desk, we were surprised to find her computer gone. A clean square outlined in dust was the only reminder of the computer that used to be there. The scavengers had apparently come for the big equipment.

"Edison, I don't believe this. All of her stuff's been removed, taken by other people."

"Not so, Ken. Her plants are still here. Do you want a philodendron?"

I gave Edison a dirty look.

"Sorry. I don't know who would take that machine. All of the computers the staff uses are faster and have more memory than Isabelle's."

"Well, they're all numbered. I guess we can go around the office and look for it."

We tiptoed around the office, looking at computer numbers, searching for number 23. All was quiet. The low lighting and the dark windows augmented the haunting atmosphere. It compelled us to walk softly and speak quietly, as if in a library or an ICU. The shrill ringing of a telephone broke the silence. It rang four times and then stopped. It must have been picked up by the automatic nighttime phone system, through which incoming callers could dial an extension or pick an employee from the directory. We continued our search.

We found the computer at Bryce Tolken's desk. I wish I'd thought of it earlier. Bryce had been making noises for months about needing a second computer so he could do CADD on one, while he did word processing at the other. He felt that switching between the two applications on the same system was too time consuming.

Go figure.

Now it was time to load the information from the tape onto Isabelle's hard drive. Edison said that this could be done through the network without moving the tape back-up machine. We went to the server room, and he seated himself at the keyboard. Still wearing the rubber gloves, he placed the tape into the machine and entered some commands via the keyboard. The tape began to hum and whirr. The screen before him filled with a tree chart listing the files on the tape. There must have been thirty files, all with strange looking names like "Puppylove," "Chocolate Princess," and "Brisket."

Edison fired away at the keyboard, highlighting the entire tree chart and copying the files to Isabelle's computer. We had to wait for the copying to take place. A bar graph appeared on screen and told us that the operation was 12% complete. A minute later it was 15% complete. This was going to take a while.

Suddenly I became aware of talking outside the server room. I couldn't make out the words, but one person seemed to be asking another a question. My heart went into hyper drive. The voices came closer, and there was a certain inflection, joviality mixed with disrespect, indicative of thieves. These were definitely not people I worked with. I feared Edison and I would be discovered in our clandestine task. Perhaps we could slip under the desks to hide while the tape finished copying. The screen showed 57% complete. I prayed it would hurry up. Why does it take so long? The voices grew nearer. I pictured them walking through the office, identifying which pieces of equipment they were going to pile into their truck. The screen now showed 76%.

"What time is it?" Edison asked.

"Shhh!" I said, pointing to the doorway.

Edison looked at me quizzically.

"Excuse me," a female voice said from the doorway. I turned to face a woman in her twenties, dressed in jeans and a sweatshirt, a scarf tied over her hair. "Do you mind if we vacuum?"

"Sure," I said. "Go ahead."

I took a breath. It was not the first time the cleaning people had scared me to death as I worked late. Edison looked concerned about me.

"I'm ok," I said.

"What time is it?"

I looked at my watch. "I've got 9:57."

Edison jumped out of his chair. "Nuts. The office backup is set to start at 10:00 p.m. If I don't take this tape out and put the office tape in, everything will get screwed up. The office backup won't run and in the morning they'll know something went wrong." He looked at me for input.

I looked at the monitor. 85%. I looked at my watch again. 9:58. "Edison, is there an override? Can the backup be done later?"

"Sure, but I can't get to it while this is still in process. Shall I abandon this operation and take the tape out?"

The screen was stuck on 85%. Why wasn't it moving on?

"How can we tell what time the system thinks it is?"

I asked.

"Oh, of course," Edison hit himself in his forehead with his palm. He looked back at the screen. The time was noted in the bottom right hand corner of the monitor.

The monitor read nine fifty-eight, and the bar graph had jumped to 94%.

"Ok," I said. "Watch that time on the monitor. Tell me exactly when it flips over to nine-fifty nine, then I'll track thirty seconds on my watch. When I say go, you remove the tape and put in the office tape."

"Cool," Edison said. "Now."

I watched my timepiece, and watched the time tick off. At fifteen seconds, I glanced at the monitor. 99%. At twenty five seconds, I looked up. It still said 99%. "Hold on, Edison," I said. "Give it a couple more seconds." At forty seconds, the screen still read 99%. What was the hold up? At forty-five seconds, I said, "Go, make the switch."

I glanced up, the screen said "100%—save complete."

Edison switched the tape with two deft motions. As soon as the office tape was in place, the screen went blue, and the whirring began. The nightly back-up operation had begun.

Edison picked up the tape. We left the server room and made our way over to Bryce Tolken's desk. On the way, we passed by the swamp just as the cleaning woman was entering the model building area, dust rag in hand.

Remembering the plastic wrappers, I jumped ahead of her.

"Excuse me," I said, "I've got to get something." I went over to the table that still had the zip lock bags and plastic wrap laid out. I stopped in place before I picked them up, not wanting to touch them bare handed. The woman went around the perimeter of the area, dusting computers and table tops. She sprayed the work surfaces. She seemed oblivious to what I was doing. Was she trained to not pay any attention to the employees, or was she just focused on her task? I called Edison to come over.

"Might as well put that back," I said, motioning to the tape.

Edison placed it into one of the tiny zip-lock bags, closed the top, inserted that package upside down into the second bag, and closed that top as well. Then he wrapped the plastic food wrap around the whole thing, and stuck the package into the larger zip-lock bag that I had brought to the house with me. When it was complete, Edison handed me the package, and I placed it in my pocket. He took off his surgical gloves. The entire operation must have looked funny, but when I glanced over to the cleaning woman, she was still running along the table tops, cleaning away the dust.

We went over to Isabelle's computer, and started trying to pull up the files. Each of the folders with the peculiar names had two sets of files in them: one set word-based documents like correspondence or notes of some kind, the other a set of graphics such as photographs or images. Every file was password protected.

We tried a host of passwords, related to what we knew about Isabelle. Her birth date. Mother's name. Daughter's name. Her middle name. The name of the street she lived on. Nothing worked. After spending fifteen minutes on that endeavor, I said, "Edison, let's put these files back onto a tape, and then get this original one back to the house."

"Can't put it on tape until the office back-up is done."

"How long will that take?" I asked.

"Nightly back-up has been running four to five hours."

I took a deep breath. "It's almost 10:30 now."

Edison nodded.

"Well, we can take this tape back to Isabelle's house now. Then later, we can make a tape of that stuff." I pointed to the computer sitting on Bryce's reference table. "We just have to get those files off that computer before Bryce gets in tomorrow."

Edison's eyes grew wide. "I've got it. I can get the zip drive from the swamp, and load these files onto a zip disk. That'll work fine. I'll erase the files from Bryce's computer. Then I can use my computer to keep working at cracking the password. "

"Good thinking, Edison. I'm anxious to get this tape back in place. Can you do all that while I drive to the house and take care of this tape?"

"Sure."

I turned, checked my pocket for the tape, and began my exit. I'd just turned down the aisle to the back door, when I heard running behind me. I turned around to find Edison coming toward me. "You're going to need this," he said as he reached into his pocket and extracted Isabelle's key.

I took the key swallowing hard. We looked at each other, unspoken wishes of good luck passing between our eyes.

"I'll see you later, Edison." I said.

Isabelle's street was deserted. The night was dead quiet, sky bright and clear, lifeless tree limbs reaching up to grasp stars too far out of reach. Parking the car two doors down from the house, I shut the engine off. I sat observing houses, cars and the street to get a feel for who was up, who was watching, and who might be interested in my movements.

A low light in the house kitty-corner across from

Isabelle's flickered blue light across what must have been the living room wall. Television. Homes to each side of Isabelle's were dark. Five vehicles were parked on the street. Light shone through the two sedans, without revealing any heads in them. The three SUV's––who could tell? They all had dark windows. I waited ten minutes. No one got out or in. My toes started getting cold. Just as I reached over to open my door, a car entered the street from the other end. I decided to let the car pass before I exited. It proceeded slowly down the street and I noticed the silhouette of larger mirrors on either side of its body. A police cruiser. I bent down, deciding this was a good time to clean the floor beneath my passenger seat. Under the seat next to me, I removed two squashed Wendy's drink cups, a straw wrapper, and one of those triangular plastic sandwich containers that you get at the convenience store when you buy an egg salad sandwich cut diagonally.

Luckily, there was a balled up Burger King bag under there too. I stuffed the trash into the bag. The police car slowly made its way past me, crunching through the snow. Still in my leaned-over position, I checked the drink holder in the console, removing several used napkins and tissues, and placed those in the bag as well. No other trash caught my eye, so I raised myself back up in my seat. I looked into the rear view mirror. The street was empty. I scanned the houses around me. The TV was still going in the house two up from my right. I didn't see anyone in the window. The watcher must have been glued to his seat.

An additional ten minutes passed. My feet had turned to icicles meanwhile. When nothing noteworthy had transpired, I left the car and walked across the street to the house. I entered through the rear door as before. Once I reached the refrigerator, I replaced the tape package underneath the ice cubes where we had found it originally.

I checked to make sure everything was left as I had found it and then exited via the rear door. Leaving more footprints in the snow along the driveway made me nervous, but there was nothing to be done about it. Continuing down the drive, I kept an eye out for movement along the street. Everything was quiet as before. The TV was still casting eerie blue flashes of light on the wall in the house across the street. I reached the sidewalk, about to cross the street, when a car turned onto the street at the end of the block. I waited briefly, deciding whether or not to cross before he passed. My feet felt the vibrations in the sidewalk from the bass in the car. Teenagers. I bent down to tie my shoe, letting the car cross in front of me. Then I sprinted across the street, got in my car and hit the road.

I didn't breathe until I was back on Twelve Mile. The shops along the street—including Ray's Coney—were closed, dark buildings with unadorned windows that revealed black interiors. The ride was quiet. Preferring the silence to the radio, I focused on collecting my thoughts and bringing down my heartbeat. The heater came on relatively quickly, though the car must have been parked at Isabelle's for a half hour. The phone rang and I almost jumped out of my skin.

Is it possible to get aerobic exercise by merely making your heart race, without actually doing physical exercise? I felt like I was getting a real workout.

It was Edison. "I got it, Ken. I figured it out."

"The password?"

"Yes. It's jockeys."

"What? Jockeys?"

"Ken, I remembered Isabelle telling me that her dad used to play the horses. I was looking through those file names, they were all so weird. The one that hit me was

'Chocolate Princess.' Isy had told me when she was a kid her dad used to take her to Hazel Park Raceway. He had a real gambling addiction. I guess that's why her mom drank so much. Anyway, every time she went down there, she begged for a chocolate bar. Well, the owner of one of the horses used to call her the Chocolate Princess. Later, he named a horse for her. I went through the list, and realized that I'd heard of some of these horses. Then, I tried to think of a password related to the fact that these were horses. I used the breed of horse, the name of the owner's farm. Finally, I tried the name of the jockey. Bingo. For each horse, the password is the name of the jockey."

Amazing. "Good work, Edison. You know the names of all those jockeys? I'm impressed."

"No, I don't. I just tried Willy Brane for Chocolate Princess. It worked. Then I had to go on to the Net to find the others. But listen, Ken, you're not going to believe what this is. There's a lot of dirt here."

"Dirt? What kind of dirt?"

"The kind you use for blackmail."

"Huh? Are you sure?"

"Yes. Pictures, letters, notes. Isabelle must have had a couple dozen people on the hook."

I whistled low. That's where she got all that money she was sending down to her sister. Big dreams.

"Edison. I bet somebody on that list killed her." Silence at the other end. "Edison?"

"Yeah, I'm here. I'm just looking through the names. Guess who's on this list?"

"Tell me."

"Robert Westin."

Chapter 21
Diary of the Dead

According to the tape, Isabelle was blackmailing Gwen, a fact which Gwen had already revealed to me. Isabelle had kept a sort of diary. A periodic recording of the events in her life, it was punctuated by her discovery of "useful information"—her words—and a recounting of the devious ways she turned the information into cash. Of course, the tale was sordid and without any kind of moral justification, but I found it truly fascinating. I was mesmerized by the way Isabelle would learn a certain little fact, ferret out the details, and turn it into profit. This diary, written like a kind of autobiography—I don't know if Isy planned on selling the manuscript one day or if she wrote it to amuse herself—would make a hit movie.

She discussed her trip to Crystals with her boyfriend that fateful Monday:

Jay's men had constructed some special brickwork inside, on the second floor, that he wanted to show me. So we went inside, staying near the center of the building, where a skylight over a large atrium lit up the structure like the rack of lights over third base at Comerica Park. While Jay went to use the bathroom, I wandered over to the parking deck entrance, where the light streamed in. When I looked out, I saw Gwen holding a gun, pointing it at a man. They were speaking, but I couldn't make out the words. She shook the gun at him. Next, I saw the man stumbling backwards, down a hole in the parking deck floor. I didn't know what had happened. It looked like Gwen had shot the man, but I didn't hear anything. He sure stumbled backward though. There wasn't any need for Jay to know about it, so I faked being ill and sent him for some aspirin. Jay was gone for 45 minutes. I watched as Gwen ran down the stairs and examined the man. He didn't move. I didn't know if he was dead or what. She then retreated to her car.

What surprised me was when Edison showed up a little while later and removed the man from the deck. He must have been dead, because Edison stuffed him in the back of the company pick-up truck. I got a picture of that one. I suppose that he had copped the body for some mortuary project or something. It really got interesting a few minutes later, when Robert and Andrew showed up! When Jay returned with the aspirin, I made him take me home. I then scooted over to the office in time to see Edison pull up with Robert. I wondered if the man was still in the truck, but he must have been. I was itching to take a look, but not in broad daylight, in the office parking lot. I watched to see if Edison would come back after it, and was surprised to see Wally bounce out and take the truck away. What an interesting turn! I followed him for a while, then he seemed to have some trouble with the truck and pulled into a repair shop.

I went to the shop Wednesday to scope things out, and then went back later that night with a couple of guys I know. A few bucks and they'll do anything. I had them help me break in. We checked out the truck, and— sure enough—the guy was still lying in there. Stiff as a board. The guys helped me move the body out, and stick it in the junkyard behind the shop. I took some photos for my collection. Having control of the location of the body would be much more valuable than merely knowing about it.

Edison is so stupid. What was he thinking moving that body? What a nut. And unsteady at that. I learned that when we went out a few times. I thought it wiser not to blackmail him, as there's no telling what he would do if I did.

I was sorry that Edison read what Isabelle wrote about him. It wasn't very kind. Isabelle was a very selfish person. Using everything she'd learned about people to her advantage, and then criticizing them as unstable.

I listed the blackmail victims on a little piece of notepaper, and stuck it in my wallet, between my driver's license and Red Cross card.

The information on Robert was startling. There were names, dates and places where Robert had rendezvoused with the wives of some of our clients. The photographs, while not as compromising as they could have been—no one was naked—indicated close relationships that I'm sure the husbands would have been shocked to see. Of course, it would have cost the firm in lost clients. I had no idea Robert was that kind of womanizer. I'm sure Gwen didn't know either.

I sat back, my head reeling. My watch said 2:15.

"Edison, let's go home. It's been a long day."

"What a day it was."

"Oh, Edison, did you put the stuff on tape?"

He tapped a zip tape. "It's all right here."

"Maybe you should delete the files from the computer. Isabelle was killed for what's on that tape. Let's just have one copy."

Edison handed me the zip tape. "You keep it then. I'll erase what's on the machine."

I put the tape in my pocket. I couldn't help noting that Edison had done a major part of the work that day.

We walked out together and climbed into our

separate cars. When I arrived at home, I quietly unlocked the back door, holding my breath until I'd examined all of the closets, nooks and crannies for hidden visitors. Everything seemed to be in order. I extracted the detective pack from my briefcase. Lowering the shade on the bathroom window, I removed the medicine cabinet from the wall, and placed the zip-tape in the wall cavity along with the detective pack.

The sewer pipe was fresh, shiny steel. Elliptical in cross section, it stood about eight feet high and was twelve feet wide. The corrugations made it difficult to walk on. Even with boots, gaining the proper footing was difficult. My flashlight cast a powerful, strong yellow beam that pierced the darkness, bouncing off the reflective metal. The light showed that the pipe went on for a long, long distance. As I walked on, I began to notice the vibrations. The floor of the pipe carried a small tremor, a deep rumbling announcing a faraway event. Tiny oscillations tickled my feet through the thick soled boots. As I walked on, my flashlight began to glow dimmer. The tremors grew larger in intensity, until the walls as well as the floor of the pipe shook. I became aware of muddy water leaching into the bottom of the pipe. It undulated with the vibrations. The dark water pushed up over my feet. My flashlight grew dim as the rumbling grew louder. I began running, splashing my way forward. The rumbling became a roar. It dawned on me that the vibrations and the deafening clamor were due to the sewer pipe being put into service. Probably millions of gallons of sewage pushed down the pipe toward me. I ran flat out, holding my dimming flashlight before me, stumbling across the uneven flooring. I came to a dead end, blocked by a solid barrier of clammy earth. I turned around as a wall of roaring sewage bore down on me.

I awoke drenched in sweat, head throbbing and feet icy. I lay back on my pillow, cold and wet with perspiration.

What had I done to deserve this? I lay in bed for several minutes before my breath calmed. My mind, however, was another matter.

After the showering and shaving rites, I went to the kitchen. The sulfur smell I noticed first. The heavy odor made me want to gag. My eyes fell upon the source, scattered on the kitchen table. Perhaps a hundred used wooden matches lay on the white plastic laminate surface, permanently marred with countless burn marks. Cupboards and drawers were in disarray. My briefcase was intact, as was the refrigerator. The battery from the smoke detector in the adjacent hallway lay on the floor. The rear door was unlocked. Had I forgotten to lock it?

Uneasy, I ran to the bathroom. The zip-tape and detective pack were intact behind the medicine cabinet.

Nervous and fatigued, I paused to consider the meaning of this event. During my poking around, I had touched a nerve. The killer had been here, searching. What did I have that would be of interest to him?

There was nothing to make breakfast out of, and I couldn't force myself to stay in that room. A drive-thru breakfast was fast and easy, but grease for breakfast was not the answer, with my gut tied in knots.

Wilson's Family Dining offered up some hearty oatmeal, which came with brown sugar, milk, and toast. My order came to the table quickly and they kept my coffee cup filled. Seventeen minutes and four dollars and sixty-seven cents later—including tip—I was on my way.

Robert was in his office. I paced directly to the door, walked in and closed it behind me. I sat in his guest chair and said, "Robert, we have to talk."

His expression, which could be so enchanting with clients, was sour, as it was so much of the time in the office. I don't know what special quality Gwen ever saw in him. But that was beside the point here. We had to have it out once and for all.

"Robert, we've had our differences, but something has come up, and I must have answers." He opened his mouth to speak. I held up my hand in protest. "No, we've got to have a discussion right now."

"But listen here, Ken, I've got a meeting in—"

"No." I raised my voice. I was tired and frustrated. "No, listen. Your meeting will have to wait. I've got to talk to you about Isabelle."

"Not this tie-tack business again." He picked up the phone.

"The last time we talked, I didn't know she was blackmailing you." Robert set the phone down and looked at me. "Or that she was blackmailing Gwen." Comprehension spread across his face. I'd gotten his attention. I sat back in my chair, and took a breath. "Robert, here are the facts as I know them. Isabelle saw Gwen accidently kill Barry Hart. She decided to use this information to her advantage, and blackmailed Gwen for a couple thousand dollars. Gwen came to you and you told her to keep quiet."

Robert kept his eyes trained on me.

I continued. "What Gwen didn't know is that Isabelle was blackmailing you too. It appears that Isabelle had a knack for getting her hands on information that people didn't want known. Isabelle found out that you had been seeing the wives of some of our clients. She threatened to go to Andrew, as well as the clients themselves. You were desperate to keep that quiet."

The rumbling inside erupted with a bang. "That little

bitch! That information would have ruined me. It would have ruined the firm. Who did she think she was? Coming in here. I gave her a chance. She had a respectable job, and that's how she repaid me?"

"Is that why you killed her?"

He moved forward in his chair and glowered at me. "Kill her? No, you've got that part wrong. I didn't kill her. Certainly the notion intrigued me, and I can't say I'm sorry she's not around to make my life a living hell, but I didn't kill her. I couldn't...do that."

"But you did go to see her. The tie-tack I found on her carpet."

"Yes, I went to see her. To persuade her to drop her little game. And I wanted to see exactly what information she had on Gwen. I had to find out how damaging that would be."

"I can't help thinking that the firm is better off, without that information coming out," I said.

"Of course it is. It was a terrible thing that happened. Barry's accidental death, and Gwen's hand in it. But I don't solve things by killing people. Am I sorry she's dead? No. But I didn't kill her."

I couldn't think of anything else to say. I stood up and reached for the door. "Oh, Robert, one more question. Did you happen to erase the photos Edison took at the jobsite that day? The day Gwen...the day of the accident?"

"Yes, I took care of them. I thought there might be something on there to implicate Gwen and the firm. I had to destroy them."

I walked out of Robert's office with an uneasy sense of satisfaction. My gut told me he was, finally, telling the truth. I was relieved that the owner of the firm I worked at was not a killer.

Now what?

Reaching into my back pocket, I pulled out my

wallet to retrieve the list of names I'd copied down the night before. I pushed my finger behind my driver's license to retrieve the paper. Nothing. I pulled the license out. Maybe I put it behind the Red Cross card. Not there either. I took the wallet apart, looking through every card and paper. The list was gone. I was flabbergasted. Was it taken last night? *They went into my wallet?*

I mentally reviewed the list of names as I remembered them. Of the people who were familiar to me, one of them struck me as odd. I called Edison, and asked him to come over to my cube.

"You look like death warmed up," he said.

"Thanks, I feel like it, too. Tell me something." I quickly decided not to tell him about the latest developments involving someone breaking into my house. "Do you have any idea how to go about doing a financial check on someone?" As much as Edison got around, I figured that if he didn't know, someone in his network of people would.

"Aubrey Kensington, at Great Lakes Financial. I think they're in Rochester Hills."

"She could find out discreetly?"

"She'll do it without anyone finding out. Not even her boss."

"Ask her to do a check on Jester Cromwell."

Edison's eyes grew wide. "Jester the Truffle King?"

"One and the same."

Question marks sprouted all over Edison's face.

"Let's just say I'm playing a hunch. Do you think you can get it today?"

"Sure, if she's in. Sometimes she leaves town for some meeting or another. I'll see what I can do."

After lunch, I was checking my voicemail messages, when Edison came bouncing into my cube and lowered himself into my guest chair. He ran his finger around the rim of my candy dish. There were two pieces remaining: a red and white peppermint and a Mary Jane. He didn't look pleased. Clutched in his other hand was a note with numerous scribbles on it.

I hung up the phone and pulled open my snack drawer. The candy drawer was as empty as my refrigerator. As soon as this trauma was over, I'd go shopping. "I'm sorry, Edison, I'm fresh out of candy."

His puppy dog face resembled a Basset hound.

"Give me some information, and I swear I'll fill up the dish with your favorite kind of candy."

"Rolos?"

"Anything you want."

"Ok." He looked down at the scribbled notes in front of him. "Ok, here's the story. Jester Cromwell has no money. He mortgaged his house to put up the money for his chocolate shop. No assets. No stocks. No property other than his house."

"What about his other store? Didn't he have a fishing outlet of some kind?"

"Fish World. Went under six months ago. Sold to pay off the debts."

"So he had no money and no cash flow. No wonder his clothes are ancient. That's all he's got left."

"Ken, what does this mean?" Edison was confused.

"It means he had motive, Edison. Somehow—I don't even know how—he passed the financial review at The Circle Group. They're generally very good about screening tenants for solid financial backgrounds. A shop owner's financial resources have to be strong enough to undergo a few ups and downs. They don't want stores folding all of the time."

"Didn't you tell me his niece worked for the mall?"

"Bingo, Edison. Yes, Mary works for the mall as their tenant coordinator. She could have fixed it." I put the tips of my fingers together and closed my eyes.

"Here's what we have. Mary fixes it so that her uncle can get in. Now Jester's got a lot at stake: he can't let the store go under, because it's his only means of financial support. He also can't let it fold because it would come to light how his niece helped him. And the information that Isabelle held over him certainly would have had people boycotting the store. He would have been ruined and so would Mary."

"If he's in that desperate financial shape, how would he even have paid the blackmail?"

"He couldn't," I said. "He didn't have the money to pay, and he couldn't let the information come out. He was between a rock and a hard place."

"Sounds like motive."

"Yes, Edison, it's a prime motive. Thanks for your help on this."

"What are you going to do?"

"I'm going to give that some thought. I don't know exactly how to approach him, but I need to talk to Jester." I thought about his face, jowls hanging. "This is big."

"Tomorrow? We could go down in the morning." He turned his hopeful eyes toward me.

"No, Edison. I can't take you with me. You have helped me so much getting to this point. You had the brainstorm of looking in the ice cubes for the tape, and you're the one who broke the password. Gwen's going to be very grateful."

Edison smiled broadly, like a happy dog waiting for a treat from his owner.

"But as for talking to Jester, it's too dangerous. I can't let you go with me."

His smile faded. "But I can help. You need some back up. We could do it together." His big eyes pleaded.

"No, I'm sorry Edison. I don't know how he's going

to react. If you got hurt...I couldn't...." I took a breath. "Edison, everyone's got their own special talents. You have gotten us this far.... I'll let you know how it comes out."

Edison's chubby face affected his pitiful look. "Well, fine. I have some work to do around here anyway. Let me know if you change your mind," he said. "Oh, by the way, I told Aubrey you'd find her financial analysis of Jester Cromwell very interesting, and that you'd show your appreciation by taking her to lunch."

I agreed and Edison left my office. I picked up the phone and called Wally.

"Wally, did you say you had a gun collection?" I said. "How'd you like to help Gwen out? I've got an idea and I need your help."

Chapter 22
The Voice of Vengeance

The grey sky showed no signs of life. Clouds blended one into the next—a continuous dull mass, spread across the sky from horizon to horizon, encompassing life and stillness in its path. The grey expanded to one vast nothingness.

Lawns were covered in drab white snow. In the diffused light, the edges of leafless trees and grey road were subdued and desolate. Squarish pellets of rock salt from the previous day's snow treatment dappled the road. The car before me kicked up a steady stream of fine mist, requiring periodic activation of the wipers. The dirty salt water left dull streaks on the glass. Winter in Detroit. A grey scene under a grey sky observed through a grey windshield.

The oppressive atmosphere did nothing to assuage the overwhelming feeling of dread that had settled in my throat. The previous evening had gone uneventfully—no more burnt offerings appearing out of the darkness. But I wasn't quite settled on how to approach today's showdown. Facing killers is not what I do. Give me a curtainwall to detail. Let me evaluate roofing alternatives. That's what I was trained for. I had no clear understanding of how to proceed. Somehow, I would confront Jester with the blackmail material. How would he react?

Was I stupid?

Within forty-five seconds, give or take, Wally could get to me once the pager was activated. In that amount of time, a bullet could have made its way from one side of my body to the other.

Turning the blackmail tape over to the police, along with my suspicions about Jester, *had* crossed my mind. After twice incorrectly confronting Robert, however, I lacked confidence that my deductions were accurate now. And there was the matter of the tape. When I handed that evidence over, I would have to admit sneaking around, entering the dead woman's house, and searching through her things. Of course, I'd have to 'fess up eventually, but all things considered I thought I would be in a better position if the murderer could be pointed out at the same time.

I parked between the mall addition and the three-story concrete parking deck. This is where it had all begun. I found some strange sense of "rightness" in the possibility that it would end here.

Wally pulled his car in next to mine. We huddled next to the building in the cold wind, exchanging our final thoughts. We tested the equipment. I pushed the redial button on my phone, and his pager rang. It was as right as it was going to be.

The metal service door was unlocked. Wally waited just outside, and I entered the dimly lit space.

The clammy air in the service corridor made my throat stick. My skin felt it, too, like a soiled blanket spread over me. I moved slowly along the concrete floor, wet with today's footsteps. Reaching the back door to Jester's shop, I stopped. Deliberately, I checked for the phone in my pocket. *Nerves or OCD?* At the first sign of trouble, I'd hit the redial button, activating Wally's pager. He would come charging in, carrying his preferred Smith & Wesson.

I hesitated at the door. I took a deep breath.

The door flew open. I sidestepped quickly and felt the breeze as the door nearly caught my face. My heartbeat vaulted to a sprint.

Ted Bylund stood there, one hand in the pocket of his blue jeans. His timid brown eyes looked up and his torso jerked in surprise when he got a glimpse of me. "Sorry, Ken; I didn't know you were there."

I breathed deeply, then shrugged in acknowledgment.

"Were we supposed to meet today?" He pulled up the sleeve on his overstuffed parka and looked at his watch. "I've got to run uptown to get some hardware. I'll be back in a couple of hours." His dirty blonde bangs clung to his forehead like they were pasted there.

I just want to get on with it, I thought. Out loud, I said, "No, Ted, I just have some business with Jester."

He shuffled by me, his work boots clunking on the concrete in the empty hall. "Well, he's in there."

Poised outside the truffle shop's back door, I waited until Ted reached the end of the hallway and exited. Cold January air rolled in as the outside door cycled through the closing action. I prayed Wally would give Ted a reasonable reason for standing out in the cold by the back door.

As I turned to enter the chocolate shop, the door moved and my head twitched back. Missed me again! I looked up to find Mary standing before me. Her eyes registered recognition, then repulsion. Wordlessly, she flung her ebony hair back, and I sidestepped as she moved to pass. Her cold stare sent shivers through me. She marched down the corridor on 4-inch heels, toward the mall construction.

Shrugging myself to action, I turned and entered the storage room, checking to leave the door unlocked. The handicap accessible toilet room was directly opposite. To the left, electrical panels. Wire shelves to my right held paper goods. Beyond the shelving was a small work area, containing refrigerators and a white solid-surfacing countertop for preparing the chocolates.

As I walked toward the office, sandwiched between the toilet room and the sales area, I turned to note that the remainder of the floor-to-ceiling glass had been installed. Through the glass I observed Mary hustling across the mall area to the jewelry store on the other side. Unpleasant feelings stirred as I recalled her kiss-off letter. I was glad she hadn't spoken to me just now. Unfortunately, she still worked for the mall and we'd cross paths again. She stopped to hand an envelope to the construction worker at the jewelry store.

The door to the office was ajar and the work light was on. I felt once again for the phone in my right-hand pocket, then stepped forward. Jester was sitting at the desk, facing the door. Twangy strains of country music emerged from a small black radio behind him. Jester was writing in what must have been the store's ledger. The folds of his eyelids came down over the tops of his light brown eyes. His heavy cheeks were red with broken blood vessels. He wore a red and yellow plaid sport coat over a brown shirt with no tie.

The sparsely decorated office held only his desk and two chairs: the one he was sitting on, and a metal folding chair against the wall next to the door. A shelf secured to the wall behind him contained three picture frames. Two displayed famous quotes, each claiming to hold the key to success. The third contained the photo of Jester with Mary that I'd seen earlier. I considered what I was about to say to this man, who was the uncle of my most recent ex-girlfriend. As he lifted his eyes to me, I felt the tension in my gut tighten. I reached into my pocket and clutched the envelope containing the blackmail materials. His eyes held fatigue—no, not exactly, desperation perhaps? The whites of his eyes were bloodshot and filmy. I hesitated. What was I about to do?

Don't get fooled, I told myself. *This man killed Isabelle*. I remembered her silky blonde hair falling away from her lifeless face, smooth and creamy as porcelain and jolted to attention.

I pulled the envelope from my coat's inside pocket with my left hand, keeping my right finger on the redial button in my pocket. I laid the envelope on the desk. Did I hear a sound, over the static-filled music from the radio? I stopped, listening. *Get on with it*, I commanded myself. Jester glanced at the flat manila wrapper, then at me. "What's this?" he said slowly with bewildered interest. He picked up the packet and opened the flap, peeking inside.

"There are some photographs of you taken in a hotel, in Canada, I think. The young lady's name is Elaine. She runs an operation called Elaine's Sweet Escorts."

Jester shuffled through the photographs. Shots of Jester frolicking with a large breasted blonde in a bath of chocolate, the confection dripping from various parts of their anatomies. "Where did you get these?" His face grew pale.

My finger was ready for any sign of aggression.

"They were hidden on a tape at Isabelle's house. From her notes, it appears that this is material she was blackmailing you over. Apparently the photos were taken a couple of years ago. With the Jester Truffle shop opening soon, you couldn't afford to have this information come out." Jester's eyes grew hollow, as if he was looking inward. "And, I'm guessing, you didn't have the money to pay her, either. So what were your options, Jester? Let the information come out? Or maybe, silence the voice that could make your life miserable?"

The sinking expression on his face spoke volumes. Beaten, defeated, he sank into the chair, put his hands to his face and began to weep. Guilt rushed over me in waves. What had I done? The photos revealed his indiscretion, and their presence on the desk in front of us was proof that what should have been a private matter was now known by another. Namely me.

I stood there in a stupid state, as Jester continued to sob into his hands, shoulders shaking. I felt like crawling under the carpet. I hadn't known how to approach a killer. Now I didn't know what to say to a broken man, whose mistakes of the past I had just rubbed in his face. Isabelle's notes indicated that she had purchased these pictures from the owner of the establishment, who regularly took photos of the activities in her rooms.

Bittersweet words sung by a haunting female voice sputtered from the radio, providing a backdrop to the soft sobs of a man brought to his knees by an overzealous architect.

My left hand reached to pick up the envelope. Jester extended his hand, grasping my wrist. Surprised by the sudden action, my right finger jerked, pushing the button that would bring Wally in.

Jester looked up at me.

"Why?" his tired eyes looked at me questioningly. "What did I do? What does this mean to you?"

I hesitated. How could I explain? "Jester, I found these things in Isabelle's house. It was obvious that this is the kind of thing that no one wants to come out. I thought maybe you'd explain how she got to you. What she wanted from you. What she expected in return for keeping this quiet."

His eyes fired up. "Why, this is none of your business, Ken. What makes you think that I'd be at all interested in discussing this with you? You've got some gall coming in here and bringing this up. And you with my niece!"

I felt about ten inches tall. All of Jester's grief stirred

up for no good reason. I stood motionless, waiting for some explanation to come to me.

I heard a crash behind me, followed by a loud groan and metal clattering. Spinning on my heels, I saw Wally spread out on the floor in the prep area, next to overturned wire racks, his face bloody. Mary stood over him, sent a two-foot pipe wrench clanging to the floor, then bent to pick up Wally's silver pistol, and trained it on him.

"Get to your feet, Cowboy," she commanded.

"What the...." Wally scrambled to his knees, touching his forehead, his fingers coming away bloody. "Ow, man, that hurts." He looked up at Mary. "You could kill a man like that."

"Shut up," she screeched, tilting the gun up and down, indicating to Wally that he should finish getting up.

Instinctively, I started out of the office toward her.

"Stay where you are!" she shouted at me, alternating the gun between Wally and me. She moved to a shelf nearby and picked up a roll of duct tape from among some construction supplies.

Jester gasped. "Mary, what are you doing? Is that a gun? I don't.... What's this about? First Ken drops these photos on my desk, now you come in here knocking people in the head and waving a gun around." He sat back in his chair, eyes unfocused.

"Uncle, I'm sorry to involve you in this." She looked at him easily. To Wally, she said, "Put your arms out." When he didn't comply, she raised the gun to his head. He put his arms out in front of him. "Now, put your wrists together."

Seeing that she was going to be occupied taping up his hands, I inched toward her.

She angled in my direction. "Stop where you are! Get back in the office. Your turn will come." I stopped.

Using her teeth and her left hand, she taped Wally's wrists, while maintaining her grip on the gun. Next she prodded Wally into the office.

"Sit down," she commanded. Wally sat down on the metal folding chair next to the door of Jester's office. I stationed myself on the opposite side of the doorway.

Mary pointed the gleaming gun in my direction. "Your friend here was just sliding in the back door. Lucky I saw him before he hurt somebody."

Turning to Jester, she said, "I was hoping to keep you out of all this, Uncle Jester. We've got a little business to take of, Ken and I. You should have never been involved. You just take care of your little chocolate shop. Everything's going to be all right." Her thick black hair, pulled back in a severe sweep held in place with a tortoise shell barrette, was slightly undone. Her dark eyes flashed with unbridled rage.

Wally spoke up. "It ain't gonna be all right. The bitch just whacked me in the head." His forehead sported a jagged gash over his left eye. "Probably left a trail of blood all over the storeroom. Cannoli, you sure can pick 'em!"

"Shut up Wally!" Mary motioned with her gun. "Or I'll hit you again."

Jester was aghast. He stood up behind his desk. "I want to know what this is all about. Someone tell me right now."

Mary looked compassionately at her uncle. "Uncle, I never wanted anything to happen to you. You were so lonely after Aunt Anna passed, I thought this chocolate shop would be just the thing to keep you busy. We had a good time planning this, didn't we? All those wonderful truffles and chocolate confections. Remember when we traveled all over town, trying the chocolates from those other shops? Every time we spent an afternoon together, I felt closer to you. I love you. I wouldn't want anything to happen to you.

"It was just by luck, I happened to be here the day Isabelle left that package of trash for you. I knew it was bad news. I could feel the vibrations from the bundle. When I opened it, the room darkened right before me. She was a wicked, wicked woman, calling out from the darkness itself. How did she think she was going to harm this sweet man?" She motioned toward her uncle. Her voice stern, she said, "Ken, why couldn't you have left it all alone? There wasn't any reason for you to go poking around Isabelle's place. What was the point in that?"

"You?" I said, dazed. "You were there that...night?"

"The first couple of times I stopped by the house to check things out, the police were there, or had it under surveillance." She was flippant. "Later, the place turned into *Grand Central Station*—first you and Edison, then Isabelle's relatives."

The pieces were finally falling into place. "You were concerned that someone would find Isabelle's records and the records of your uncle's...indiscretions," I said. "You discovered us there and slashed my tire."

"You came out too fast." Her face turned hard. "I would have flattened them all," she said through her teeth. She turned to her uncle. "See, I told you he was smart."

"So you broke into my house...and burnt my table," I accused.

"I had to find that material. Something told me you'd discovered it first. The table was a small price to pay for making me go out of my way to search your house, too." She ran her hand along her hair.

"What made you think to look in my wallet?" I asked, curious.

"Personal interest. I wanted to see if you had a picture of *her*." Mary pouted.

"Who?" I puzzled. "You thought—Gwen?"

"Don't say her name!" Mary screeched.

I shut my mouth.

Mary continued. "Picking through your cards and things, I found something much more interesting. A list of names. *What could that be about? I pondered.*" Her face suddenly grew cold. "Oh, why did you have to meddle? Why did you have to go after Isabelle's filthy notes? Once she was gone," she glanced at the envelope on the desk, "all this trash had no one to bring it to the light of day."

"You killed her?" It was more of an accusation than a question. I was unsettled. I had not seen this side of Mary.

"She had to be put down. She could not have been allowed to sully Uncle Jester's reputation. She was the devil's hand. Such darkness. Didn't you feel it? You worked side-by-side with her."

"Mary," Wally piped up, "he didn't see the devil in you either, bitch."

Mary turned a pair of cold eyes to Wally and said, "I told you to shut up!"

"Gwen's gun," I said. "You killed Isabelle with Gwen's gun?"

Mary smiled, a glow of satisfaction in her eyes. "Yes. What luck! I was out on a cigarette break, checking out the new construction, and I stumbled across the pistol a couple of weeks ago. I knew it would come in handy, but I had no idea how wonderfully it would work out. For some reason, Isabelle recognized it when I pulled it out. You should have seen the puzzlement on her face. *Gwen's gun*, she said. *You've got Gwen's gun?* Fate shone upon me that day. To get rid of Isabelle and Gwen at the same time? How fortunate! I dumped the pistol where I knew the police would eventually find it."

Wally began coughing and taking deep wheezing breaths between robust, deep coughs that moved his entire body. I thought he was choking. He rocked back and forth in his chair. As he proceeded with his thrashing around, I became aware of a rasping sound coming from the ceiling above us. A metallic, hollow straining sound. A high pitched creak. Moving my eyes upward, I snuck a look at the ceiling. I noticed the water stains in the 2-by-4 perforated ceiling tile. The metal ceiling grid was moving ever so slightly. What was going on?

"You keep still!" Mary shouted.

She grabbed Wally's arm, digging her nails through the green down-filled coat. He probably felt nothing, but Mary's energy was strong. Wally sat back, then stuck his legs out, sliding down the chair like some high school punk. Mary stood back and leveled the gun at him.

In my peripheral vision, I saw one of the sections of ceiling grid begin to bow. With a sudden implosion, the ceiling came crashing in, broken pieces of white acoustical ceiling tile flying. A huge grey body dropped down on Mary, limbs flailing, dark hair spraying about. The unannounced form and Mary fell to the floor in a heap. The gun spun about, clattering under Wally's chair. He sprang up, turned and dove for the gun with his confined hands. Wally, sprawled on the floor, clutched the weapon and aimed it at Mary from his position on the ground.

Edison, covered in dust and white crumbled ceiling tile, lay on top of Mary. He spoke first, as he slowly crawled to his knees. "I found that leak," he was breathing hard. "In the piping to the water heater."

Mary was trying to push Edison off her legs. "Get off me. You're hurting me. Get off."

Edison untangled himself from Mary and stood up,

brushing off his clothes. Mary limped to her feet. Wally kept the gun trained on Mary. "Stay right there," he said. "Move a muscle, and I'll blast you." He gestured with the gun.

Jester and I stared at Edison, covered in white dust. Edison continued, "Ken, I knew you were too busy to check on that water leak that Jester's been worried about. I thought I'd just see what I could find. You didn't want me tagging along while you came over here, so I considered staying at the office and straightening up the model building area. Then it occurred to me to use the time to check out that leak. It had to be in the piping up there. You know, there's not much room to work in the ceiling space. Why do we put those heaters up there anyway? I know they're out of the way like that, but that ceiling won't hold a repair person either."

Edison.

What a character.

Chapter 23
Emerging Endings

I've decided to employ a bit more caution when I contemplate welcoming a woman into my life.

Mary, I discovered, blew up my garbage can the night we argued on the phone. A week earlier, she'd detonated an explosive device in Earl and Margie Bostonian's trash can as retaliation for their moving into the house that Mary and I had prepared for the holidays. In addition, it was apparent that Mary punctured Gwen's tires after stopping at my house to find Gwen and I sharing a glass of wine.

Subsequent to her discovery of Isabelle's blackmail material in her Uncle Jester's office, Mary arranged to meet Isabelle at the jobsite, ostensibly to deliver the blackmail money. Isabelle canceled her trip to Indiana. Instead of a payoff, she received a bullet in the chest. Mary then proceeded to cut up Isabelle's clothes and scatter them all over the building and grounds.

Mary was convicted of first degree murder.

Charges were filed against Edison, stemming from his act of relocating the body, and obstructing justice by hiding his actions from the authorities. The sentences were suspended, and he promised not to move any more dead bodies.

For my part in it, two conditions were examined for prosecution. It's hard to tell which was the more serious crime: not revealing the fact that Edison found a dead body, or acting like some dime store detective unearthing information through questionable means.

For my indiscretions, I received a harsh talking to by Lieutenant Coogan, who threatened to make sure that charges were filed. The paperwork never surfaced.

Barry Hart's body, along with the plastic and cardboard from the truck, was found in the junk yard behind Valley Auto Repair and Parts.

Gwen's unsettled life suffered another blow by preliminary indications that the D.A. would charge her with involuntary manslaughter. A period of intensive investigation followed. Eventually, Barry's death was ruled accidental.

Robert left the firm out of public disgrace and moved out of state. My understanding is that he's started a firm specializing in the design of drive-through additions to fine dining establishments.

The firm went through a period of recovery after the publicity. Most of the firm's clients returned when Gwen was cleared, and Andrew campaigned heavily to improve client confidence. We were able to retain the Six Forks Mall commission, on the condition that project management was handled by Jeff Smartain out of our Florida office. The "hit team" would do a good job of it.

Andrew has undertaken the task of persuading Gwen to accept a partnership arrangement. While Andrew has been relentless in his pursuit of her consent, Gwen is reluctant to commit herself to such a sizable obligation. We'll see where that goes.

I spent a good couple of hours shopping and stocking my refrigerator with breakfast and dinner food. The three pounds of Rolo's I brought into the office to stock my candy dish were a big hit (but only lasted four days).

What began with Edison drawing me into an impossible situation—a situation that only seemed to get worse every turn it took—ended in a profound lesson. Sometimes the people you go out of your way to help, will help you out as well.

Gwen thanked me for helping to clear her name. We came to share an unspoken bond, forged in desperate times, that drew us nearer to one another while simultaneously blocking us from the closeness I once desired. Periodically, warm silent glances pass between us, neither of us knowing precisely how to proceed.

Edison reminded me that Aubrey Kensington was still waiting for the lunch I owed her for performing the financial check on Jester Cromwell. And Sharon Webster called me twice the following week to inquire about getting together over dinner.

Somehow, I had not the slightest shred of desire to begin a new relationship.

THE END

ABOUT THE AUTHOR

 Christian Belz has been a practicing architect in Metro Detroit for 28 years, with experience in retail, educational, and industrial projects. He is Vice President of Detroit Working Writers. He won the Grand Prize in Aquarius Press's 2011 Bright Harvest Prize for his short story *Chambers*. Christian's fiction has appeared in *Writers' Journal, The Story Teller Magazine*, and Wicked East Press's anthology: *Short Sips, Coffee House Flash Fiction Collection 2*. His poetry has been published in *WestWard Quarterly* and *Yes, Poetry*.

Christian is one of the co-authors of *The 28-Day Thought Diet*. His blog *Real :) life, love and growth* can be found at ChristianBelz.org.

The Accused Architect is the first of the Ken Knoll Architectural Mysteries. Look for Christian's author page on Goodreads.